PATRICIDE

PATRICIDE

Elizabeth Fackler

Five Star
Unity, Maine

This book is a work of fiction. Names, characters, places and incidents are either the product of the author's imagination or, if real, used fictitiously.

Five Star Mystery
Published in conjunction with Tekno Books and Ed Gorman.

March 2000

First Edition, Second Printing

Five Star Mystery Series.

The text of this edition is unabridged.

Set in 11 pt. Plantin by Minnie B. Raven.

Printed in the United States on permanent paper.

Library of Congress Cataloging-in-Publication Data

Fackler, Elizabeth.
Patricide / Elizabeth Fackler.—1st ed.
p. cm. (Five Star Standard Print Mystery Series)
ISBN 0-7862-2363-4 (hc : alk. paper)
1. Police—Texas—El Paso—Fiction. 2. Police—Family relationships—Fiction. 3. El Paso (Tex.)—Fiction. I. Title. II. Series.
PS3556.A28 P38 2000
813′.54—dc21 99-059538

PATRICIDE

Chapter One

Detective Devon Gray parked his city-issued sedan circumspectly at the curb and took a deep breath, knowing he was about to walk into the chaos of murder. The house looked like his father's, a red rock box set high off the street with a flight of stairs leading to the front door. Every room was brightly lit, none of the drapes closed, and the gyrating blue lights of the squad cars attested to an emergency within.

Threading his way through the uniformed patrolmen milling in the yard, Devon nodded a silent greeting, avoiding the eyes of the curious neighbors, then climbed the stairs to where a rookie was standing guard, looking inordinately proud of his uniform. Though they hadn't met, the rookie evidently knew Devon because he didn't ask for identification but merely said, "Sergeant Brent's in the living room, sir."

Devon started through the door then stopped, surprised to find himself in the kitchen. White metal cabinets over green formica countertops, a large gas stove and a small refrigerator. On the gray formica table, books were stacked on a red spiral notebook beside a black purse. The top title was *Stories of Today and Yesterday.* Three aluminum chairs with padded plastic seats matched the pearly gray of the table top. No dishwasher or microwave, not even a garbage disposal in the sink, which was empty and scoured clean. Two doors on swing-through hinges, one in front of him, past the refrigerator, the other to his right, beyond the sink, both open.

"Turn right," the rookie said.

Devon nodded and walked into the dining room. A massive dark table with eight chairs tucked underneath, a bronze chandelier throwing an amber light to shimmer off the glass doors of a built-in china cabinet in the far right corner. To his left an alcoved mirror over a hutch, also built-in, a black telephone beneath the mirror. The whole room was painted a soft green, the carpet rose-colored, thin beneath his feet. A wide arch opened into the living room. The same carpet, same green walls and high ceiling, built-in bookcases at the far end filled with Reader's Digest Condensed Novels flanking a recessed window with sheer yellow curtains open between heavy maroon drapes. Looking out the window with his back to the room stood a uniformed patrolman, slate gray trousers with a dark stripe on the legs, dark blue shirt, the large silver shield on his left breast pocket reflected in the pane of glass.

Also in uniform, Sergeant Brent stood in the middle of the room like an armed pillar of authority, the amber light from the chandelier reflecting off the scant metal of his gunbelt and coating the walnut hues of his complexion with honey tones. On the sofa sat a small, thin woman, maybe twenty years old. She wasn't crying.

Meeting Devon under the arch, Brent whispered, "She's the daughter. Found the body. Name's Anne Truxal."

Devon nodded, watching the daughter. Her shoulders were hunched under her white blouse, no jewelry or makeup, her dark hair cut short, a deep, lustrous brown, her face set with determination to maintain control of her emotions as she stared into a blackened hearth built of the same red rock as the exterior of the house.

Brent asked, "Want to see the body first or talk to her?"

"See it," Devon answered.

"Excuse us, Miss Truxal," Brent said, speaking up. "We'll be right back."

She swiveled her head to look at him, shifted her gaze to Devon, then looked at the empty hearth again.

Brent led him through the kitchen, out the other door and into a hall which ended abruptly on the right with closed french doors, their panes covered with tight white curtains. Brent turned left. The hall was painted the same green, dimly lit by a small lamp suspended from the ceiling. At the turn of the hall, the bathroom door stood ajar, the white porcelain commode stark in the shadows. To the left of the bathroom was a bedroom, cherry four-poster bed neatly made with a dark chenille spread. Brent turned right and stopped. The victim lay on the floor of the hall, sprawled on his back with his eyes open, his arms thrown wide, his chest bloody. His belt was unbuckled.

Brent said, "Name's Theodore Truxal."

In front of the victim were two doors adjacent to each other at the end of the hall. One was open, the other only slightly ajar. To Devon's right a door stood open to a laundry room, more green formica counters, the white washer and dryer visible through the crack between the door and the wall. He looked at the corpse again. "Time of death?"

"Coroner's not here yet," Brent answered, "but the body's not stiff and rigor mortis sets in at three to four hours."

Devon nodded, knowing Brent was reciting a fact gleaned from his preparations for taking the detective test. "Weapon?"

"Shotgun. Both barrels from not more'n six feet. Haven't found the gun, though."

Devon looked at the door ajar six feet directly in front of

the body. He stepped over the corpse, careful to avoid the blood, and used his pen to push the door all the way open then switch on the overhead light. The room smelled faintly of cigarette smoke. One single bed, neatly made, a maple bedside table and matching chest of drawers, a small desk on spindle legs, a bookcase of wooden crates, literary fiction and one shelf of anthologies bearing titles like *Modern American Drama*. A Modigliani print on one wall, a woman's elongated face, Picasso's Mother and Child in blue on another. The closet door was open. Inside, he saw skirts and blouses, a few dresses, one with Size 7 showing on the label, a jumble of kneeboots and sneakers on the floor, on the shelf neat stacks of sweaters and sweatshirts, all dark colors. Turning around, he again caught the lingering scent of tobacco smoke, so looked for an ashtray. Not seeing one, he walked across to the bedside table and threaded his pen through the oval handle on the drawer, sliding it open. Nestled among a collection of barrettes and ribbons was a small, dirty ashtray holding two cigarette butts. On the filters of each, blue letters spelled out VANTAGE next to a tiny bullseye.

Devon closed the drawer with his pen, walked out and stood in the open door of the other room. It was considerably larger. Two single beds, one with a stuffed pink poodle propped against the pillows surrounded by a collection of well-worn dolls. An old mahogany chest of drawers, what his grandmother would have called a chiffonnier, nothing on top of it. The closet was closed and the knob not yet dusted for prints. He looked at Brent. "I'll talk to the daughter now."

As they walked toward the kitchen, Devon again saw the curtained french doors at the end of the hall. "What's in there?"

"Family room," Brent said. "Door to the back porch."

Meeting Brent's eyes as they entered the kitchen, Devon said, "Thanks," dismissing him. Brent stayed behind as Devon walked through to the living room. The daughter was sitting as if she hadn't moved since they'd left her, the officer still standing at the far end of the room, apparently looking out the window but probably watching the woman in the reflection. She was watching Devon now.

He sat in the wing chair closest to her and smiled sympathetically as he took his notebook from his inside jacket pocket. Her face was round, her nose snubbed, a red rash marring the bottom line of her lower lip. Her eyes were dark brown, glazed with shock and confusion. "I'm Detective Gray," he began. "Your name's Anne, is that right?"

Watching him write it down, she said, "With an *e*."

He added the *e*, then asked, "Are you the victim's daughter?"

She nodded.

"I understand you found the body?"

Again the silent nod.

"Can you tell me about finding it?"

"I told the other policeman," she argued.

"Yes, I know, but I need to hear it from you, Miss Truxal."

She sighed, staring into the blackened hearth.

"When did you find your father?" he asked gently.

She shrugged, looked at the mantle clock, then said, "An hour ago."

He looked at his watch. "That would be around six?"

She nodded, lowering her gaze to the cold, empty hearth.

He wrote: 6 pm 5-21-93. "Do you live here?"

She shook her head. "Someone should tell my mother."

"Where is she?"

"They went on a church retreat."

"Who's they?"

She raised her eyes, and he saw a flash of anger heightening their acuity. "My mother and sisters. I came home to study for finals, thinking the house would be empty, you know."

He nodded, wondering if she was irritated by his questions or if her anger had a deeper source. In a more friendly tone, he asked, "Do you live on campus?"

She shook her head. "I live at 224 Schuster. Apartment B."

He wrote it down. "When did your mother and sisters leave for the church retreat?"

"Four-thirty is when Mom said they'd leave."

"Do you know where the retreat was being held?"

"Up by Cloudcroft. The Baptist Church has a camp up there."

"Do you have a number where they can be reached?"

She shook her head. "The church will know. Glory Baptist on San Antonio Street."

"What're your sisters' names?"

"Elise and Sunny."

"How old are they?"

"Elise is fifteen, Sunny's nine."

"How old are you?"

"Twenty-four."

"Attending UTEP?"

She nodded.

"What are you studying?"

"Elementary education."

"Any other brothers and sisters?"

"I have a brother, Teddy. He's married and lives up by Veterans Park."

"What's his wife's name?"

"Wanda."

"Any children?"

"Petey. Peter. He was a year old last September."

Devon scanned the notes he'd taken, then said softly, "Tell me about finding your father."

A tremor shuddered down her body. She crossed her arms beneath her breasts, pulling her blouse tight over their curves. "I came home to study," she said, her voice flat. "When I drove into the garage, I saw Daddy's car, but the back door was locked, so I came in through the kitchen. I don't have a key to the back door since Mom changed the lock. I left my books and purse on the table and walked toward the bathroom. I saw him on the floor in the hall." She shrugged.

"What did you see, Miss Truxal?"

Her eyes were dry as she bit her lip before speaking. "He was just lying there. I could see he was dead."

"How'd you know that?"

"His eyes were open, and he wasn't breathing."

"Did you touch him?"

She shook her head, one vigorous shake.

"Then what did you do?"

"I went to the bathroom," she said.

"To do what?"

She looked up as if he were stupid. "I had to go."

"Did you close the door?" he asked, trying to visualize her sitting on the commode staring at her father's corpse.

"Of course!"

He nodded, though it wasn't any easier to picture with the door closed. "Then what?"

"When I came out, I looked at him again."

"What did you see, the second time you looked at him?"

"He'd been shot."

"You didn't notice that the first time?"

"I guess I did."

He nodded. "Then what did you do?"

"I called my brother. He wasn't home, so I called the police."

"And said what?"

"That someone had shot my father."

"Did you love your father?"

She stared at him a long moment, then whispered, "No."

Gently he asked, "Why not?"

She looked into the hearth. "I just didn't like him."

"That's okay," Devon said. Now her eyes brimmed with tears, meeting his. "What phone did you use," he asked, "to call your brother and then the police?"

"The one in my mother's room."

"Didn't your father live here?"

She shook her head and the tears fell onto her cheeks. When she wiped them away, he noticed her nails were bitten past the quick.

"Where did he live?" he asked.

"At his hotel."

"Where's that?"

"Downtown. The Cristo Rey."

Devon nodded, knowing the hotel to be a dive for old men. "Were your parents divorced?"

"Just separated."

"Did he have a key to this house?"

"Yes."

"Do you think he knew your mother and sisters were going on the retreat?"

"I don't know."

"Would that have made him angry, their going?"

She shook her head. "He was proud they're religious."

"Do you think they are?"

She shrugged. "They go to church."

"Do you?"

She shook her head.

"How about your brother? Did he know they were going?"

"Yes."

"Do you think maybe he went, too? And that's why he wasn't home when you called him?"

"Teddy wouldn't go."

"Why not?"

"He goes to his wife's church."

"Why did you call your brother before calling the police?"

She bit her lip again. "I guess I wanted him to tell me what to do."

"But you knew what to do, didn't you."

She just looked at him.

"You knew you had to call the police."

"I guess I wanted him to be here," she said.

"Have you tried calling him again?"

She shook her head.

"Where were you before coming here?"

"In class."

"What was the name of it?"

"Political Correctness in the Elementary Classroom."

Devon suppressed a smile. "Who's the teacher?"

"Dr. Cooper. Jane Cooper."

"Can witnesses verify you were there?"

She stared at him.

"Did you see anyone you know in class?"

"Yes," she said.

"Could they verify you were there?"

She nodded.

He smiled. "Why don't you call your brother now?"

She stood up fast, as if she'd been sitting on a spring. He watched her hurry toward the phone in the dining room, then he asked, "Miss Truxal, does anyone in your family keep a shotgun in the house?"

She pivoted into an abrupt stop. "No," she said, her voice shaky. "Teddy hunts, but he keeps his guns at home."

"Go ahead and call him," Devon said, smiling kindly.

She disappeared behind the arch, then he listened to the rotary dial of the phone, thinking this family had quit buying things about twenty years ago. He looked around the room again, seeing a photo of a baby on the mantle. Petey, no doubt. Besides the gold sofa and two matching wing chairs, there was a green naughehyde recliner in front of the television next to the front door. A green and orange afghan was draped across the back of the chair. Behind it were more french doors leading into the family room.

Devon stood up and saw the doors didn't close with a knob but a bar-handled latch. Using his pen to push one down, he opened a door and stood peering into a large pine-paneled room with a maple bedroom desk, a chair from the kitchen set, a worn brown sofa and modular blond coffee table, a cardboard box of toys for a toddler. The windows were covered with only sheer curtains, the back yard dark.

Behind him, the daughter said, "Teddy, this is Anne. I'm at Mom's." A momentary pause, then she said, "Daddy's dead. Someone shot him." After a moment she said with a small, squelched sob, "Please." She hung up. Devon resumed his seat.

Sergeant Brent walked through the dining room and

across to Devon in the wing chair. "The coroner's here and wants to know if it's okay to remove the body now."

"Not yet," Devon said.

"There's press outside. What should we tell them?"

"That we haven't notified next of kin." Devon beckoned him closer and spoke in a near whisper. "Call the Cloudcroft police. Ask them to send an officer to the Baptist camp to tell the family, and ask the officer to watch how they take it."

Brent nodded, then left briskly.

Anne Truxal came back into the room and sank into the opposing wing chair. "My brother's on his way," she said.

"How long will it take him to get here?"

She shrugged. "Twenty minutes."

He watched her a moment, sitting limp in her chair, then he asked, "Miss Truxal, could you make me some coffee?"

As he'd expected, she seemed relieved to have something to do. "Of course," she said, again rising as if she'd been sitting on a spring. Or like a puppet, he thought, dancing on strings habitually jerked. He watched her walk out, then looked at the officer still standing by the window. The officer turned around, expectant of orders. "Go outside," Devon said, "and tell Brent the brother will be arriving soon."

The officer moved eagerly. As he passed, Devon said, "On your way through the kitchen, shut the hall door, but don't touch it with your hands."

The officer nodded and left. Devon relaxed into the curve of the chair, closed his eyes a moment and allowed his mind to fall slack, letting the information he'd gathered tumble through without judgment. Jumping to conclusions was the nemesis of detective work. Gather all the facts, then assemble them, hold your mind in stasis until the right moment, then pounce.

Sliding his notebook and pen back into his pocket, he stood up and walked through the french doors into the family room and through the open back door to the porch. Another officer stood at the bottom of the stairs in front of a screen door. Devon nodded at him, then asked, "Any sign of forced entry?"

"No, sir," the officer said.

"What's in the garage?"

"The victim's car and the daughter's. We searched 'em both but didn't find anything suspicious."

"Have you searched the yard?"

"Yes, sir. It's surrounded by a six-foot rock wall."

"Is there a gate?"

"One by the garage. It's locked with a padlock but could be climbed."

Devon gestured at the door behind him. "Was this locked?"

"Yes, sir. The front one too. The daughter let us in through the kitchen."

"Any windows open?"

"No, sir. The house was shut up tight, as if the family meant to be gone a while."

Devon nodded and retraced his steps to the living room. He stood in the middle of the carpet and looked around, not seeing anything he hadn't noticed before except his reflection in the far window. To distract his mind, he studied himself as if he were a suspect. 5'10", 175 pounds, brown hair and eyes, a pleasant, clean-shaven face and non-threatening demeanor, wearing jeans over scuffed brown boots, a pale yellow shirt under a tan corduroy jacket showing wear at the elbows. No wedding ring. No scars, distinguishing marks or peculiar traits. Mr. Nondescript, the type of Anglo seen everyday on the streets of El Paso, his dress western without being cowboy, of good enough quality to denote employment but not an exceptionally high salary, his manner the right degree of nonchalance to foster the impression of a man without much ambition or passion, a man pushing middle age with neither bitterness nor satisfaction. His soft belly attested to a fondness for beer, the lack of flash in his belt buckle signified a disinterest in playing the stud to lonely fillies in honky-tonks. In other words, a man the observer knew next to nothing about because the subject chose not to tell him. His appearance could as easily be a study in obscurity as genuine mediocrity, except for his eyes. If Devon Gray were a criminal meeting the eyes he met now in the window's reflection, he'd keep his mouth shut. To the adept observer, intelligence was impossible to disguise. And in Devon's experience, criminals were adept observers.

The killer of Theodore Truxal could be a simple burglar who'd noticed the family was leaving. The thing wrong with that was there wasn't much worth stealing in this house. Even desperate burglars didn't break and enter without some assurance the take would be worth the risk. But then no one had broken into this house. And in his six years as a detective, Devon had never heard of a burglar carrying a shotgun to work.

In Devon's lexicon of values, the only unforgivable motive for murder was money. If a man was killed for any other reason he usually deserved it. Yet justice wasn't Devon's job. It was discovering the perpetrator, no matter what motivated the crime. The fact that the victim's daughter hadn't cried over his death didn't mitigate Devon's responsibility to pinpoint whoever had pulled the trigger. At the moment he suspected the victim's son, only because he hadn't been home when his sister called for help. But Devon shelved that suspicion, holding it in abeyance until he could meet the man.

When he arrived, he was tall and thin, sandy brown hair cut short, dressed in sneakers, jeans, a white tee-shirt and an open Levi jacket. Devon watched through the dining room as Teddy Truxal greeted his sister in the kitchen. They didn't touch but merely looked into each other's eyes in silence, then Anne led him into the living room. "This is my brother," she said. "Teddy, this is Detective Gray."

Teddy extended his hand, his blue eyes wary, blurred with neither grief nor shock.

Nodding an apology to Anne, Devon led Teddy through the family room into the hall by coaxing, "Will you come with me a moment?"

The corpse had been covered with a sheet. Watching Teddy, Devon told the officer to take the sheet completely off. The son looked down at his father with no apparent emotion despite the savage destruction of the wound, the ashen gray of the dead man's face, the unbuckled belt probably indicating he was innocently on his way to the bathroom when someone intervened. Gently Devon asked, "Is that your father?"

Teddy Truxal nooded.

Softly Devon asked, "Do you own a shotgun, Teddy?"

He shook his head.

"Did your father or anyone else keep a shotgun here?"

"No," he said.

"What kinds of guns do you own?"

"A .22 Remington and a .44 Winchester, both rifles, and a .357 handgun," he said so quickly his answer sounded rehearsed.

"Your sister tried to call you when she first found the body," Devon said, feigning compassion for her lack of success. "Where were you?"

"What time was that?" Teddy asked, meeting his eyes.

Devon smiled, recognizing the wiliness of his prey. "Around six o'clock."

"Is that when he died?"

"We won't know for sure until we get the coroner's report. Six o'clock is when your sister says she discovered the body."

"Don't you believe her?"

"I have no reason not to," Devon answered.

"Sounds like you don't though," Teddy said.

"I try to keep an open mind until I have all the facts," Devon said, surprised at how intensely Teddy Truxal maintained eye contact. "Where were you at six o'clock?"

"Having a beer with a friend."

"Where?"

"Rosa's Cantina."

"On Doniphan?"

"That's right."

"What's your friend's name?"

"Earl Carter. We work together."

"Where's that?"

"Border Steel."

"What do you do there?"

"I'm a mechanic in the fleet garage."

"Did you love your father?"

Teddy's face reddened but he didn't drop his gaze. "Can we talk somewhere else?"

"After you answer the question."

Teddy looked down at the corpse. "He was a sonofabitch."

"In what way?"

"I feel sick," Teddy said. "I need to sit down."

"All right," Devon said easily. "Go on back to your sister.

I'll be along in a minute." He watched the man turn stiffly and walk away, then he took out his notebook and wrote down Earl Carter, Border Steel, Rosa's Cantina, and the kinds of guns Teddy admitted to owning. Looking at the officer, Devon said, "Tell Brent he can take it out now."

"Yes, sir," the officer said, dropping the bloodied sheet over the corpse again.

Devon found the brother and sister sitting across from each other in the dining room. They each had a white cup of black coffee steaming in front of them, and there was a third cup at the end of the table. The saucers were sitting on placemats, brown and yellow flowers against the dark wood. Devon sat down over the third cup as he smiled his thanks at Anne. He took a sip, then returned the cup to the saucer, watching Teddy, who no longer looked sick.

"I won't keep you much longer," Devon said, hearing the gurney come into the kitchen. Neither of the people in front of him gave any indication they heard it. He sipped his coffee again, then asked, "Do you know of anyone who might want to kill your father?"

Teddy and Anne met each other's eyes, then Teddy shook his head. Devon looked at Anne. "No," she said.

"We've called the Cloudcroft police," Devon said, "to notify your mother and sisters."

"Thank you," Anne said.

Devon noted they both held themselves as rigidly as if they were braced for a whack on the head to come out of nowhere. "It's my job to discover who killed your father," he said, "but as of right now, I haven't much to go on."

Teddy's shoulders dropped a notch. Anne gave no reaction whatsoever.

"It strikes me, however," Devon said, "that he won't be missed by his family." When they answered only by looking into their cups, he added, "At least not by the two of you."

"You don't know what we're feeling," Anne accused, her eyes bright with anger though still dry.

"That's true, I don't," Devon said in a conciliatory tone. "But there's no evidence of forcible entry into the house, which probably means he was killed by someone who had a key. Do you know of anyone outside your family who has a key to the house?"

Anne looked at Teddy, who shook his head.

"It's possible," Devon said, "that when your father came in he left the door unlocked and someone followed him, but that would indicate a person who had reason to kill him, not a burglar surprised in the act. It's not unusual for a man to have fatal enemies and his children not know who they are, so I'm not ruling that out."

"What are you ruling out?" Teddy asked sharply.

"Nothing, right now," Devon answered. "Not even that you have good reason for your apparent lack of grief." He smiled into their startled faces. "I assume you're anxious to help me find the killer."

They both nodded woodenly.

"Good," he said, seeing their eyes warm at that tidbit of praise. "I'm afraid the crime lab people will be here for at least an hour yet, dusting for fingerprints mostly. It would be helpful if you could check for anything missing, but since neither of you actually lived here, your mother and sisters will probably be able to tell more easily than you if something's been taken. If it has, of course, that would add credibility to the surprised burglar theory."

"And if it hasn't?" Teddy asked.

"Then we have to look for another motive," Devon said.

"Maybe the burglar was interrupted before he had a chance to take anything," Teddy said.

"Maybe," Devon agreed. "But most burglars don't carry a shotgun. If he found the gun in the house then used it to kill your father, I could understand that. But you've both told me there wasn't one here."

Teddy and Anne met each other's eyes, their coffee growing cold in their cups. The phone rang, making both of them jump. Though it was directly behind Teddy, Anne got up and walked around the table to answer it.

"Hello," she said, her voice shaky. Then, "Yes, he's here." She held the receiver toward her brother. "It's Mom," she said.

Devon watched Teddy stand up and take the receiver from his sister, who hovered nearby as if she could hear her mother's voice.

"Mom?" Teddy said, then, "Yeah."

Anne shuddered, watching her brother.

"She's okay," he said, then after a minute, "Don't you feel up to driving?" He listened. "No, you're right." Another pause before he asked, "How's Elise?" As Teddy listened to his mother's answer, Devon waited for him to ask about his other sister, the baby of the family. But when Teddy spoke again, all he said was, "We'll be here." He hung up and met his sister's eyes. "The Cloudcroft police are driving them home."

Anne nodded.

"It's a two-hour drive," Teddy said, facing Devon.

He stood up. "I'll be on my way. If there's anything else you think of that might help the investigation, make a note of it, will you?" They both nodded dumbly. "I'll be back tomorrow to talk to all of you. Like I said, the lab people will be here a while longer yet, but they should be gone before your mother and sisters arrive." Again they both nodded. "Your father's body will be taken to the morgue at

Thomason Hospital. You can tell the funeral home that." They looked chagrined, as if they'd committed an oversight by not asking. Devon took a card from his pocket and laid it on the table. "Here's my number. Call me anytime. If I'm not in, they can always reach me." He gave them a sad smile. "You'd think after having gone through this so many times, I'd have some wise parting words to offer, but I'm afraid I don't."

Anne laughed weakly. Teddy didn't crack a smile. Devon extended his hand. "Until tomorrow," he said.

Teddy took a step back at the same moment he accepted the handshake. His palm was sweaty. Devon started from the room then turned around in time to catch them exchanging an apprehensive look. "If you can think of anyone who knew him," Devon said gently, "and also owned a shotgun, it might give us a lead."

"Most of the men in El Paso own shotguns," Teddy scoffed.

"You don't," Devon said.

"I'm not that kind of hunter," Teddy said.

"Only go for the big game?" Devon teased.

Teddy frowned. "Deer and elk," he said. "I don't bother with birds."

"Where do you hunt?"

"New Mexico, usually."

"Near Cloudcroft?"

"No, that's the Mescalero reservation. I usually hunt in the Gila."

"Do your sisters ever go with you?"

Teddy shook his head.

"Not even for target practice?"

"Are you asking," Teddy replied tersely, "if my sisters know how to use a gun?"

Devon smiled. "Yeah, I guess I am."

"What's there to know?" Anne demanded, her voice slightly shrill. "All you have to do is pull the trigger."

"And hit the target," Devon answered, watching Teddy.

"Neither of my sisters has ever held a gun," he retorted.

"Which one of them has?"

"I just told you, none of them."

"You said neither," Devon said. He looked at Anne. "Do you know how to use a gun?"

"I watch TV," she said.

Devon nodded. "Reality's a bit different, isn't it?"

Teddy snorted. "Are you suggesting Anne killed him?"

"At this stage of the investigation," Devon replied softly, "I can't disregard anyone."

"Including me?" Teddy asked, a little too loud.

"Unless your alibi checks out."

"It will," he replied between clenched teeth.

"So will mine," Anne asserted.

"Good," Devon said, again seeing a slight warmth of gratitude in their eyes. "Depending on the time of death, and the time your mother and sisters arrived at the church retreat, hopefully I'll be able to eliminate all of you as suspects. Believe me, I'd rather it happen that way."

This time Anne's shoulders hunched down a notch as if in relief, but Teddy's stayed rigid. Devon smiled again. "I'll see you tomorrow," he said, walking through the kitchen and out the door.

Most of the squad cars were gone, only two still casting their revolving blue lights onto the street. He walked back to his sedan, got in and started the engine. Letting it warm up a minute, he watched the dining room windows and wasn't surprised when the drapes were closed. Family of the victim usually sought privacy right after the crime. It didn't necessarily denote guilt.

Chapter Two

Devon drove slowly through the dark neighborhood. When he made the last turn and saw his house on the hill, he again thought of how much it looked like the Truxal home. But then, red rock was a common construction material in the Twenties and Thirties, and many of the older homes resembled each other. Multi-paned windows, generous front porches, red-tile roofs. With large rooms and high ceilings, they were houses designed for gracious living, but Devon hadn't witnessed an abundance of happiness within them.

He parked his sedan in front of the single-car garage, which was also built of red rock, its wooden door painted yellow a decade ago. Walking through the waist-high wooden gate into the back yard, he made a right turn into the house, entering a utility porch still boasting a milk door in the wall, though the dairies hadn't delivered milk since the Fifties. In the kitchen, he took a Budweiser out of the refrigerator and continued through the dining room, into the living room and out the front door, leaving it open behind him, to sit on the top step and look down the street.

Under a canopy of mulberry trees, the asphalt curved downhill toward Mesa, the main artery on the west side of town, which meant west of the Franklin Mountains, the last rumple of the Rockies. Mesa was a neon strip illuminating the sky, the Rio Grande Valley and the mesa for which the street had been named obscured in darkness beyond the glare of car lots and fast food restaurants. Devon popped open the can and took a refreshing sip of cold beer, then heard Laura call from behind him, "Connie?"

"No, it's me," he said over his shoulder.

Emerging from the hall to stand in the shadowed living room, Laura looked tired, her thin face creased with the wear of being married to his brother. Her dark hair was pinned with a barrette behind her neck to fall halfway down the back of her faded red sundress. "Are you hungry?" she asked. "I made a pot of chile for supper. I could heat it up again, if you like."

"Sounds good." He smiled, then watched her disappear into the kitchen. She turned on the light, illuminating the walnut dining room table and chairs his parents had bought soon after they moved into this house. Their carpet had been torn out, leaving a wood floor in need of refinishing, but other than that not much had changed. Devon had lived here alone for over ten years. Then Connor came back from California with his wife and kids and Devon invited them to move in. He figured the house was as much Connie's as his, though the will hadn't stipulated that.

Laura's bare feet whispered on the wood as she came to stand behind the screen door. "Rough day?" she asked.

"The usual," he answered between sips of beer.

She came onto the porch and sat on the rock wall, leaning against the pillar. "Connie's boss called this morning and said he hadn't shown up for work. I haven't seen him all day."

Devon took another drink. "Where're the kids?"

"Misty said she was gonna study with Arnette, and Eric's hanging out with the guys, whatever that means. Prob'ly nothing good."

Devon drained his beer and crumpled the can in his fist.

"Want another?" Laura asked.

"No, thanks," he said, watching the shadows thrown by

the streetlight dance on the asphalt beneath the trees.

"You think Misty's really studying?" Laura asked plaintively. "I remember being thirteen and telling my mother I was gonna study with a girlfriend. But what we were really doing was meeting boys in places we weren't s'posed to be."

"Sounds like more fun," Devon said, giving her a smile.

"Till she gets pregnant," Laura answered.

"Haven't you given her the lecture on safe sex?"

"I tried, but she said she'd already heard it in school." She sighed deeply. "You're lucky you don't have kids, Devon. They're a pain in the butt."

"So are parents sometimes," he teased.

She laughed. "Yeah, I know. My old man was, that's for sure. But Misty and Eric love Connie more'n me. I think it's 'cause in his heart he's still a kid like they are." She sighed. "This is his fifth job in two years, Devon. If he gets fired from this one, I don't know who'll hire him. Do you?"

Devon shook his head.

"How come you two turned out so different?" she asked.

"We started out different," he said.

"Your father never liked Connie. Don't you think it would've made a difference if he had?"

"It was the other way around," Devon said. "Connie never liked the old man."

"All little boys like their fathers."

"I met one tonight who called his a sonofabitch."

"A little boy said that?"

"Well, he wasn't so little. Twenty-one or thereabouts. But the way he said it made me think he'd felt that way a long time."

"Was the father getting him out of jail and that was how he thanked him for it?"

"No, the father was murdered."

"By his son?" she whispered.

"I don't know yet."

"There's a lot of that happening now. Kids killing their parents. Scares me to death."

Devon nodded, watching the shadows. "Did you ever think about killing your father?"

"Sure. Those years Connie was in prison, Daddy was always giving me grief about it and there were plenty of times I wished I could just blow him away so I wouldn't have to listen to it anymore."

Devon remembered those years. He'd kept in touch with his older brother, writing letters that were never answered, and he spent every Sunday with Laura, who was still living with her parents as if her husband were a specter who'd come and gone, leaving only a son in his wake. Eric was three when Connie came home from prison and moved his wife and son to an apartment in the lower valley to which Devon was never invited. He was a cop by then, and Connie avoided his company. Laura sent him a photo when Misty was born. Devon had sent a check in lieu of a present, merely because he had no idea what to buy for a baby, but Connie returned the check with a simple scrawled note saying no thanks.

The same month his parole was up, he moved his family to California. Then Devon began receiving long lonely letters from Laura complaining that Connie was having trouble keeping a job and they were living in poverty. Devon had sent her small amounts of cash through a neighbor because she asked him to, promising she'd tell Connie she earned the money babysitting.

Devon had thought he understood what drove Connie to create a self-image built on being an outlaw, and Devon's belief that he could convince a few young men that pride and autonomy were possible inside the system had been most of his motivation to become a cop, even though he hadn't been able to change his brother. Now Devon didn't believe in much of anything except doing his job well. He had a better conviction rate than any other detective in Homicide, and he was proud of that, if nothing else.

He turned around to study the face of his brother's wife as the shadows flickered across her cheeks, the light catching in her eyes. "But you never did kill your father," he said.

"Only 'cause I knew someday I'd get away from him," she scoffed. "Murder's something a person don't ever leave behind. My Aunt Celia told me that and I believed her. She said *her* daddy used to come into her bed at night, and all a girl can do when her father's a problem is hold her head up high and get out as soon as she can." Laura laughed bitterly. "Course back then I thought there was someplace to get. Now it seems no matter where you turn it's more of the same."

Devon tried to give her an encouraging smile. "At least you married a man who stays out of his daughter's bedroom."

"He stays out of the whole damn house most of the time."

"It's not you, Laura. It's his memories of this place."

"Yeah, I know. But I'm not about to move into some ramshackle apartment and have the landlord hounding us for rent all the time. In California, we had our power shut off every other month 'cause we didn't pay the bill. Least here it's stable. That's important to kids."

Devon looked away, knowing it was important to Laura too.

"I know it's your salary we're living on," she said softly.

"Don't think I don't know that, Devon. Sometimes I wish Connie would disappear and you'd take his place." When he didn't say anything, she laughed to cover her embarrassment. "I wouldn't even have to change my name."

He watched the shadows on the asphalt dancing in the same patterns he'd seen growing up, only then it had been his father sitting behind him on the porch complaining about Connie. His father had sat in a rocker smoking cigarettes, the scritch of the runners on the floor falling silent when he flicked his butts into the street. Watching their embers die as his father began another litany of grievances, Devon hadn't had any more of an answer then than he had now. Connie was just restless, needing a high voltage of excitement in his life. To follow in his father's footsteps would have meant spending his days in the copper smelter and his evenings smoking cigarettes on the porch. It was an honorable life, but the dreariness didn't make for drama.

"I guess that chile's hot," Laura said. "You ready to eat?"

In his room upstairs, Devon switched on his answering machine and listened to the messages. Lieutenant Dreyfus wanting to know why Devon hadn't filed his report on the Truxal murder. An Officer Malone from Cloudcroft saying he'd be at Chuy's in Canutillo till ten if Devon wanted to talk. Devon looked at his watch and saw it was nine-thirty. As he walked back downstairs, he could hear the TV in the living room where Laura was watching a sit-com, the canned laughter rattling in the emptiness of her silence.

Devon drove north on Interstate 10 and took the Transmountain turnoff west, then turned south again on Doniphan. Although surrounded by lush fields feeding off the river, Canutillo was a tawdry collection of cinder block buildings and dusty trailer parks. A haven for cattle rustlers at the end of the last century, it had grown without the benefit of zoning into a hodgepodge of small factories and stores catering to people without much money. A mile south of the business district, Chuy's Cafe was in a hundred-year-old adobe next to a FINA gas station.

The parking lot held two pickups past their prime and one brown sedan that reeked of being a cop car. Devon parked his own ominously nondescript sedan next to it and walked into the cafe. Two couples lingered over late suppers. At the bar, one man sat with a half-empty mug of beer in front of him.

The man was dressed cowboy, jeans and lizard boots, a big bucking-bronco belt buckle, a black cotton shirt with the sleeves rolled up to reveal a silver bracelet on his right wrist, a turquoise-studded watchband on his left. He wore his hair long for a cop. It was a dirty blond, his eyes pale blue, and he neither appeared to be armed nor sported a badge, but since he'd had to cross the state line to take the family home, Devon hadn't expected him to be in uniform.

Devon walked over to him. "Malone?"

Malone stood up and offered his hand with a smile. "Devon Gray?"

Devon nodded, shook with him, then took the next stool. When the elderly Hispanic bartender raised his eyebrows, Devon ordered a draft, then studied Malone as the old man filled a mug from the tap. Malone was in his mid-twenties, with a thin sarcastic smile and an avaricious hunger behind his pale eyes. He looked to be the kind of man who enjoyed trouble, the exact kind Devon would never hire if he were running a police force.

His beer arrived and the old man retreated to the other end of the bar where he stood with his arms folded, staring at the door as if hoping for more customers. If the old man had been the one Devon was seeking information from, he'd start out with small talk, probably covering the slowness of the night's business, the weather, UTEP's winning basketball team and the state of the economy before honing in on his intentions. But Malone was an Anglo so all that protocol was neither expected nor necessary. "What'd you see?" Devon asked.

Malone chuckled, a snide, high-pitched snicker of derision. "The oldest girl's a looker. I watched her in the rearview all the way down here."

"That would be Elise?"

"Elise, yeah. The other one, Sunny, is fat with a face full of misery."

"She's nine, right?"

"Sounds right. Elise looks to be sixteen going on thirty."

"Fifteen," Devon said.

Malone grunted.

"What about the mother?"

"A cupcake. Fat, blond, peach complexion. The kind of garage we'd all like to park our car in when we get old."

Devon doubted that he could get Malone's mind out of his pants, but he asked anyway, "How'd they react to the news?"

Malone took a pack of Marlboro's out of his shirt pocket and offered one to Devon. He shook his head. Malone lifted one with his lips straight from the pack, returned the pack to his pocket and fished out a Zippo, flicked the flame and sucked hard, then set the lighter on the counter with a smack as he exhaled a jet of smoke. "They didn't seem surprised," he said.

"What was missing?" Devon asked.

"Tears, for one thing. Didn't shed nary a one."

Devon nodded. "Maybe they're just a family good at hiding their feelings."

Malone shook his head. "Elise's got eyes you can read like a book. She looked scared. The fat one, Sunny, she carries a blankie. Kept it to her nose the whole ride down. The mother was so cheerful you'd think I'd told 'em they'd won the lottery."

Devon watched him finish his beer and signal the old man for another. When he'd brought it and retreated again, Devon said, "Give it to me blow-by-blow."

Malone took a deep drag on his cigarette and exhaled through his nose, knocked the ash into a dirty ashtray, then said, "When I got there, they were in a sing-along. Jesus Loves Me, stuff like that. I told a dude who was an usher or some such that I needed to speak to the man in charge, then I waited for him to get loose of the sing-along. It was happening outside, and I looked over the singers but couldn't pick out the family I wanted. I picked out Elise, though. Like I said, she's a looker. Long blond hair, skinny with big tits, the way I like em. I don't like big butts. Even though she was sitting down, I could tell she'd fill her jeans just right."

"Was she singing?"

"Oh yeah. They all were. The whole crowd. The chief honcho let someone else lead the next song and came over to me. I told him I needed to speak to the Truxal family, that there was an emergency at home. So he goes back and picks his way through the crowd right to that pretty little girl." Malone laughed. "I couldn't believe my luck."

"How'd they look when he spoke to them?"

"Well, I was watching Elise. The honcho, he bent over to speak to her mother, and he kind of stuck his ass right in Elise's face, and she looked plumb disgusted. I had to laugh 'cause he was kind of a paunchy dude, you know?"

"You couldn't see the mother's face?"

Malone shook his head. "When they got up and followed the honcho, their back was to the light so I couldn't see much then either." He paused to grin. " 'Cept the way Elise filled her jeans."

"All of them followed the minister, not just the mother?"

Malone nodded. "I took 'em over to a log and had 'em all sit down, and I told 'em we'd gotten a call from the El Paso police that there'd been an accident in their home, that we'd been asked to let 'em know. I didn't say a murder, I figured that'd be hitting 'em with too much too fast."

Devon nodded. "What they'd say?"

"Nothing," Malone answered, stubbing his cigarette out. "They just watched me, waiting for the rest. Like they knew there was more to come." He shrugged. "So I gave 'em the more. I said we'd received information that Mr. Truxal had been shot. And the fat girl, Sunny, she asked, 'Isn't he dead?' She sounded worried that maybe he might not be." Malone gloated a moment, then sipped at his beer.

Devon asked, "Did you tell them he was dead?"

"Yeah, I said we heard he was." Malone pulled his cigarettes out again, lit one, and returned the pack and lighter to his pocket. "I said I was sorry, you know, the formula things you say in such a situation, and then I said my shift was over and I'd be glad to drive 'em home if they wanted. The looker, Elise, she said they had their own car, but the mother said someone there would bring it along and she'd be pleased to accept my invitation. Like I'd asked her to a dance or something. She kept smiling real big, but I think she's just one of them women who smile no matter what."

"Did you see any marks on any of them?"

Malone turned his head and looked straight at him a

minute. "You mean like bruises?"

Devon nodded.

Malone shook his head. "The mother, she said she wanted to call home 'fore we left. So I waited, and five minutes later they were back, suitcases in tow. I put 'em in the trunk and we headed out."

"They all sit in back?"

"The girls did, both of 'em up against the doors like they didn't want to touch each other. The mother sat in front."

Devon sipped his beer, watching the smoke Malone exhaled bounce off the bar and waft over the other side before it rose again. "They say anything?"

"Not the girls. The mother talked pretty near the whole trip. A shit shoot, you know. Laughing about what the neighbors would think if they saw her in a police car—though I brought 'em in an unmarked sedan—and asking about the radio and how I liked being a cop and all that stuff you get from civilians."

"The whole two hours?"

Malone nodded. "I brought 'em across White Sands 'cause when I asked what side of El Paso they live on and they said the west side, I figured no use going over that Spaghetti Bowl y'all got down below Chaparral. I don't like that much, not with so many drunks on the road. Being up in the sky like that, you ain't got no options. So I come through Cruces, and when we crossed the line, I asked if they wanted to stop at the tourist station and use the bathroom. The mother said no, they could wait. I looked in the mirror and met Elise's eyes. I swear I'd get her in bed if she wasn't jailbait. The fat one, she just kept her blankie close to her face and never looked at me after we were on the road."

"What happened when you got them home?"

Malone shrugged. "The mother told me where to turn and all, all them windy streets and half a block this way, block and a half that, up to the bottom of the mountain where their house is. What do you call that mountain?"

"Crazy Cat," Devon said.

"Yeah." Malone took a drag on his cigarette and knocked the ash off, then sipped at his beer. "I stopped in front of the house and got out and opened the door for the mother. I would've done the same for Elise but the girls didn't wait, just walked up the sidewalk and up them steps. There was a man in the door waiting for 'em. I asked the mother if she wanted me to come in. She said no, that man was her son and they were all right. She thanked me for the ride and told me to drive careful going home. That was it." He took another drag on his cigarette, which was burning into the filter, then stubbed it out. "I watched till they got in the house. Then they closed the door and I figured wasn't no use standing there staring at a closed door, so I drove back up here and called you. That was an hour ago."

"How many beers have you had?" Devon asked.

Malone laughed. "This is about my fourth."

"You plan on driving back into the mountains tonight?"

He laughed again. "I've driven that road so many times I could do it blindfolded. Yeah, I'll be all right."

"Well, watch yourself till you cross the line."

Malone looked at him with the bravado of a mock challenge. "You saying New Mexico's soft on drunk drivers?"

Devon shrugged. "Is there anything else you can tell me about the family?"

Malone shook his head. "Can't think of nothing. If I do, I'll give you a call."

"Appreciate it," Devon said, pulling a card out of his pocket and laying it next to the overflowing ashtray.

"I envy you," Malone said.

Devon thought it was because his card had detective in front of his name and Homicide Division beneath the police logo, but he asked rhetorically, "Why?"

"For spending time with Elise." Malone snickered. "She's a centerfold waiting to be photographed. If she'd been of age, I might've tried to maneuver her mama into driving down with the fat one and letting me take Elise by myself. I got the feeling Elise would've jumped at the chance."

Devon finished his beer, quietly set the empty mug down, then watched the man when he asked, "You think she's experienced?"

"Oh yeah." Malone chuckled. "Struck me like Eve in the garden offering Adam the apple." He nodded emphatically. "Makes a man understand why Adam ate it. Hell, it could've been a turd she was offering, which might be the origin of shit-eating grin."

"But you've surely seen your share of pretty girls," Devon said tongue-in-cheek.

Malone laughed, not catching the sarcasm. "This one, though, she's like sin incarnate walking on two very fine legs."

"Must've been more to it than looks," Devon pressed.

Malone stared back a long moment, then nodded. "I get what you're after. Yeah, there *was* more to it. She swaggered with challenge, like she was thinking 'go ahead, touch me, you bastard, and I'll cut it off,' the kind of look that makes a man ache to get her begging for it. You know what I mean?"

Devon managed to smile as he laid a ten dollar bill on the bar and stood up. "Thanks," he said, "see you around."

When he was halfway toward the door, Malone called, "If you get up to Cloudcroft, come say howdy."

Devon waved with another smile, then escaped into the cool, smokeless air and took a deep breath. As he walked toward his car, he was thinking that with men like Malone wearing badges, it was no wonder citizens felt the need to find their own justice with a shotgun.

Rosa's Cantina was in Sunland Park, about seven miles below Canutillo. Devon drove south on Doniphan toward the bar where Teddy Truxal had said he shared a beer with a friend while his father was being murdered. At one time, Doniphan had been the only road between El Paso and Las Cruces. It had been dirt then, traveled by men on horses taking a full day to make the trip. Now the same forty miles was less than an hour's drive, but the sights along the way had deteriorated considerably. Both sides of the road were cluttered with a hundred years of unzoned development, trailer lots interspersed with ancient adobes boarded up.

Devon tried to imagine the mindset that would accompany needing a full day to travel forty miles. If he were Pat Garrett, who'd been a famous lawman in both Cruces and El Paso, and he needed to make the trip on business, he would've had a full day to ponder the complexities of his problem. A day listening to nothing more than the plodding of his horse's hooves, meadowlarks in the mesquite and cottonwood trees. Ten hours to let his thoughts explore not only the problem at hand but his entire life and how all the repercussions of past decisions influenced the one he was about to make. Devon couldn't see that the compression of time fast travel had given humanity was of much benefit, and it amazed him that the acceleration hadn't yet quit. Now even air mail was obsolete and FAX machines were required equipment for any business making the cut.

Rosa's Cantina was a cinder block building that hadn't existed ten years ago and bore no resemblance to its namesake. Probably there had been a Rosa's Cantina in El Paso of the 1880's, the time Marty Robbins' song immortalized, but it hadn't been this Rosa's. This one had been named after the song, which Devon guessed was part of the problem of modern life: it took its inspiration from the glorified memory of a romance no one had ever lived, providing a script of heroism but failing to supply any props. If Devon had owned Rosa's Cantina, he would have tried to augment the fantasy, giving the place a wooden floor, a decorative tin ceiling with a few stray bullet holes for effect, and hanging posters of famous gunfighters on the walls. The only thing the owners of Rosa's had done was put Marty Robbins' song on the jukebox.

The floor was bare cement, the walls nude cinder block without any posters whatsoever. Other than the fluorescent jukebox, the only furnishings were a few mismatched tables with torn chairs. The bar was a horseshoe keeping the clientele away from the bartender, a dowdy woman selling canned beer and bottled wine coolers for three dollars a shot. Her name was Tulles, and Devon knew she worked twelve-hour shifts.

At eleven-thirty this Friday night, her only customers were men who had stopped in for a brew on their way home from work and hadn't yet made it out the door. They hung on each other in drawn-out, drunken demonstrations, of farewell while Tulles gained beauty as the neon lights of the beer ads blurred her customers' alcoholic haze into the softening kindness of a drunkard's dream.

Devon stopped at the jukebox, dropped a quarter in the slot and punched the number for *El Paso*. When the opening chords drowned out the customers' vows of eternal loyalty to men they probably didn't like sober, Tulles grimaced to hear the song again. Devon laughed and ordered a Tecate.

She took the beer from the cooler, opened the can and nestled a slice of lime in the notch, then slid it toward him.

"Thanks," Devon smiled, dropping a five on the bar. "How you doing?"

She shrugged with a laugh, showing her bad teeth.

He cast his gaze over her pudgy figure dressed in stained purple sweat pants and an orange-flowered blouse with gaping buttons. "You get prettier every time I come in here, Tulles."

"You must be living an ugly life then," she answered.

"You should've been here last night," Tulles said. "One of them wild young cowboys knifed another. Ay, *Americanos,* they are violent people."

"Mexican men never knife each other, do they?" he teased.

"No, they use machetes." She grinned, then asked, "How is your wife?"

"Fine," Devon said.

"The other day your brother told me you have no wife."

"That's why she's fine," he answered. " 'Cause I haven't married her yet."

"Hah!" she grunted. "There is nothing more pitiful than a woman with no husband." She paused for effect, then said, "Except a woman with a husband."

He smiled. "Do you know Teddy Truxal?"

She shrugged.

"About twenty-one, twenty-two. Anglo, tall, thin, light brown hair, blue eyes, works at Border Steel."

"Maybe I know him. So what?"

"Was he here tonight?"

"All nights are the same to me. All men also."

"He said he was here with a friend of his. Earl Carter. They work together. Teddy said they had a beer after work."

Her eyes narrowed. "Are you asking as a cop?"

He nodded.

"*Sí,* he was here with his friend Earl Carter. They come after work two, three nights a week."

"What time were they here tonight?"

"Right after they get off work. They have . . ." she stopped to count in her mind, "three Coors each. Then they leave." She shrugged.

"Can you pinpoint the time?"

"It was still light outside. I remember seeing the sunshine when they open the door and wishing for a window in here."

Devon nodded. "How's Raul?"

"That *cabrón.* I wish I never marry him and never come to El Paso."

"Then you wouldn't be working here," he teased, "and we would've never met, Tulles."

"You think that makes my day?" Her dark eyes flashed with fun. "I could trade him for you, then I would be telling him what a *cabrón* you are."

Tulles turned away to give one of the drunks another beer, waiting patiently while he fumbled through his pockets for money. He gave her a twenty. Going to the till, she looked at Devon, then gave the man thirteen dollars in change. Coming close again, she hissed, "See what you do! I could have made ten dollars just now."

"You made four," he smiled.

She squinted her eyes. "Do you hear him complain?"

Devon listened but heard only Marty Robbins so shook his head.

Tulles laughed. "Ay, Devon, your wife will be a lucky woman. Not like the wife of your brother. For her I feel sorry. He was here with that bitch Lucille. What you think he sees in her, eh?"

Devon shrugged.

"Don't you think she's ugly, Devon?"

"She can't hold a candle to you," he answered. "When was Connie here?"

"Earlier tonight. He left Lucille at the bar so I have to look at her face while he talked with Teddy Truxal and Earl Carter. They whisper in the corner, like men plotting murder."

Devon met her eyes. "What time was Connie with 'em?"

"Time!" she scoffed. "You gringos run by the clock. I don't know what time, but Connie no stay long. The other two stay maybe another hour, *más o menos*."

"You sure it was Connie?"

"I never forget a man I fuck. It happen long ago, but I remember every time he walk through the door what he feel like inside me. Is he fucking that Lucille now?"

"I don't know," Devon said.

Tulles laughed again. "Ay, Devon. Why else would he take her around and buy her beer, eh?"

"Maybe they were reminiscing about old times."

"Nobody comes here to do that, *hombre*. This is a place only for getting drunk. You want another beer?"

He shook his head. Marty's song ended.

Tulles mocked, "One lee-tle kiss, then goodbye bitch."

Devon gave her a smile, left the five on the bar and took the wedge of lime with him to clean the bad taste from his mouth. As he slid behind the wheel of his department-issued sedan, he had the distinctly unpleasant suspicion that the reason for Connie's absence from work today was connected to meeting Teddy Truxal inside Rosa's Cantina.

Chapter Three

He drove to headquarters in Five Points and parked his sedan in the basement garage, then took the elevator up to the detective's bullroom on the third floor. Only Carl Snyder was there. They nodded at each other but didn't speak. Sitting down behind his desk, Devon pulled his notebook out and scanned his notes. At the end he wrote: Tulles Ortiz, confirmed Teddy at Rosa's with Carter, 5-21, 5-6 p.m. He let his pen hover over the next line, knowing he should add that Connor Gray had been seen talking with Truxal and Carter during the time of Teddy's alleged alibi. If Devon included that in his report, though, two things would happen: he'd be taken off the case, and Connie would be harassed because of his record. Devon dropped his pen and leaned back in his chair, watching Carl Snyder type a report with two fingers.

Making up his mind, Devon turned on his computer, called up a blank Homicide Report, and pecked out the preliminary information, giving the date, his name and badge number, the name of the victim, address of the crime, time of his arrival on the scene, the names of the two people he'd talked with and their relation to the victim. Under the heading Further Action, he typed: verify alibis; interrogate rest of family a.m. He routed an electronic mail copy to Chief, Crimes Against Persons, Eyes Only, then saved it in his open file. Detective Snyder didn't look up as Devon left the bullpen. In the garage he signed out a sedan identical to the one he'd turned in except that it had a full tank of gas, then he drove home.

Connie's Dodge Ram was in the driveway. Devon parked behind it, allowing enough space for Connie to back out around him. The garage was reserved for Eric's black Shadow, a gift from both Connie and Devon on the kid's seventeenth birthday last year. Eric was meticulous about keeping it shiny, so the men had ceded him the garage, pretending to do it begrudgingly but both feeling pleased with Eric's pride of ownership. Last summer Devon got Eric a job with City Parks and he'd earned enough to pay his insurance for the year. The bill was due again in August. Eric would graduate from high school in June and he'd told Devon he'd find a job on his own right after that. But Devon expected to renew the policy when the time came, suspecting if he didn't, nobody would.

The house was dark when Devon let himself in the back door. Taking a beer from the refrigerator, he carried it unopened upstairs. His room was of a commodious size, with a wood floor, rows of high windows on two walls, a walk-in closet and a tiny bathroom at the end opposite the stairs. Other than the double bed graced with a brown dust ruffle and a comforter printed with a jade and brown Egyptian motif that Laura had charged at Dillard's on Devon's account, the only furniture consisted of a straight-backed chair next to the small table holding his phone and answering machine.

Devon hung his jacket in the closet, then stood in the dark working on his beer as he looked west across the neighborhood to the neon end of Mesa glowing in the distant sky. When he heard Connie coming up the stairs, he reached into the bathroom and flipped the switch to give them some light, then turned to watch his brother sidle around the corner.

"Talk to you, bro?" Connie asked.

"Sure," Devon said.

Connie dropped onto the end of the bed as Devon lifted the chair out of its corner and set it in the middle of the room. When he turned around again, he saw Connie had been looking at the gun he wore on his belt in the small of his back. He smiled at his brother as he straddled the chair.

Connie was thirty-five, a year and a half older than Devon, an inch taller and ten pounds lighter. His dark hair was tucked behind his ears to brush against his shoulders, which were bare now because he wasn't wearing a shirt, only jeans. Devon could see the front curves of the tattoos on his well-developed biceps. Though he couldn't read them from this angle, he knew the one on the right was an arrow-pierced heart bearing the name LAURA, on the left a rattlesnake coiled to strike with BORN TO LOSE underneath. That one always made Devon wince when he saw it. "What's up?" he asked.

"Eric ain't come home yet," Connie said. "Laura thinks I should go find him."

Devon glanced at his watch. "He's been out after midnight before."

"Yeah, but he's s'posed to be grounded," Connie said with a self-conscious smile.

"What for?"

"Fighting in school last week."

Devon sipped his beer. "You got any idea where to look?"

Connie shook his head.

"Who's he hanging with these days?"

"Don't know," Connie said.

"If you found him," Devon asked, "what would you do?"

"Laura wants me to whip him, but I ain't gonna."

Devon kept quiet, though the kid obviously needed some discipline.

"Dad beat the shit outta me," Connie said, "and never laid a hand on you. I think that speaks for itself."

"I felt Dad's belt more'n once," Devon said.

"Twice maybe?"

"More than that." Devon smiled. "What do *you* think Eric needs?"

"A better world."

Devon chuckled. "We could all use one of those."

"What can I say to him, Devon? Keep yourself clean so you can sweat for some rich man's profit? Or get dirty and be like me, bouncing from one shit job to another?"

"Are you bouncing again?"

Connie stared with anger in his eyes. "What'd Laura tell you?"

"Just that your boss called wondering where you were."

"I hate that job. I don't care if he cans me."

"What'll you do for money if he does?"

With a grimace of annoyance, Connie muttered, "I came up here to talk about Eric."

"Okay," Devon said. "Unlike you, he seems to be following in his father's footsteps. I don't know how to stop him any more than I did you."

"Seems you should, being a cop and all."

"We're not big on prevention."

Connie leaned back on his elbows, staring out the windows over Devon's head, though Devon knew he wasn't seeing anything but dark sky. Devon asked, "Have you told him what prison's like?"

Connie shook his head.

"Maybe you should."

"I know I should. It's just that I want him to see my good side, not listen to me bellyache about how my old man was right and I fucked up."

"The old man wasn't right," Devon said.

Connie met his eyes.

Devon shrugged. "What worked for him would've been hell for me or you. I think it was hell for him, but telling your sons to become grunts for the sake of making an honest living isn't offering much."

"What is there to offer?"

"Staying out of jail seems a good enough motivation for just about anything, even working in a copper smelter."

"That's a negative, though, see, Devon? It's saying *don't* do something, not what he *should* do."

Devon nodded. "Well, what he should do is go to school so he can get a job that isn't grunt work. Other than that it's all negatives: don't knock up your girlfriend, don't mess around with drugs, don't hang out with bad company. I guess the other side of the coin is marry a woman 'cause you want to instead of 'cause she's pregnant, keep your mind sharp 'cause you're gonna need it, and be careful choosing your friends 'cause you'll probably turn out like they do. Can't you tell him that?"

Connie's eyes softened. "Coming out of my mouth, that'd sound like don't do what I did. Why don't you tell him?"

Devon sipped his beer, then said, "He doesn't want advice from me."

"But you've made a success of yourself," Connie argued.

"Have I?" Devon scoffed. "Living with my brother's family 'cause I don't have one of my own, spending my time mopping up murders and sending people to jail for doing what I might do in their situation? That doesn't sound like anything to aim for."

Connie watched him finish his beer, then said, "You're

not living with us. We're living with you."

Devon smiled, crumpling the can. "Kind of hard to tell the difference."

"Well, hell, you could get married any day of the week."

Devon shook his head. "I have yet to see a cop's wife who's happy. More misery the world doesn't need."

With a crafty smile, Connie asked, "Who're you sticking it to these days?"

Devon grinned. "I stop by Rosa's and take Tulles into the back closet every now and then."

Connie laughed. "I hope you wear a rubber."

Devon laughed too. "Have you seen her recently?"

Connie shook his head and stood up, then moved to the window to look down at the back yard. "Goddamn," he whispered. "Eric's sitting out there smoking a cigarette. At least I hope it's tobacco." He smiled at Devon. "See you later."

Devon nodded and listened to him descending the stairs, then the back door opening. He heard his brother say with a laugh, "If it's legal, you can do that inside, Eric."

After a minute the back door closed and the house beneath Devon was silent.

Elise Truxal was the most beautiful girl Devon had ever seen. Her features were delicately chiseled, her eyes a cornflower blue, and her pale blond hair fell in silky curls nearly to her waist, small enough for a man to circle with his hands. Her legs were long in baggy jeans which didn't hide the seductive curve of her hips, and her breasts were generous beneath an equally baggy, gray tee-shirt. Her lack of makeup, like her grungy clothes, only served to heighten the allure of her rampant blossoming into womanhood.

Devon sat at the dining room table in the Truxal home,

watching her through the open kitchen door as she brought him a cup of coffee. She placed it carefully in front of him, then retreated to lean against the built-in hutch, the mirror above it reflecting the platinum gold of her hair. Devon thought Officer Malone had been dead wrong about this girl. Though her beauty was apparent, she kept her distance like someone who had already been badly hurt by men, not displaying any of the challenge Malone had found so enticing. Elise watched Devon shyly, and though he knew he was missing a chance that probably wouldn't come again, her pained vulnerability stopped him from questioning her while they were alone. She looked as tender as the opening buds of a spring plant, encouraging him to add thorns to the armor of her camouflage, not peel it away in the glare of interrogation.

"This must be a difficult time for you," he said.

She shrugged, sending a wave cascading the length of her hair, her face assuming an expression of studied indifference he suspected was habitual.

"You're an extraordinarily beautiful young woman," he offered. "Do you realize that?"

Again the shrug, as if her shoulder had an uncontrollable tic. "Sometimes," she said. "When I walk in someplace and everyone stops what they're doing to watch me. It isn't all it's cracked up to be, though."

He nodded, remembering the books he'd seen in her room, the literary novels and collections of plays, and realizing he was looking at the rare phenomena of a beauty with brains. "I can understand that someone as sensitive as you might feel uncomfortable receiving so much attention."

Her defensive edge slackened a notch. "You want something in your coffee?"

He looked down at the full, steaming cup, having forgotten it. "No, black's fine," he answered, giving her a smile. "Do you like Modigliani and Picasso because they distort feminine beauty?"

She stared at him, then sassed, "Yeah," defensive again, probably because now she knew he'd been in her room.

"They're usually a more mature taste," he said, giving her another smile. "But then I noticed you're also fond of the theater of the absurd."

"I'd like to be an actress," she conceded, "but I figure all I'd get is dumb blond roles."

"You could always dye your hair," he suggested.

She lifted a strand and studied the ends. "I've thought of it," she said, dropping the lock to bounce against her waist, "but Zane says there's no sense in destroying natural beauty."

"Who's Zane?"

"My boyfriend."

He clucked with regret. "And I was just about to ask you out."

She laughed. "You wouldn't do that."

"You're right. I wouldn't."

" 'Cause I'm a suspect, aren't I?"

He shook his head, hiding his surprise. " 'Cause you're under age."

She laughed again, then drawled with the saccharine sarcasm of a southern belle, "Well, who knows, Mr. Gray. Maybe we'll meet again in three years when I'm legal."

"I'll say my prayers," he joked, thinking maybe Officer Malone hadn't been wrong after all: she was a chameleon who changed personas as easily as shifting gears in an automatic. Her youth made him suspect she wasn't totally in control of her presentation but gave her audience what she thought he wanted. That could be dangerous in the wrong company, lethal if the man wanted a fight, and Devon caught himself wondering if her father hadn't coaxed her too far into a scene in which he erroneously believed he was writing the script. Taking his notebook out of his pocket, he asked, "What's Zane's last name?"

"Gray," she said.

He met her eyes.

"Just kidding." She laughed. "It's Kalinsky."

He smiled at her joke. "Where does he live?"

"The Sunset Apartments on Mesa."

He wrote it down and was sipping his coffee when her mother came into the room with Sunny, a nine-year-old girl with the same coloring as her sister but nowhere near the beauty. Sunny's flaxen hair was cropped into a Dutch boy that didn't flatter her plump face, which was red and pinched, though Devon didn't think it was from grief. Even though she didn't look directly at him, he could see her eyes were clear, displaying no evidence of recent tears. The rag of a blanket she held was a tattered piece of cloth that had once been yellow but was faded to beige, and she wore a robe of green velour with gold metal stars scattered across the yoke.

The mother was a combination of both girls. Long-legged and blond and wearing a housedress that matched her blue eyes, she was plump and her complexion the peaches and cream Malone had admired. Her eyes were weak and watery. Again Devon didn't credit it to tears because of her seemingly sincere smile as she herded her daughters to sit down for a discussion of murder. When they were seated around him, Elise on his left, Sunny on his right, Mrs. Truxel at the end facing him, she said gaily, "This is all of us, Detective Gray."

"Where's Anne?" he asked.

"She went back to her apartment to study. College exams, you know, don't wait for anything."

Devon was fairly certain Anne could have them postponed for the death of her father, but he didn't argue. "And Teddy?"

"Home with his wife," Mrs. Truxal chirped. "They'll be here soon."

Devon nodded. "Well, I have just a few questions to ask you, Mrs. Truxal. I hope you won't find them too upsetting."

"We're ready," she said, squaring her shoulders against the chair as if they were about to play charades.

He lifted his pen and held it over his notebook. "What time did you leave for the church retreat yesterday?"

"Five o'clock," she answered without hesitation.

"Was Mr. Truxal here when you left?"

"If I'd known he was coming, I would have waited long enough to say goodbye," she answered with no apparent sorrow that she'd lost her last chance to do that. She laughed softly. "I never knew when he was likely to show up."

"Were you separated, or did he live at his hotel just for the sake of his business?"

Mrs. Truxal blinked, appearing to Devon as if she were feigning stupidity. But that wasn't an unusual mannerism for women of her generation. Finally she said, "There was nothing wrong with our marriage, Mr. Gray."

"It was a happy one?"

"Completely," she said.

Because two of her children had denied feeling any affection for their father and Elise had merely shrugged at Devon's expression of sympathy, he suspected Mrs. Truxal's answer was the biggest lie of her life, unless that was yet to come. Gently he said, "His death must be a great loss to you then."

"God doesn't give us burdens we're incapable of carrying," she answered.

Devon nodded, though he'd seen many people undone by burdens no one could carry. He clicked the point of his pen into and out of its casing, then asked, "Where did you go when you left at five o'clock last night?"

"To the Glory Baptist Church on San Antonio. We met in the parking lot before leaving on the retreat."

"Did everyone drive their own car?"

"There was a bus, but we hadn't planned on staying the entire weekend, so we took our own car. Many others did the same."

He nodded. "What time did you arrive at the church?"

"It must have been about five-fifteen. We drove directly there."

"Did anyone see you arrive?"

"Most everyone, I imagine."

He glanced at Sunny, who was holding her blanket to her nose. Elise was staring at the table as if she weren't paying attention. "In cases like this," Devon said, laying his pen beside his notebook, "the first suspicion is that the victim was killed by a burglar surprised in the act. Have you noticed anything missing?"

"He took my silver dollars," Elise nearly whispered.

Devon looked out the window, remembering Connie's adolescent hobby of collecting old coins and feeling unhappy that the connection had come so quickly to mind.

Mrs. Truxal said, "Elise had a collection of silver dollars started by her grandfather. She has one for nearly every year going back to 1840."

Devon looked at Elise when he asked, "What did you keep the coins in?"

Slowly her blue eyes turned to him, a flicker of fear deep

in their depths, the same fear he'd often seen behind the bravado in Connie when they talked about their father. "A leather notebook specially designed for coins," Elise said, "so you could see both the front and the back."

"How big was this notebook?"

"Regular size."

"Like a school notebook? That size?"

She nodded.

"What color was it?"

"Black," she said.

He made a note. "Every year between 1840 and now?"

She shook her head. "I was missing a couple that were real expensive, and then some years they didn't mint any."

"Do you have any idea of the worth of this collection?"

"Oh, a lot," Mrs. Truxal said. "Some of those coins were worth several hundred dollars a piece. The whole collection was worth thousands, wasn't it, Elise?"

She shrugged, sending a ripple through her hair again. "I liked it 'cause it came from Grandpa."

"Where did you keep it?" Devon asked sympathetically.

"In my desk in my room," she said.

"In the drawer?"

"Yes."

"Was it locked?"

"No."

He remembered noting how neat the room had been on the night of the murder. If a burglar had taken the coins, he'd either known where to look or been extremely lucky. "Who knew you had this collection?"

Elise stared at him, an odd uneasiness behind her eyes.

"Only the family," Mrs. Truxal said.

"Did Zane know about it?" Devon asked Elise.

She nodded.

"Any of your girlfriends?"

"I don't have any girlfriends," she said.

He noted the anger in her voice. "Why not?"

"The last time I brought a girlfriend home, Daddy shamed me in front of her."

"Elise!" Mrs. Truxal reprimanded.

"How did he do that?" Devon asked softly.

"He'd asked me to run the vacuum that morning," she said. "I vacuumed the living room but didn't do the hall. He came into my room without knocking and yelled at me for not doing the hall. I told him I didn't know that was what he wanted, and he called me a lazy bitch and told me to do it right then. I did, but he kept yelling at me all the time I was doing it, calling me awful names. Later, my girlfriend said she wouldn't let anyone talk to her like that, and I asked how I was supposed to stop him. She said she just wouldn't take it, and she acted like I was stupid for taking it, so I thought I didn't need to hang out with anyone who thinks I'm stupid and I didn't speak to her again."

Devon looked at Mrs. Truxal, who laughed girlishly and said, "Well if you'd done what you were supposed to in the first place, Elise, none of that would've happened."

"Were you home at the time?" Devon asked her.

"I was at work," she said proudly. "I'm a senior clerk in the county tax assessor's office."

Devon nodded, then gave Elise a smile of commiseration. "So as far as you know, only Zane and your family knew of your coin collection?"

"Zane didn't take it," she answered.

"Probably you're right," he said gently. "But it's my job to make sure. Can you understand that?"

"I guess," she said, tossing her head as if in disbelief.

"When was the last time you looked at your coin collection?" he asked.

"Last week," she said.

"Do you think someone could've taken it between then and last night?"

"How could I know that?" she retorted.

"I didn't ask if you knew someone had," Devon answered with measured calm, "but if someone could have."

"I suppose," she said.

"Is it possible someone in your family borrowed the collection without telling you?"

"It was mine," she said. "If they took it, they stole it."

He nodded. "I'll run a check on the coin dealers in town to see if anyone's tried to sell a similar collection. Do you have a list of the coins?"

She shook her head. "It was in the book."

He nodded again, then looked at her mother. "Is that the only thing missing?"

"Yes." She smiled, as if trying hard to please.

"Do you keep any guns in the house?"

Mrs. Truxal shook her head. "I don't believe in guns, and even if I did, I wouldn't have one anywhere near children."

"That's wise," he said, though he thought not believing in guns was akin to not believing in evil, a creed which didn't affect reality. He also thought her children were old enough to understand the danger of guns, which made him wonder if either of her daughters still at home were suicidal. "Do you have any reason to think your son might have left a shotgun in the house? Maybe one he used for hunting and for some reason left here?"

"I wouldn't allow him to do that," she said.

"Who has a key to your house, Mrs. Truxal?"

"Only the family."

"You and your children?"

"Of course."

"And Mr. Truxal?"

"Yes."

"No one else?"

"Teddy gave Wanda a key. She's his wife."

He nodded. "I know this is a difficult question, Mrs. Truxal," he said softly, "but it would help if you could think of anyone who might want to kill your husband."

"I wouldn't know about that," she said.

"What do you mean?"

"He had business associates I never met. I don't know how they felt about him."

"Did he ever mention anyone being angry with him over something?"

She shook her head.

"Any other relatives in town?"

"No," she said. "We moved here from Missouri shortly after we were married. My husband was in the army then, stationed at Fort Bliss. All my family's in Missouri."

"And his family?"

"They're there too."

"Are you in touch with them?"

"We exchange Christmas cards."

"You haven't written or spoken to any of them recently?"

"No," she said.

"Had your husband?"

"No."

"Are you certain?"

"He would've told me. He told me everything."

Devon nodded, though he doubted any husband told his wife everything. "How often did you see him?"

"He came home for breakfast."

"So you saw him only in the morning?"

"He came in the evenings sometimes too, but he always came for breakfast."

"He'd leave her a tip," Elise muttered with scorn.

Devon looked at her.

"A quarter by his plate when he left," she said, her eyes sharp with ridicule.

Mrs. Truxal laughed. "My bingo money," she said.

"Did you see him at breakfast?" he asked Elise.

She shook her head. "I didn't get up till he'd gone."

He looked at Sunny. "How about you, Sunny? Did you eat breakfast with your father?"

She shook her head, still holding her blanket to her nose.

He smiled, trying to reassure her. "Was he a good father?"

She looked at Elise, which surprised him. He looked at her too, while also watching Sunny in the mirror. Sunny seemed confused by the question until Elise winked, making her giggle behind her blanket. Devon looked directly at her again.

"He was okay," Sunny said.

"Did he spank you?" he asked softly.

"He was their father," Mrs. Truxal bristled.

Devon nodded, not taking his eyes off Sunny. "When did he last spank you?"

"I don't remember," she said, hiding behind her blanket again.

"Was it a long time ago?"

She shook her head.

"Was it last week?"

"He hit me last week," she whimpered.

"For what?" he coaxed.

She dropped her blanket away from her face and looked at Elise as she said, "He told me to set the table. I was getting up to do it but he didn't think I was fast enough, so he hit me."

"Where did he hit you?"

"In my ear," she whimpered, raising a hand to cup her left ear. "It bled."

He looked at her mother. "Did you take her to the doctor?"

"It stopped bleeding right away," she said. "I can't afford to take my children to the doctor for every little thing."

He looked at the girl holding her blanket in front of her face again. "How does your ear feel now, Sunny?"

"Okay," she whispered.

"Can you hear through it as good as the other?"

She nodded.

He looked at Elise. "When was the last time he hit you?"

She shrugged.

"Did he ever hit you?"

"What are you suggesting?" Mrs. Truxal asked with a nervous smile. "All fathers discipline their children. At least good ones do."

He nodded, then looked back at Elise. "Do you think your father was a good one?"

She glared at him with hostility.

"I'm on your side, Elise," he said gently. "You can tell me the truth."

"You're not on my side," she retorted. "You're a cop trying to figure out who killed my father."

"Did you kill your father?"

"I wanted to!" she shouted. "What do you think of that?"

"Elise!" her mother whispered.

"Why did you want to?" he asked.

She met his eyes, tears glimmering on her lashes.

"Did he spank you often?" he asked softly.

"Yes," she said between clenched teeth.

"And that made you want to kill him?"

She nodded, the tears falling across her cheeks.

"That's okay, Elise," he said. "We've all felt that way about our fathers at one time or another."

Sunny whimpered, "I wanted to kill him too."

He looked at the obese little girl with the pinched red face half-hidden behind a rag of a blanket. "Did you kill your father, Sunny?" he asked with a friendly smile.

She shook her head. "Neither did Elise."

He looked at Elise. "No, I don't think she did," he said.

Elise raised her head higher, letting her tears fall unhindered as if for effect. Devon didn't like thinking that, but there was an odd light of triumph in her eyes that made him uneasy. "Tell me about the last time he spanked you, Elise."

"It was the same night he hit Sunny's ear," she said. "I'd already gone to bed and he came into my room without knocking and looked at the book I was reading. He didn't like it."

"What was it?" he asked with a sympathetic smile.

"A biography of Oscar Wilde," she said defensively.

Devon tried to pigeonhole Wilde. "He was an English playwright, wasn't he?"

She nodded. "But he was gay, and Daddy thought the book was dirty."

"So he spanked you for reading it?"

She nodded. "He tore the book up first."

Mrs. Truxal said with a gloating smile, "I would have taken it away from her myself if I'd known what was in it."

He studied her a moment, then looked back at Elise. "How did he spank you. With his hand?"

"His belt," she said, raising her head higher again.

"On your bottom?"

She nodded. "He pulled my nightgown up to do it."

"Were you wearing panties?"

"Mr. Gray!" Mrs. Truxal protested, her smile finally gone. "This isn't necessary."

"I'll be the judge of that, Mrs. Truxal," he said firmly. Then he looked back at Elise.

She shook her head.

"How many times did he hit you with his belt?"

She shrugged. "I wasn't counting."

"It lasted half an hour," Sunny whimpered from behind her blanket. "I watched the clock."

Devon looked at her, then back at Elise. "Was he hitting you that entire time?"

"He'd stop and yell a while," she said, "then he'd start up again."

"What did he say when he yelled?"

"That I was a slut," she answered bitterly. "A whore with a dirty mind, an oversexed bitch."

Devon sighed and closed his notebook, using the gesture as a stall to gather his thoughts. He was remembering the many times he'd listened to his father whip Connie, how the old man would grunt each time the belt fell, and how as the years passed Connie's cries had diminished to whimpers and then a silence loud with hatred. Pulling his thoughts back to the present, Devon recalled the open belt on Theodore Truxal's corpse. Rather than being on his way to the bathroom the night he was murdered, as Devon had originally thought, Truxal might have been unbuckling the weapon to punish his daughter. "Why don't you girls go along," Devon said, "and let me talk to your mother alone?"

They both lurched from their chairs and nearly ran from the room. Carefully he lifted his cup and sipped at the cold coffee, then he set the cup back in its saucer and met the mother's eyes. Her lips were pressed tightly together, her cheeks drained of color. Trying to keep judgment out of his voice, he said, "Most people would consider that what your husband did to his daughters went beyond parental punishment and became abuse."

"Not most people I know," she said.

In his mind he counted to ten, then asked, "Did he ever strike you?"

"All men hit their wives at one time or another."

"That's not true, Mrs. Truxal. What concerns me here is that you're teaching your daughters it's acceptable for a man to take his disappointments out on his family."

"That's what families are for," she said. "We share each other's pain *and* happiness. It's a whole package, Mr. Gray. Do you have children?"

He shook his head.

"Then you're not one to criticize, are you?"

"Maybe not," he conceded. "But it's my job to discover who killed your husband. It's not my wish to pry or to judge, but a crime has been committed. In this case, I'm an advocate for the victim, and the fact that right now I don't feel much sympathy for him doesn't change my duty."

"If you're looking for a criminal," she said, "I suggest you question the scum, not a good, church-going family."

He smiled sadly. "You'd be surprised how many criminals go to church."

"Not my church," she said.

"Mrs. Truxal," he asked, losing patience, "did your husband ever have sex with his daughters?"

"No," she whispered. Then, her voice gaining strength, "He had too much honor to do such a thing. Instead of defiling his memory, you should be catching his killer."

"That's what I'm trying to do, Mrs. Truxal."

"By making Elise admit she hated him? Do you think that will help her in the days to come? He was a hard man in many ways, but he wasn't as bad as you're implying. If he'd lived, Elise would have come to understand that what he did came out of his love for her. Someday she may still be able to understand that. But aggravating her hurt won't help her."

"I'm sorry I've upset you, Mrs. Truxal. I'm just doing my job."

"You have a callous way of going about it," she said.

"Maybe I think it was callous of you not to take your daughter to the doctor after your husband struck her in the ear so hard it bled."

"If you paid my bills, I'd listen to what you think. But since you don't, I don't care to hear it."

Devon stood up, returning his notebook and pen to the inside pocket of his jacket. "It's a shame it all comes down to money, isn't it?"

The kitchen door opened, and he turned to see Teddy walk into the house. A young woman walked in behind him, carrying a toddler. Teddy came forward, extending his hand with a cautious smile. "Detective Gray?" he said in an inquisitory tone.

Devon smiled, shaking his hand. "Is this your wife?"

"Yeah," Teddy said, half-turning toward her. "Wanda, this is Detective Gray."

"Hello," she said nervously, holding her child close. She was a pretty woman with a soft, round face marred only by the broad bridge of her nose which attested to its having been broken some years past. Her brown hair was short and worn in wispy curls, her eyes a buttery brown. "Say hello to Mr. Gray, Petey," she cooed to the child. "He's a police detective."

The child stared warily.

Devon smiled at the boy, then looked at his father. "Maybe we could meet later?"

Teddy shrugged. "When?"

"How about noon at Denny's on Mesa?"

"All right," Teddy said.

"Good," Devon said. He turned to nod at Mrs. Truxal. "I'll keep you advised of further developments."

He walked out, feeling tension follow him until he closed the door. As he descended the steps to the street, his sense of foreboding was akin to what he'd felt as a kid whenever he left his brother alone in the house with their father. Devon tried to convince himself it was only the similarity of family politics which kept bringing Connie to mind, that a mutual interest in old coins or a coincidental conversation in a cantina didn't mean anything, but the need for the argument only increased his suspicion that Connie was more than peripherally involved.

Chapter Four

He drove north on I-10, then took the turnoff to the Scenic Heights subdivision between the interstate and the mountains. A new neighborhood of modest homes, the yards were native cactus and decorative gravel. In the 3500 block of Toltec, he saw a man working under the hood of a blue Chevy pickup backed into the driveway. Devon parked his car and walked over. Flashing his badge, he said, "I'm looking for Earl Carter."

"You found him," the man said, carefully wiping his hands on a filthy red rag. Carter was in his early twenties, a heavy-set, dark man who hadn't shaved that morning, dressed in a black sweatshirt with the sleeves cut off and grimy jeans over workboots. He kept scrubbing his hands with the rag, though it seemed saturated with all the dirt its fibers could collect.

Sensing Carter's discomfort, Devon gave him a friendly smile and said, "I'm here about Teddy Truxal. Do you know him?"

Carter finally dropped the rag on the fender of his truck. "We work together."

"I'm investigating his father's murder."

"Burglar, wasn't it?" Carter asked, squinting his eyes.

"What makes you think so?"

"Stands to reason. TV news said he was home alone." He studied Devon, then asked, "You don't think so?"

"I don't know yet. When was the last time you saw Teddy?"

"Yesterday at work."

"You both get off at the same time?"

"Yeah. Four-thirty."

"That was the last you saw him?"

Carter hesitated before saying, "We had a beer after work."

"Where was that?"

"Rosa's Cantina."

"What time did you get there?"

"Quarter to five."

"How long did you stay?"

"An hour, maybe a bit more."

"See anyone else there?"

"Tulles. She's the bartender. She knows us."

"No one else?"

Carter hesitated, then said, "Teddy ran into someone he knew. Fella called Connie Gray." His eyes narrowed, connecting the names. "He a relative of yours?"

"It's a common name," Devon said. "How long was this Gray with you?"

He shrugged. "Fifteen minutes."

"What'd the three of you talk about?"

"The basketball playoffs."

Devon smiled. "Who'd you bet on?"

Carter dug a crumpled pack of Winstons from his pants pocket, took a cigarette out and pulled a book of matches from the cellophane around the pack, lit his cigarette and left the pack and matches on the fender by his rag. "It was a dollar bet among friends," he said, exhaling smoke. "Is that against the law?"

"Technically," Devon paused to smile, "but gambling's not my jurisdiction. I work Homicide."

Carter looked down as he sucked hard on his cigarette,

then he met Devon's eyes again and asked, "You checking Teddy's alibi?"

Devon nodded. "Have you known him long?"

"Just since we've been working together, 'bout a year now."

"Did you notice anything odd about him yesterday?"

Carter shook his head.

"What'd you talk about before this Connie Gray showed up?"

"The usual bullshit. Work. Family."

"What'd Teddy say about his family?"

"His wife wants a new TV they can't afford." He took a drag on his cigarette. "His kid, Petey, is starting to talk."

"Nothing about his sisters?"

Carter shook his head.

"Did you know he has sisters?"

"Guess he's mentioned it."

"Nothing sticks in your mind?"

"One of 'em goes to UTEP. The other two are still at home. That's all I know."

"What about his father?"

"He owns a dive hotel downtown."

"Did he and Teddy get along?"

"I don't know anybody likes his father much. Comes with the territory, you know?"

"Can you remember anything particular Teddy said about his father?"

Carter shook his head.

"Nothing about how he treated Teddy's sisters?"

"He didn't talk about 'em much."

"What'd he say when he did talk about them?"

Carter thought. "The oldest ones goes to UTEP like I said. The middle one's his favorite, a real beauty queen, according to him. The little one's fat, has a blankie." He dropped his cigarette and ground it out with his heel. "I don't know, man, I didn't pay much attention, you know?"

Devon nodded. "You never met any of them?"

Carter shook his head.

Devon looked toward the house, tan stucco with fake green shutters. "You married?"

"Yeah."

"Kids?"

"Two sons," he said proudly.

"Any brothers or sisters?"

"One of each."

Devon met his eyes. "If you found out your old man was fucking your sister, what would you do?"

Carter stared hard. "Was that the case with Teddy's old man?"

"I don't know. What do you think he'd do if it was?"

Carter pulled another cigarette out and tapped the end on the fender, then struck a match. Turning his head to exhale, he muttered, "I don't know the dude well enough to say."

"You've been working with him for a year, having a beer after work coupla nights a week. Does he have a temper?"

"Doesn't everyone?" Carter muttered, squinting through his smoke.

Devon nodded. "This fellow Gray. You never saw him before last night?"

"Never."

"He just happened to run into Teddy there?"

"Seemed that way."

"Any money change hands?"

"The playoffs ain't over yet."

"So that was the gist of the conversation, a bet on basketball?"

"Yeah."

"Who'd you bet on?"

"I didn't bet," Carter said, veiling his eyes. "It was just 'tween them."

"Who'd they bet on?"

"This dude Gray," Carter snickered, "bet on the Sixers."

Devon thought. "Will they make it to the playoffs?"

"Not without a miracle."

Devon smiled. "Maybe he likes long shots. Who'd Teddy bet on?"

"The Bullets."

"Not much better."

"Two losing bets if I ever heard 'em," Carter agreed. "The only thing I could figure is it was a private joke."

Devon nodded, but he didn't think it had been a joke. Sixers and bullets could both be construed to have lethal connotations, and he couldn't help wondering if they hadn't been code words closing a deal. Looking at the man who'd missed the message, Devon asked, "Does Teddy own a shotgun?"

Carter's eyes narrowed. "He hunts."

"You ever go with him?"

Carter shook his head.

"Who does?"

"I don't know."

"He told you he goes hunting but never mentioned who he went with?"

"Maybe he did." Carter took a long, slow drag on his cigarette, then said, "Maybe it was the sister's boyfriend. Zane something or other. He has a shotgun."

"How do you know?"

"Teddy said he borrowed it last winter."

"Did he mention returning it?"

"I don't remember."

"You ever meet Teddy's father?"

"Yeah, once."

"What'd you think of him?"

"I didn't like him."

"Why not?"

"Teddy and me went downtown to help his old man haul a trailer outta the parking lot of his fleabag hotel. When we got there, Teddy had the wrong kinda hitch on his truck. His old man started yelling, calling him stupid for having that kinda hitch. Teddy, he just stared at him a minute, then he stomped into the hotel to get something and we took off. Teddy said that was the last time he'd try to help his old man do anything."

"What'd he go into the hotel to get?"

Carter shrugged. "Nothing I could see."

"When did this happen?"

"April."

"April what?"

Carter thought, then smiled. "It was the third. I remember 'cause that's our anniversary and my wife was pissed off I was helping Teddy 'stead of spending the day with her."

Devon smiled. "Did she get over it?"

"Oh yeah. I made up for it that night. Dinner at a fancy restaurant and all."

Devon nodded. "Has Teddy said anything about his father since then?"

"Nothing that sticks in my mind."

Devon extended his hand, signaling that the interrogation was over. "Thanks, Earl."

Carter visibly relaxed, shaking hands, then asked, "You think Teddy killed his old man?"

"I don't think anything yet."

Carter nodded. "I'd give odds Teddy didn't do it."

"Why?"

"If my old man yelled at me the way Teddy's did, I would've flattened him. Teddy, he just got in his truck and peeled rubber outta there. That kinda anger held inside sours your gut. Me, I let it out so it'll blow over. If you don't, it festers."

"Maybe into murder?"

Carter looked at him hard. "Maybe," he finally said. "But I'd never pin Teddy for it. I've known a few dudes who crossed that line and killed someone, but it wasn't their first time fucking up, you know? They got in fights all along 'fore they crossed that line. Teddy, he turns the other cheek."

Devon nodded. "Thanks, you've been a big help." When he got back in his car and looked in the rearview mirror, Carter had disappeared, probably to call Teddy unless Devon missed his bet.

He drove south and took the downtown exit to Chihuahua Street, a dilapidated neighborhood between the bus station and the Amtrak terminal. The Cristo Rey Hotel was a five-story brick building just south of Overland. Pancho Villa had once filled the top floor with his entourage, but the decor had no doubt deteriorated since then. Now the floors were covered with linoleum and the windows with venetian blinds that didn't hang straight. Permeated with the smell of ammonia from a disinfectant detergent, the lobby was occupied by old men who looked as if they'd lost every battle as well as the war. A large screen TV was vibrant with color, tuned to a Mexican soap opera though the men watching were Anglo. No one was behind the desk.

Devon rang the bell, noting that not one of the old men reacted to the sound, which explained how they could watch a TV show broadcast in a language they didn't understand. Half the action in Mexican soap operas took place in bedrooms, and Devon guessed the men translated the stories into private memories of women they'd left behind. He was watching the actress begging her lover not to leave her alone again—Devon's Spanish was good enough to understand that much though he missed why the lover felt so impelled to leave—when a whiff of perfume caught him unawares. Its musky scent matched the sultry beauty of the actress, and for a second he wondered if Mexican TV had surpassed American technology. Then he turned around and saw a woman watching him from behind the desk.

She was in her early thirties, plump and pretty though her eyes were red from crying. He showed her his badge and introduced himself. "Come this way, please," she whispered, indicating with a graceful lift of her hand for him to meet her in the hall.

Turning into the dark corridor, he felt as if he were entering a brothel, though he guessed that was a remnant of the soap opera's bedroom scene mingled with the woman's perfume. She opened a door and gestured for him to come into the office. It was small and cluttered, though clean.

"Please sit down," she said. "You have come about Señor Truxal, no?"

"Yes," he said, taking a seat on one end of the worn, brown leather sofa.

"I was his housekeeper," she said, fresh tears in her eyes. "What is it you wish to know?"

"Why don't you sit down?" he suggested kindly.

She sat at the other end of the sofa, leaned over her knees and held her face in her hands as she cried. Devon watched her, feeling relief to finally see someone shed tears. He didn't think he would have liked Theodore Truxal, but that someone cared enough to mourn the man's passing helped Devon remember it was his job to avenge the victim. Each muffled sob from his housekeeper strengthened Devon's resolve. When she eventually stopped crying, wiped her eyes and blew her nose, then looked at him, he gave her an encouraging smile.

"I'm sorry," she sniffled. "He was a good man."

Devon nodded. "Had you worked for him long?"

"Three years," she said. Then with surprising honesty, "We lived as man and wife."

Devon guessed that probably meant she wasn't paid a salary, though he immediately chided himself for his cynicism in the face of her evident love. "I'm sorry for your loss," he said.

She sighed deeply. "What is it you need to know, señor?"

He took his notebook from his pocket. "Can I have your name?" She looked frightened, so he quickly put it back and said, "I have nothing to do with *la migra,* señora."

She studied him a long moment, then said, "Alejandra Guerrero." She smiled sadly. "Ted called me Alex."

He nodded. "How did you hear of his death?"

"I hear on the news on TV this morning."

He winced. "That must have been a shock."

Suppressing fresh tears, she whispered, "His wife is very sad, no? And his *niños,* his children?"

"Yes," he lied. "Can you tell me, Señora Guerrero, if there was anyone here in the hotel, or someone connected to his business in another way, who might have wanted to kill him?"

She shook her head. "He was a good boss, good to the men who live here. He was kind to everyone, and often he played checkers with the old men in the lobby. He gave them each a bottle of wine for Christmas, and a free Thanksgiving dinner too, turkey and pie and everything. Every year he did that. This hotel is not a fancy place, but we keep it clean, and for the old men who live here, it is their home. He would always say that if not for the grace of God, he would be one of them, and he wanted to make it nice for them here. Many times he picked up homeless young men off the street and brought them here, gave them a bath and a bed for the night. Many times he did that. He was a good man, señor."

Devon nodded. "Did you ever see him drunk?"

She snorted delicately. "He was a man," she said.

Devon smiled. "Was he a happy drunk?"

"No, he was sad. *Muy triste,* very sad."

"Did you ever see him angry?"

"What person can live life without feeling anger?"

"Nobody," he said. "Did he ever get violent when he was angry and drunk?"

"No," she said. "Sometimes he would yell at the old men, when one of them peed in the hall or something like that. But he would only yell, that is all. The men who do that can't help it. They lose control sometimes, on their way to the *baño.* Ted knew that, but sometimes he was impatient with them. Ask any of the men, they will tell you the same: he was good to them." She gave him another sad smile. "If you ask, though, you will have to shout. Most of them are deaf. Even when you are not angry, you have to yell at them."

Devon stood up. "Well, thank you, Señora Guerrero. You've made my job easier."

"Why is that?" she asked, puzzled.

He didn't tell her the truth, he simply said, "I can eliminate you and the old men as suspects."

She shook her head. "These men have no strength to hurt anyone. And I loved him."

He nodded, starting for the door.

"Señor?" she petitioned.

He turned back to look at her still sitting forlornly alone on the sofa.

"What will happen to the hotel now? Will his family sell it?"

"I don't know," Devon said.

"He promised to take care of me," she said. "Did he leave that he said so in writing?"

"I don't know," Devon said again. He took his notebook out of his pocket and wrote down the name of an attorney specializing in the rights of illegal aliens. "Go see this man," he said, tearing the page out and giving it to her. "He's an *abogado.* He'll help you."

"Gracias," she whispered.

"De nada," Devon said, thinking it was truly next to nothing he'd given her.

He walked out past the old men watching the same actor being petitioned for mercy from another beautiful actress. Back in his car, he drove north again and took the Resler exit off the freeway to Mesa. A mile further north, he pulled into the Sunset Apartments, three two-story buildings in a horseshoe around a central rectangle of thick foliage. The name Kalinsky was on the first mailbox, but when he got to the door of Apartment 1, there was a scrawled note saying the manager was at the pool. Devon knocked, thinking Zane might be inside alone. When he didn't get an answer, he walked toward the garden surrounding the pool.

A kid maybe sixteen, wearing jeans without a shirt, was vacuuming the pool. He was tall and rangy, with a good tan and curly red hair. As Devon walked through the gate, the kid stopped work and watched him approach with solemn, brown eyes.

Devon flashed his badge and asked, raising his voice over the whine of the vacuum, "Are you Zane Kalinsky?"

The kid nodded.

"I'm here about Elise's father," Devon said.

Zane went back to work, carefully dragging the vacuum nozzle along a straight line at the bottom of the pool.

Following him away from the noise of the machine, Devon said, "He was killed last night."

"Couldn't have happened to a nicer guy," Zane muttered.

"You hear it on the news?"

He shook his head. "Elise told me this morning." He walked away again, maneuvering the vacuum.

Devon followed him. "Did she call you?"

"No, she was here," Zane said, his eyes on his work.

"What time?"

"About an hour ago."

"Was she crying?"

Zane turned around and studied him without rancor, then continued his work, walking away again. Devon watched him, thinking the kid had an edge he hadn't seen before on anyone so young. It was neither the tough-guy pretense common among gang members, nor the chip often seen on abused kids. Zane's was different, a quiet calm in the center of himself that seemed to keep the world from affecting him much. Devon could understand why Elise would find him attractive; his calm could be a still point in the chaos of her world. He waited until Zane had finished the job and turned off the vacuum; then they met each other's eyes across the sudden quiet. "Let's go inside," Zane said.

Devon followed him back to Apartment 1. Zane pulled a crowded keyring out of his pocket and unlocked the door, walking in first and leaving it open behind him. As Devon stepped in and closed the door, Zane disappeared into another room. The apartment was furnished cheaply, the painting on the wall a machine-manufactured desert scene of saguaros. Zane came back in less than a minute pulling a blue tee-shirt over his head. He ran a hand through his hair to straighten it, then nodded at two stools in front of the breakfast bar dividing the kitchen from the living room. "Have a seat," he said.

Devon sat down. Zane walked into the kitchen and took a cup out of the drainboard. "Coffee?"

"Thanks," Devon said.

Zane took another cup from the cabinet, filled them both from a pot on the burner of a Mr. Coffee, slid Devon's cup toward him and stood leaning against the refrigerator sipping at his own. "Elise told me you'd be coming," he said.

"In reference to what?" Devon asked.

Zane shrugged. "She said you wrote down my name."

"Are you sleeping with her?" Devon asked.

Zane sipped his coffee before saying, "That's none of your business."

"Murder makes everything connected to it my business," Devon answered.

Zane took another swallow of coffee, set the cup down and crossed his arms over his chest. "Yeah," he said.

"How long has it been going on?"

"Since the end of last year."

"Do you love her?"

Zane dropped his lashes to hide his eyes as he nodded.

"Did she talk to you about her father?"

"Some," Zane said.

"What'd she say?"

"That he lost control when he was drunk."

"Did it happen often?"

"I don't think the man was ever sober."

"Did he rape her?"

Zane stared a moment before saying softly, "She said no."

"But you think he did?"

Again he hesitated. "I know he hurt her a lot."

"Spanked her, you mean."

Zane made a sound of disgust in his throat. "Beat her with his belt 'cause she's pretty."

"Why would that make him beat her?"

"He knew she wasn't a virgin."

"Did she tell him?"

Zane shook his head.

"Did he catch you together?"

Again he shook his head.

"How'd he know then?"

"He checked," Zane said.

"What do you mean?"

"Stuck his finger up her to find out."

Devon tried to conjure an image of that happening, but he couldn't make it jell into any semblance of paternal concern. "She tell you that?"

Zane nodded. "She said he told her it was the same as giving her an enema when she was a kid, but it wasn't hardly the same, was it?"

"No," Devon said. "How'd you feel when she told you?"

"Pissed off."

"What'd you do about it?"

"Nothing. It happened before I met her."

"She wasn't a virgin when you met her?"

Zane shook his head.

"How many other boys has she been with?"

"I never asked."

Devon looked over his shoulder, trying to gather his thoughts. "Where are your parents?"

"They live in Fabens."

He looked back at the kid. "You live here alone and manage these apartments by yourself?"

"I've been doing it since I was fourteen."

"How old are you now?"

"Sixteen."

Devon was beginning to understand why the kid seemed so mature. "Where'd you meet Elise?"

"In school."

"Coronado High?"

Zane nodded.

"Are you a good student?"

"I might be, if I wasn't always falling asleep in class."

Devon nodded. "Play football?"

The kid shook his head. "I don't have time for that."

"Being a kid, you mean?"

Zane shrugged.

Devon pulled his notebook out, opened it on the counter and flipped through the pages, pretending to look for a notation that in reality he hadn't bothered to write down. "I understand you loaned Teddy a shotgun."

"That's right," Zane said.

"Did you get it back?"

Zane nodded.

"When?"

"Coupla weeks after he borrowed it."

"When was that?"

"Like you said, last winter."

"Did I say that?"

Zane flinched. "That's when it happened, whether you said it or not."

"Do you still have it?"

"In the bedroom."

"Can I see it?"

Zane hesitated, then walked in and came back carrying a double-barreled Remington. When he handed it over, Devon opened the breech and sniffed the chamber, smelling the fresh powder indicating it had been recently fired. "You mind if I take this with me?"

"What for?" Zane asked, shifting his weight from one leg onto the other.

"Theodore Truxal was killed with a shotgun."

Zane looked at the gun. "Not that one."

"Ballistics can prove it, one way or the other," Devon lied, knowing shot pellets were impervious to analysis, so all ballistics could prove was the gun had been recently fired, something he already knew.

"I didn't do it," Zane said.

Devon closed the breech and laid the gun on the counter, watching the kid. "Protecting Elise from further abuse would be an understandable motive."

Zane kept quiet.

"Where were you," Devon asked, "between five and six last night?"

"Here," Zane said.

"Alone?"

He nodded.

"Anyone see you, talk to you on the phone?"

Zane shook his head.

"What kind of vehicle do you own?"

"An '89 Dakota longbed."

Devon wrote it down. "Color?"

"White."

"License?"

"1623QU."

"Texas?"

"Yeah."

"Ever been in trouble with the police?"

"No."

"Before this morning, when did you last see Elise?"

"Friday in school."

"Didn't see her after school?"

Zane shook his head.

"Did you know her father beat her last week?"

A tremor of sadness washed across the kid's face. He walked back into the kitchen, picked up his cup and rinsed it under the faucet, set it in the drainboard, then leaned against the refrigerator again. "She told me," he said.

"Did that make you mad?"

"Wasn't anything I could do about it."

"You could have killed him so he couldn't do it again."

Zane stared at him, but there was no anger in his eyes, no fear of being trapped, only a profound sorrow. "I could have," he said, "but I didn't."

"Who did?"

Zane shook his head.

"Elise?"

Zane looked down, studying the floor as he said, "I've thought of that." He raised his eyes. "But I don't think, if she did, she could keep from telling me."

"What she'd say when she told you it happened?"

Zane shrugged. "Just that someone shot her old man."

"Those were her words? Someone shot my old man?"

Zane nodded.

"Was she crying?"

He shook his head.

"Did she sound glad?"

"Scared."

"For herself?"

"Yeah, but only 'cause she wanted him dead. Now that he is, she feels it's partly her fault for wanting it. But that doesn't mean she did it."

Devon nodded. "Could Teddy have done it?"

"I don't think so."

"Why not?"

Zane grimaced with one side of his face. "He doesn't like killing things."

"You mean, when you went hunting together, he didn't kill anything?"

Zane shook his head. "He just liked walking through the country, you know. Being out there in the quiet."

"Did you kill animals?"

"I've bagged a few deer."

"When was the last time you fired this gun?"

"Not since before I loaned it to Teddy."

"And he gave it back last winter?"

"Maybe it was spring. I don't really remember."

"But you're sure it was quite a while ago?"

Zane nodded.

"Does anyone else have a key to your apartment?"

"Elise does."

"Don't your parents?"

"Sure, but I haven't seen them since Christmas."

Devon put his notebook and pen away, then stood up holding the gun in his left hand. "Do you have any objection to my taking this gun to the lab?"

Zane shook his head.

"Just one more question," Devon said. "Do you smoke?"

"No," Zane said.

"Does Elise?"

"She never has with me."

"Okay," Devon said, extending his hand. "Thanks for talking to me."

Zane shook his hand, looking as if he wanted to say more.

"Anything else you want to tell me?" Devon asked.

Zane smiled with chagrin. "I thought for a minute you were gonna arrest me."

"If having a motive for murder was proof of guilt," Devon smiled back, "we'd all be in jail."

Zane laughed.

"I'll be in touch," Devon said.

"I'll be here," the kid answered.

Devon walked around to the carports and saw the Dakota parked in the space reserved for Apartment 1. The license was the same as Zane had told him, the hood cold. In the next stall was a '92 Taurus. Devon wrote down the license of the Ford, then walked back to his sedan, caught the Resler ramp onto the freeway and drove southeast toward Five Points. He numbed his mind to anything but maneuvering through traffic at high speed, enjoying the nip and tuck of physical motion. At headquarters, he entered the shotgun into ballistics, wrote a request for the men on the beat to check coin dealers for anyone selling a collection similar to Elise's, then left again, driving west on Montana.

Waiting for a light to change, Devon let himself think about Zane Kalinsky. He liked the kid and was hoping ballistics could somehow prove Zane's gun hadn't been the murder weapon. But Devon could understand how Elise could motivate a man to murder, and it was all too easy to picture Zane, with his calm demeanor, pulling the trigger without a second's hesitation. Devon could even figure the scenario: Elise hadn't gone on the church retreat, she'd stayed home and entertained Zane in her bedroom. Her father, parking in the garage and walking through the back yard, had heard the unmistakable sounds of sex from behind Elise's window. He'd walked down the hall unbuckling his belt in anticipation of inflicting punishment for what he maybe thought was masturbation. But the couple in the bedroom heard him coming. When her father opened the door to Zane's gun, he'd taken a few steps back before Zane pulled the trigger. If Teddy hadn't returned the shotgun but had left it with Elise, it all could have been an unfortunate chain of circumstances leading to the fatal moment.

If Zane drove Elise to the church parking lot before the group left for the retreat, it's possible nobody would have noticed she hadn't arrived with her mother. Or maybe someone had noticed, because Devon hadn't questioned any of them yet. But he couldn't help thinking, if that scenario was how it happened, why Zane wouldn't have invented a reason for having recently fired his gun and concocted an alibi. He was a smart kid who would've anticipated being questioned.

If Zane hadn't been the one to pull the trigger, he might agree to lie about when the gun was returned. But even being asked to do that should have alerted him to its being the murder weapon. Devon's other supposition was that someone had used Elise's key to either take and return or merely return Zane's gun. Why had they returned it? They could have simply reported it missing, which would lend credence to the surprised burglar theory. That hadn't happened. Someone had taken the gun back, knowing it would point the finger at Zane. Did that someone assume Zane had an alibi? Or not care that a kid took the fall for a murder he didn't do? If that someone was Teddy, and he'd killed his father to shield his sister, framing her boyfriend didn't seem the logical next step to protecting her.

But if that someone was a stranger who'd been hired to commit murder, he wouldn't likely care for the finer points of the sister's sensibilities. Maybe he knew Zane had a shotgun and that Elise had a key to his apartment, so he got hold of the key, slipped in while Zane was out, took the gun, used it, and put it back. It was convoluted but possible. If he knew Elise, he could have copied the key without her knowing. If she was sleeping with someone besides Zane, for instance. That someone would have access to her purse.

Certainly her brother did. Teddy could have copied the key without her knowing, given it to the hired killer, sacrificing Zane, maybe thinking Elise was too young to have a lover anyway, and if her lover was sent to prison for killing her father, maybe Teddy would see that as a step toward keeping his sister in line. It was hard to say what religious people could accommodate as being right. Elise's mother accepted as parental punishment acts Devon considered brutality.

But for any of this to be feasible required believing the murder had been premeditated, and there was something about the victim's unbuckled belt which smacked of impulse. He had been walking down the hall, not on his way to the bathroom, as Devon originally thought, but on his way to punishing his daughter, and someone stopped him. Eliminating Teddy for the sake of argument, Devon hadn't for a minute suspected Anne. Under the circumstances, it would have been too easy for her to simply leave the scene and let someone else find the body. He couldn't believe either Mrs. Truxal or Sunny was capable of committing the murder,

Mrs. Truxal because her religion taught her to submit to her husband, Sunny because she seemed too wimpy to strike back even when it was justified.

He felt differently about Elise. That gleam of triumph in her eyes when he said he didn't believe she'd done it continued to nag him. Still in all, murder wasn't generally a woman's crime, so his instincts pointed to Teddy. Earl Carter had said Teddy was too passive to cross that line, but Devon suspected he might. And maybe, if it hadn't been Devon's brother making that suspiciously phony bet on the playoffs with Teddy, Devon could admit that what had been happening in Rosa's Cantina was a contract for murder.

Chapter Five

When Devon walked into Denny's, Teddy Truxal was sitting in a booth in the non-smoking section. He stood up when Devon approached, and they shook hands, assessing each other warily.

"So what have you found out?" Teddy asked as soon as they sat down.

"Not much," Devon answered, turning his cup over for the waitress coming with the coffeepot.

"Would you like to see a menu?" she asked.

"Just bring me a burger and fries," Devon smiled.

"How about you?" she asked as she refilled Teddy's cup.

"Nothing, thanks," he answered.

Devon watched Teddy tear open a packet of half-and-half and pour it into his coffee then stir it with a spoon until it was uniformly muddied. "Your alibi checks out," Devon said.

Teddy's pale blue eyes flashed with relief. Then they glittered with scorn as he asked, "Did you really think I'd kill my own father?"

"It's been known to happen," Devon said.

Teddy looked at the traffic on Mesa backed up behind the light, then returned his gaze to Devon and waited.

"The preliminary coroner's report said your father died between five and five-thirty yesterday afternoon. Cause of death was both barrels of a shotgun fired into his chest from not more than six feet away."

Teddy dropped his gaze to stare into his coffee.

Devon sipped his, then said, "I understand you borrowed a shotgun from Zane Kalinsky a few months ago."

Teddy met his eyes with new worry. "I thought I was in the clear 'cause of my alibi."

Devon nodded, thinking Teddy was having a hard time believing it, which to Devon's mind meant he was guilty of something. "When did you return the gun?" he asked.

"Coupla weeks after I borrowed it," Teddy answered.

"When was that?" Devon asked patiently.

"Sometime in March."

"Do you think Zane could have killed your father?"

Teddy stared at him a long time before saying, "Zane's only a kid."

"Kids commit murder."

"He didn't do it."

"Are you sure?"

"How'd he get in the house? And why would he want to when Elise wasn't home?"

"Maybe she was entertaining him in her bedroom," Devon suggested, "and your father interrupted them."

An odd combustion of emotions flared behind Teddy's eyes. Devon read them as both guilt and fear, but Teddy answered earnestly, "Elise was with my mother."

"Are you certain?"

"My mother doesn't lie."

"Okay," Devon said, "Elise was with your mother, but whoever used that shotgun was standing in the door to her room, and the only thing reported missing is her coin collection. There's probably a causal relationship between those two facts. Who outside the family knew about the coins?"

Teddy shook his head, his eyes ablaze with guilt.

"Zane did," Devon pointed out. "And since her room wasn't messed up, whoever took them didn't have to do any looking."

"So you think Zane broke in to steal her coin collection?" Teddy scoffed.

"There's no evidence anyone broke in," Devon said. "Maybe he has a key. Elise has one to his apartment."

Teddy looked unhappily surprised. "Did she tell you that?"

"No, he did."

When Teddy looked out the window again, Devon wondered why he felt it necessary to avert his eyes now. A brother's concern over his sister having sex wasn't anything to hide, unless Devon was reading everything wrong. "How'd you feel about her sleeping with Zane?" he asked.

Teddy shrugged, the nonchalance of his gesture belied by the anger in his eyes. "She's always been willful."

"Is he her first boyfriend?"

Teddy shook his head, looking out the window again.

"Was your father molesting her?"

Teddy jerked back to stare at him hard. "No," he said.

"You sure?"

"My father had a lot of faults, but he wasn't a pervert."

Devon sipped his coffee, then asked softly, "Did you know he was sleeping with his housekeeper?"

"Are you gonna tell my mother that?" Teddy asked testily.

"I'm not trying to malign your father, Teddy, but I'm getting a pretty complex picture of the man. That's not unusual. Most people are complex. But with your father, the reports I'm getting contradict each other."

"What do you mean?"

"Well, your mother seems to think he was a good parent, that the punishment he dealt was justified and reasonable. From what I've heard, I wouldn't call it that and I don't think too many other people would either. Both Earl Carter and Zane Kalinsky think he was a sonofabitch." He watched Teddy's eyes flare with anger even though he'd used that word himself to describe his father. "On the other hand," Devon said, "his housekeeper told me he was a good boss and generous to his tenants, that he enjoyed playing checkers with the old men, gave them Thanksgiving dinner and bought each of them a Christmas present. She admitted he sometimes lost patience with them but said he was never violent." Devon paused, then said, "It seems only his family saw his dark side."

"You think we killed him?" Teddy asked point blank.

It was a question only the most crafty killer would ask of the investigating detective, and Devon didn't put Teddy in that category. "I haven't reached any conclusions yet," he said.

They stared at each other until the waitress brought Devon's lunch. Then Teddy stood up. "I'll leave you to eat," he said.

Devon looked at him, not walking away but waiting to be dismissed. "Can I have a few more minutes of your time?"

Reluctantly, Teddy sat back down.

"Just a couple more questions," Devon said, lifting the top bun off his burger and laying the tomato and lettuce on the meat, then covering them with the bun. He licked tomato juice off his finger, watching Teddy, then asked, "Do you know Connie Gray?"

Teddy's eyes changed, flattening behind a sheen of what could have been hatred. "Is he a relative of yours?"

"Just answer the question, Teddy."

"Yeah, I know him."

"Ever do business with him?"

Teddy shook his head without much conviction.

Devon cast his fly into the rapids. "When you made that

lame bet on the playoffs last night at Rosa's, weren't you really closing a deal?"

"To do what?" Teddy asked under his breath.

Devon smiled. "Must've been something illegal."

"It wasn't."

"What was it then?"

Teddy tried to laugh. "You're fishing."

"Why don't you tell me what I caught?"

Teddy was silent.

"If it's anything short of murder," Devon said, "I'll cut the line and let it go."

"Take my word for it," Teddy said between clenched teeth.

"Can't do that. If you don't tell me now, the next time I ask will be in front of a stenographer at police headquarters."

"Then I'll have a lawyer," Teddy said, jerking to his feet. Lowering his voice, he muttered, "If you want to talk to me or anyone in my family again, bring a warrant."

"All right," Devon said. He watched Teddy walk away, then reached for the shaker and salted his fries, letting this new information tumble through his mind without allowing himself to invest too much hope in believing that whatever Connie had agreed to do for Teddy Truxal might have been legal.

The waitress came over and cleared Teddy's cup and the empty half-and-half cartons off the table. "Your friend didn't pay his bill," she said. "You picking up his tab?"

Devon turned around and looked out the far window in time to see Teddy nose his brown Ford Ranger into the traffic. "Guess I am," he said, smiling at the waitress.

She smiled too, leaving two checks on the table before walking away. As Devon lifted his hamburger and began to eat, he told himself the simplest thing would be to ask Connie flat-out what he'd agreed to do for Teddy Truxal. But Connie had already lied about being at Rosa's last night, and rather than backing him into lying again, Devon wanted to clear him of suspicion without ever letting on that he'd been under it, so the fragile friendship growing between them could continue.

When Connie first came back to El Paso, he had refused to move in with Devon despite Laura's argument that the large house in a good neighborhood was better for the kids than any apartment they could afford. The night Connie agreed to do it, he and Devon had sat on the front porch drinking beer together for the first time since before Connie went to prison. Out of the blue, Connie said, "The old man always liked you more'n me."

Devon took a while to consider his answer. Finally he said, "We spent more time together, is all."

"Why do you think that was?" Connie asked.

"You shut us both out," Devon smiled, "so we were stuck with each other."

Connie laughed. "You were too young to run with me, bro."

Devon shook his head. "I was part of what you were running from." He swished the dregs of beer around in his can. "Dad was the big part, but maybe just 'cause I listened to him you figured I was on his side. I guess the fact that I did listen made it look that way. But it was a choice I made early on, to try and patch our family together rather than tear it further apart. You acted like you wanted to rip Dad's guts open and make him spit blood. And you did that pretty well. Dad bled a lot over you."

"Aw, I was just an excuse for him to yell about something."

"He cried when you went to prison."

"Dad did?"

Devon nodded. "Sitting right there in his old rocker. Said he was glad Mom hadn't lived to see it. Then he said maybe if she'd lived longer, you wouldn't have gone so wrong. He blamed himself, but I never thought it was his fault."

"You think I was born bad?" Connie taunted half-playfully.

"No." Devon smiled. "You needed a lot of freedom to stretch out in, and that's hard to come by for a kid growing up in a city. About the only way he can find it is to break the law."

Connie laughed, flattered, then grunted thoughtfully. "Which lands him in jail."

Devon nodded. "Dad said you'd caught yourself in a trap that would never open again. Partly 'cause of Laura and Eric, 'cause taking care of them would make it even harder when you got out and found it tough to get a job. He expected you to abandon them, fall into old habits, and bounce right back in again."

"I proved him wrong on that one," Connie muttered, then drained his beer.

"He'd be glad you have," Devon said.

"I don't know. Ever since the first time I got in trouble, he was always yelling that I'd end up in prison. I think he liked being proved right."

"You're not in prison now."

"No, but I'm scrabbling for a job just like he said I would. And don't think the idea of abandoning Laura and the kids hasn't crossed my mind. The thing of it is," he smiled with chagrin, "I'd miss 'em."

Devon laughed. "Well there's plenty of room here, Connie. And Dad already paid the rent."

"You haven't taken out another mortgage?"

Devon shook his head. "The taxes run about two hundred a month, the utilities another hundred all told. I could move into your old room upstairs. Downstairs, you'd be the patriarch. Everything you thought Dad did wrong, you could redo and change the memories in these old walls."

Connie looked behind himself, through the open door into the dark house, then at the shadows on the empty porch. "What'd you do with his rocker?"

Devon finished his beer before answering. "Right after Dad died, I'd sit out here sharing a bottle of whiskey with the stars, and sometimes I swear I could hear his rocker scritching on the floor like it did when he was mad. He never did approve of drinking, you know."

Connie chuckled. "Oh, yeah."

"Well, one night, after I'd finished a bottle of Old Crow, I thought I saw his cigarette arc through the dark. Remember how he used to flip his butts into the street?"

"Yeah," Connie said.

"Well, that did it. I carried the rocker into the back yard and burnt the fucker."

"Sonofabitch," Connie whispered.

Devon laughed, standing up. "You want another beer?"

"Yeah," Connie mumbled.

When Devon came out of the kitchen with a cold can in each hand, Connie was standing in the living room looking into the dark hall. "You ever hear him around anymore?" he whispered.

Devon smiled, handing him a beer. "Not a scritch."

"Well, hell," Connie said. "Maybe I'll put Eric in your room so he grows up a law-abiding citizen, put Misty in Mom's sewing room so she grows up to be a good wife, and bang Laura in the old man's bed every night. What d'ya think of that?"

"I think you better change the bed," Devon answered. "I used it a coupla times and the springs are loud enough to wake the dead."

"I'll definitely change it then," Connie said.

After lunch, Devon went back to his office and called the Cloudcroft police, asking for Officer Malone. When he came on the line, Devon asked him to drive out to the Baptist camp and ask the minister if the Truxal family had arrived at the church parking lot together and if the minister noticed anything peculiar about any of them. Malone sounded so eager to do it, Devon suspected there wasn't much criminal activity in Cloudcroft. After he hung up, he briefly contemplated working in a small town, twiddling his thumbs at his desk while waiting for someone to break the law. He decided that proposition was even more collusive than working a big city where the bad guys didn't need any encouragement.

He called the emergency investigations clerk in the Division of Motor Vehicles and ran a make on the Ford Taurus parked next to Zane Kalinsky's Dakota at the Sunset Apartments. It was registered to a Benjamin Escalante. Devon found Escalante's number in the phone book. Identifying himself, Devon apologized for not coming in person but said he was under the wire in his investigation and would like to ask Escalante a few questions. Guardedly, Escalante told him to go ahead. Devon said he was investigating a traffic accident involving a white '89 Dakota pickup. He wondered if Escalante had noticed whether or not Zane Kalinsky's truck was in its parking space last night between five and six. Escalante said it had been there when he got home from work at five-fifteen, was there when he went out again at five-thirty, and there when he got home about six.

Other than that, he couldn't say. Devon assured him the information meant Zane hadn't been involved in the hit and run, thanked him, and hung up.

Then he called patrol and asked if anyone was checking the coin dealers in town. Told Bruce Corbett had been assigned the duty, Devon walked downstairs and left a message in Corbett's mailbox asking that the information be relayed to his home number. While he was on the second floor, he stopped in the coffee room and bought a cup out of the machine. Carl Snyder was alone in the room, eating his lunch. Devon smiled with commiseration as he carried his cup over and sat down. "Brown-bagging it these days, Carl?"

Carl nodded glumly, chewing a bite of his tuna sandwich. He swallowed, then said, "Daughter's wedding," as if those two words explained it all.

"Saw you working late last night," Devon said.

"Another drive-by." Carl shrugged. "Damn *cholos* yelled out the name of their gang 'fore they opened fire on a party. Put two kids in the hospital who'll be heroes to their own gang when they get out. We picked up the shooters an hour later, cruising around drunk with the guns still in their car. They'll be heroes too, but they won't be going home anytime soon."

Devon shook his head. "Helluva way to start life."

"Sixteen and seventeen, the shooters," Carl said. "Their lives are over." He dug into his lunch bag. "Want a cookie?"

"Sure." Devon took one from the baggie Carl proffered. It was homemade oatmeal. "Good," he said around his first bite.

"My wife makes 'em. You coming to Nita's wedding?"

"Wouldn't miss it," Devon smiled, "after witnessing your sacrifice."

Carl grunted. "You were smart not to get married and

have kids. This wedding's costing as much as a new car. I'd rather give Nita the car. Probably last longer'n the marriage."

Devon laughed.

"How's your case shaping up?" Carl asked.

"Looks like patricide," Devon said.

"A mercy killing, you mean," Carl said.

Devon laughed again. "Wait'll you see Nita standing at the altar. You'll think better of fatherhood then."

"No, I'll be thinking how much that damn dress cost." He crumpled his empty bag into a ball and threw it in the trashcan by the door. "Dreyfus was looking for you earlier."

"Guess I better see him," Devon said, standing up.

"Heigh-ho, Silver." Carl laughed, opening his thermos to pour himself another cup of coffee.

When Devon walked into the bullpen, he saw Lieutenant Dreyfus in conversation with Detective Garcia at the far end of the room. Dreyfus glared at Devon, communicating unhappiness with his scant report, but just then Devon's phone rang. The call was from Malone.

Malone said the minister thought the Truxal family had arrived at the church together, though he couldn't be certain as the parking lot was crowded and he hadn't spoken with Mrs. Truxal until just before they left. He didn't notice anything unusual about any of the family. "Said Elise seemed unhappy," Malone added, "but that she always does. He called her a wayward child who resisted her mother's efforts to bring her into the fold." Malone snickered. "I would've bet money on that."

"Did you talk to anyone else out there?" Devon asked.

"Uh-uh. You want me to go back and question 'em all?"

"No thanks," Devon said. "If I find it necessary, I'll do it when they come home."

"I did notice something odd," Malone said with the air of a man who wanted to chat.

"What?" Devon asked.

"The minister didn't know the old man was dead."

Devon didn't say anything.

"Doesn't it strike you odd," Malone asked, "that Mrs. Truxal didn't tell him the reason she had to leave?"

"Yeah," Devon said.

"Seems to me," Malone gloated, "her minister's the first person she'd tell about such a tragedy hitting her family."

"Yeah," Devon said again.

"She just told him she had to go home. He was real surprised to learn the reason."

"Anything else?" Devon asked.

"He said Elise has been in trouble before."

"Before what?"

"I don't know," Malone answered with surprise. "Makes it sound like she's in it again, doesn't it?"

"Did he mention any specifics?"

"No, he didn't," Malone said, his voice expressing regret that he hadn't thought to pursue it.

"Thanks for your help," Devon said. "Call me if I can return the favor."

"Maybe next time I'm down your way, we'll share some brews."

"Let me know when you're in town," Devon said, certain he could manage to be busy that night. When he hung up, he looked for Dreyfus, but the lieutenant was gone.

Devon turned on his monitor and typed in a general info request for anyone named Truxal. He was given a short selection of first names, two of which were Theodore and Elise. He chose Theodore and was given a list of four citations for DWI. The third one resulted in sentencing to traffic school; the fourth got him thirty days in the county jail plus a fine of one thousand dollars. It was dated two months ago, which meant Theodore Truxal had been out of jail only three weeks when he was murdered. Devon wondered why no one had mentioned that.

When he requested the info on Elise, the screen showed a missing person report filed in August of last year. She'd been categorized a runaway, then in October she'd been arrested for soliciting in Los Angeles, California, and returned home. So at the age of fourteen, Elise Truxal had tried her hand at prostitution. That she'd been working the streets proved her naiveté. With her looks, she could have been a high-class callgirl protected by a madam and earning more in an evening than Devon made in a week. He cleared his screen and turned off his monitor, then left before Lieutenant Dreyfus could nab him in the halls.

Devon drove downtown to the county lockup. He checked the records for Truxal's cell assignment, then requested permission to go inside and talk to the officer in charge of that block. His name was Antonio Najera, a big-bellied veteran who'd once been on his way up through the ranks but because of his own DWI's had been demoted to the jail, where his continued drinking had kept him for the last twenty years. "Yeah, I remember him," Najera answered Devon's opening inquiry.

"What was he like?" Devon asked.

"Madder'n piss when he first come in." Najera laughed. "Is he coming back?"

Devon shook his head. "He's in the morgue."

"Ay, *chingada,*" Najera whispered. "Who killed him?"

Devon smiled. "That's what I'm trying to figure out."

Najera laughed again. "It could've been any of his other cellmates. Nobody liked him."

"Did he make trouble?"

"Not so bad he earned discipline. But he was always complaining, yelling that he didn't belong with the other maggots. I told him, if he wasn't a maggot, he wouldn't be here, no?"

"Was there anyone in particular he fought with?"

"He didn't fight. After a few days, he settled down."

"But you said his other cellmates didn't like him."

"They didn't. He thought he was better'n them, so they harassed him. You know how it is, trip him when he's mopping the floor. Shit like that. They cursed him up one side and down the other, but only because he thought he was better'n them."

"Was he?"

"Hell, no. He owned some dump hotel downtown. Big deal. A slum landlord's no better'n the slum."

"So there wasn't anyone in particular that might've acted on a grudge when he got out?"

Najera shook his head. "There was one maggot he made friends with."

"Who was that?"

"*Chingada* name of Elvis Short. I remember 'cause of his name. Elvis, no? We called him the King of Maggots." Najera laughed.

"What was he in for?"

"Same thing: DWI. Except when they picked him up, he was holding some gold coins they traced to a robbery in Juárez. They couldn't pin nothing on him for that, though, so he got thirty days just for the DWI."

Devon nodded then held out his hand. "Thanks, Tony."

"Anytime, *hombre*. You tell my boss how I helped you, eh? Maybe he'll get me out of this maggot pit."

"I'll tell him," Devon called back, walking out.

At the records office, he found the home address of Elvis Short. It was near the border and Devon didn't think there was much chance Short would still be there, but he drove by on the off-chance. The neighborhood was one of the oldest in El Paso, built in the bowels of what had been the brothel district before Prohibition finally closed the Tenderloin. Short's address was in a low building with narrow doors facing a dusty courtyard. Through the dirty window, Devon could see the apartment was empty.

He knocked on the next door. After a moment it was opened by a woman who looked old and seasoned enough to have worked in one of the neighborhood brothels back in the Teens. She still wore an excessive amount of makeup and he could see the toes of frayed gold slippers poking out from under her fuzzy pink bathrobe. When he showed her his badge and introduced himself, she retreated a step deeper into her shadowed apartment. Enticing her with reassurances that he meant no harm, he discovered she didn't speak English. Mincing through the conversation in his gringo Spanish, which only peripherally matched the gutter colloquialisms sprayed from the mouth of a degenerate with ill-fitting dentures, he managed to decipher from her torrent of words that Short had moved out right after being released from jail, announcing to anyone who'd listen that he was moving to San Antonio. Devon thanked her and left. He was almost back on the street when a boy eight or nine years old came running after him.

"Oye, policia," he hissed.

Devon turned around and looked at the kid who wore a supercilious smirk beneath a shock of black hair falling into his metallic eyes.

"You wish to know where is Elvis?" the kid teased.

"Do you know?" Devon asked.

"Maybe, for a dollar, maybe I tell you."

Devon gave the kid a dollar.

"He moved to San Antonio all right," the kid laughed, "but not the city, the street. He's living in a room above the pawn shop on the corner of San Antonio and Ochoa."

"Thanks," Devon said.

"For another dollar, I tell you something else."

Devon studied him, thinking the kid was probably lying. "Tell me first, then I'll decide if it's worth another dollar."

The kid looked around as if an advisor were lurking in the shadows of the building behind them. He took a step closer and whispered, "He is a fence."

"How do you know that?" Devon asked.

"Hombre." The kid grinned. "A dollar only buys so much."

Devon smiled. "Yeah, and I already feel cheated."

The kid laughed before he turned tail and ran. Devon watched him disappear, then looked around. The building could have been deserted for the emptiness of the windows opening onto the dismal courtyard. He walked back to his car and drove to the corner of Ochoa and San Antonio. The store was called Sun City Coins and advertised in large letters painted on the front window that it paid cash for anything of value, but cruising by, Devon saw a closed sign hung in the door. He drove to the bottom of Santa Fe Street and walked into the Tampico. Sipping a beer at the bar, he knew everyone in the room had pinned him for a cop. Devon wondered what it would feel like to move through the world without being considered an enemy by half its inhabitants.

At five-thirty, Devon was parked at the curb in front of the public library on Oregon Street. The uniformed guard, a woman with jet-black hair worn in a rooster's comb, was opening the door for person after person leaving work for the day. Samantha Sawyer was almost the last one out.

Wearing a soft brown skirt over low-heeled shoes and her auburn hair curling against the shoulders of her yellow blouse, she hesitated just outside the door, looking for him in a moment of hope. When she saw him, her eyes shone with love and he chuckled deep in his throat, then leaned across and opened the passenger door. She half-ran to slide in with her arms already reaching to pull him close in a hug. Burying his face in the perfume of her hair, he listened to her laugh. Their public kiss was discreet, though they briefly touched tongues in hungry anticipation of the private pleasures ahead.

She closed the door as he checked the rearview mirror for traffic; then he pulled away from the curb, crossing Franklin to turn right on Main, then again on Santa Fe and up the hill to her apartment in Sunset Heights. They were barely inside before they came together in a desperate embrace, as if it had been years instead of days since they'd last seen each other. She unbuttoned his shirt as he unbuttoned her blouse while they walked toward the bedroom. Shedding their clothes, they fell naked on her bed and lost themselves in a coupling so frantic any observer would have thought their love was forbidden by propriety. But they were both single and it was only their passion which drove them.

In the fading light of dusk, they disengaged and met each other's eyes as separate entities again. They exchanged a smile of mutual self-amusement, then Samantha rolled away and reassembled her librarian's distance from reality while Devon resumed the weight of a cop's knowledge.

"So how've you been?" Samantha asked, giggling at the tardiness of their pleasantries.

"Can't complain," he answered. "You?"

She met his eyes, hers a honied brown. "I could but I won't," she said.

He leaned over her belly, kissing the softness fragrant with sex. "Where do you want to go to dinner?" he asked between kisses.

"Let's eat in," she said.

"Order a pizza again?" he teased, sitting up to meet her eyes.

She nodded.

"Why won't you let me take you to dinner?"

"I don't like being out with you," she answered.

"Ashamed to be seen with a cop?" he joked, though he suspected she was, being an ex-hippie.

She shook her head, reaching up to trace the curve of his ear. "You're different out," she said. "Watching the world all the time. I like it better when you only have eyes for me."

He cast an appreciative gaze over her slender body. "So do I," he said.

"Devon?" she whispered.

He kissed her to stop her next words, covered her again and they made love again, this time more slowly, delicately and deliciously, until they lay in the dark breathing with contentment. "What?" he asked in answer to her earlier inquiry.

"What do you want on your pizza?" she asked.

"Jalapeños," he teased, getting up and heading for the bathroom. "Onions and anchovies." He knew she hated all of those, and that she knew it was his way of telling her she wouldn't like what she wanted if she got it.

"Peppers and mushrooms," she said just before he turned on the shower.

When she joined him, having phoned in the order, he

was already finished but he stood in a steamy corner watching her wash. She lifted her face out of the spray and blinked water from her lashes as she smiled at him. "You're beautiful," he said.

"No I'm not," she scoffed, turning off the water. "Have you ever seen a truly beautiful woman?"

"Besides you?"

She laughed. "Yes."

"I saw one today," he said as he reached for a towel.

She wiped the mirror clear with her palm then met his eyes in the reflection.

"I'm investigating her father's murder," he said.

Samantha smiled sadly. "I don't know how you stand it."

"What?" he asked, draping the towel across her shoulders as he kissed her neck.

"Seeing beauty and death all mixed together."

He met her eyes in the mirror. "Isn't that what life is?"

"That's the way it is in stories. I thought real life was supposed to be tawdry and banal."

"That's 'cause you read too many books." He walked into the bedroom and turned on the light, looking up in time to watch her enclose her body in a green velvet robe. It reminded him of Sunny's robe, though Samantha's tied with a sash and was missing the gold metal stars on her breasts. She turned back to the mirror to comb her hair as he stepped into his trousers, the belt heavy with the revolver in back. He buckled the belt as he walked into her living room. Standing by the sofa, he picked up her phone and punched in his home number.

She came out while he was waiting to hear his messages. Watching her open the refrigerator to get him a beer and herself a Diet Coke, he listened to Lieutenant Dreyfus say with heavy sarcasm that the preliminary report on the

Truxal case was a bit sketchy and he expected a remedy before Monday morning. Samantha walked toward him opening his beer while he listened to the lab tech in ballistics tell him Zane's shotgun had been fired within the time parameters of the murder. She set the beer on the table as he heard Officer Corbett say a coin collection matching the right description had been sold to Sun City Coins at eight o'clock the night before by a man with BORN TO LOSE tattooed on his left biceps. The dealer said he'd paid twenty-four hundred for the collection, and had given the seller an 1888 silver dollar to start a new one. Samantha walked away as Devon listened to Laura say, "I'm calling you from downstairs, Devon. Connie lost his job. His boss just called me. But I haven't seen Connie all day. Do you have any idea where he is? Wherever it is, he's got Eric with him. I think they've left me." She sobbed. "I know you'll check your messages, Devon. Please come home when you do."

After that he heard a beep indicating the tape thereafter was blank.

He hung up the phone, sank onto the sofa and held his head in his hands.

Samantha came over and sat beside him. "What?" she whispered, running her hand up the knobs of his spine, her fingertips warm against his bare skin.

He raised his head, made a steeple of his fingers and pressed it against his mouth, sighing deeply. Then he dropped his hands and looked at her. "I have to go home," he said.

She nodded, taking her hand back.

He stood up and dug into his pocket for money, peeling a twenty off the folded bills and tossing it onto the coffee table next to his beer. "For the pizza," he said.

"I don't give a damn about the pizza, Devon," she said.

He went into the bedroom and finished dressing, then stood in the door, watching her where she still sat on the sofa, looking forlorn in her green velvet robe. "This is my life, Sam," he said gently. "If it bothers you now, do you really think you'd like it better if we were married?"

She lifted her head and gave him a smile as she met his eyes. "If we were married," she said, "at least when you went home, I'd be the one who was there." She shook her hair back out of her eyes. "Besides, I've never mentioned marriage."

He smiled. "It's one of those things that don't need to be said."

"You're cheating," she accused. "Asking me how I'd feel before you risk making the offer."

"You're right," he conceded. "I withdraw the question."

"You're good at withdrawing, Devon."

He remembered her passion from a short time before, when he'd been doing the opposite. Remembered too the sanctuary he found in those wordless moments of their togetherness. Then he thought of his brother with BORN TO LOSE tattooed on his arm, and of his nephew right now somewhere in the dark city following the lead of a man who had so little faith in his future, and unconsciously Devon looked at the door.

"Go on," Samantha sighed.

"Can I call you tomorrow?" he asked, already on his way out.

"From all the evidence," she answered, "you can do anything you want." She stood up and swept the twenty off the table, catching him as he opened the door and sliding the money into the breast pocket of his jacket. "If I was a whore," she said, "I wouldn't be so cheap."

"Jesus, Samantha, why do you say such a thing?"

"Yeah, well, when you come only to fuck me then drop twenty dollars on your way out, it kinda comes to mind, you know?"

He heard footsteps ascending the stairs and turned to see the pizza delivery boy walking toward them. Meeting her eyes, he smiled and said, "At least I didn't make you eat jalapeños."

She laughed.

"When this case is closed," he promised, "I'll take time just for us."

"Seems to me I've heard that before," she said.

"Peppers and mushrooms?" the pizza boy asked.

Devon took the twenty from his pocket and gave it to him. "Keep the change," he said, accepting the pizza.

"Thanks!" the boy gulped, hurrying away.

Devon handed the pizza to Samantha with a rueful smile. "Maybe we'll go to Mexico," he said. "Have you ever seen Acapulco?"

She held the pizza box like a platter waiting for his head. "I've heard it's where rich Mexicans take their mistresses on holiday," she quipped.

"For Mexicans it's a family resort," he countered. "It's where they go for Christmas."

"That gives you seven months," she said.

"Maybe we'll make it for Halloween," he teased.

"How about the Fourth of July?" she said acidly.

"Acapulco's hot in July."

"So's El Paso," she said.

He turned away and looked over the balcony into the deep shadows of foliage in the patio beneath him, trying to think of a pleasant ending to their repartee. But before he could come up with a parting remark, she closed the door.

Chapter Six

Laura was sitting on the wall of the porch when he parked in the empty driveway. He opened the garage door and saw Eric's car was inside, then closed it again and met Laura's eyes as he walked up the steps. She looked away when he stood close behind her.

"You still haven't heard from them?" he asked.

She shook her head, and he saw tears on her cheeks in the light from the street. The house behind them was dark.

"Where's Misty?"

"Out," she said.

"Studying with Arnette again?"

She looked up at him. "You amaze me. I mean, you heard the girl's name once. What is it, etched in your mind or something?"

He shrugged. "It's my job to remember details."

She nodded. "You hungry? I've got a whole pot of chile going to waste."

"Did you and Connie fight recently?"

"I haven't seen him long enough to fight," she said.

He sighed. "Yeah, I'm hungry."

"Thank God," she half-laughed. "If it wasn't for you, I'd swear I was dead." She stood up, looking at him from so near. "Don't you ever get hungry for something besides food, Devon?"

"Don't, Laura," he whispered.

"Why not? I feed you and do your laundry and change the sheets on your bed. You pay my rent and buy my groceries. Why not go all the way in this exchange of services?"

"You're my brother's wife," he said.

"What good does it do me when he never comes home?"

"He was home last night," he said.

"He didn't come into my room."

"When was the last time you saw Eric?"

"Yesterday. They were both gone when I got up this morning."

Devon remembered listening to Connie tell Eric to bring it inside if it was legal, then hearing the door close. He had assumed they came in. Now he wondered if maybe Connie hadn't joined his son in whatever he was doing outside. Devon moved to open the screen door for Laura.

"And a gentleman too," she quipped, brushing past him to walk into the dark house.

He stayed at the door until she turned on the light in the kitchen, then he followed her. Watching her take a large, stainless steel pot from the refrigerator, he asked, "Is there any beer in there?"

"I always keep beer for you, Devon." She smiled, putting the pot on the stove and reaching back inside for a Budweiser. "You know Connie drank Coors," she said, opening the can and handing it over, "when he bought his own."

Devon sipped at the beer. "Why was he fired?"

"He was fired this time for not showing up. Last time it was 'cause he punched out a customer. The time before that he got caught pilfering from the till. I had to beg his boss not to call the cops." She laughed bitterly. "I was afraid if he did, you'd be the one to answer the call."

"I only work homicide," he said.

"Yeah, well, who knows? Maybe Connie'll kill somebody just so you get to be the one who arrests him."

Uncomfortably, Devon said, "You make it sound like that's what he's aiming for."

She kept quiet as she turned away to light the burner under the chile.

He walked back through the living room to stare out through the screen door as he worked at the beer. Behind him, the dining room light came on and he turned around to watch Laura setting the table for him to eat alone. She was barefoot, wearing tight jeans and a snug black T-shirt flaunting a figure any man would feel proud to see on his wife.

She looked up and gave him a sad smile. "You know how pathetic this feels?"

He nodded.

She leaned against the table, bowing her head so her long dark hair hid her face as she cried. Reluctantly he walked toward her, set his beer on the table and took her in his arms, holding her close. "Shhh," he whispered into the perfume of her hair. It was a more flowery scent than the herbal fragrance Samantha wore, but the affection he felt was mingled with the same knowledge that he was letting her down, withholding what she wanted for different reasons but achieving the same disappointment. Laura raised her face and kissed him, her lips trembling against his.

"Don't," he murmured, not moving away.

She kissed him again, more deeply.

"We can't," he whispered, withdrawing mere inches. He heard again Samantha's accusation that he was good at withdrawing, but he couldn't force himself to do it now. Laura's need was too great.

"Please," she whimpered. "Please want me, Devon."

Remembering the open door and how they were standing in the light, clearly visible to anyone on the street, he took hold of her shoulders and met her eyes. "What if Connie came home right now?"

"He won't," she argued.

"Or Misty? You want her to see this?"

She shook her head. "Nobody ever comes home but you."

He pulled her close again, aching with hurt for her. "It wouldn't be right, Laura."

She sobbed, her body slackening with defeat. "I gotta stir the chile," she said, breaking free and walking away.

He sat down over the empty plate, staring through the open door to the darkness outside. In the kitchen, Laura turned on the radio and he heard Randy Travis singing, "When my phone doesn't ring, is that you not calling?" He heard her stir the chile and bang the spoon against the side of the pan; then she came to stand in the open door, giving him a wistful smile.

"I guess that's why I love you," she said, "because you're so good."

"I love you too, Laura," he answered.

"But not that way."

"You're my brother's wife," he said again.

She laughed sadly. "I remember when I was first dating Connie. You were such a quiet kid, I thought you'd never measure up to his flash but would always live in his shadow, envying him for having me. Oh yeah, I thought I was hot shit back then. If I could've seen the future, me and you in this moment, I wouldn't have believed it."

"I did envy him for having you."

"But you don't anymore?"

He shook his head. "Not because of you, though. I just don't envy Connie anything."

"He's fucked up all around, hasn't he."

"Looks like he's on the edge of doing that."

"What do you mean?" she asked suspiciously.

He kept quiet.

"Devon?" she asked. "If you had cause to arrest him, would you do it?"

He studied her. "Do you think I have cause?"

She stared back, then whispered, "You think you might, don't you."

He looked at his beer, beyond reach.

She walked over, picked it up and set it down in the middle of his empty plate. "This case you're working on. Is Connie involved?"

"Maybe," Devon said, meeting her eyes.

"Jesus," she whispered. "What're you gonna do, Devon?"

He didn't answer.

"You gonna arrest him for murder?"

"I don't know that he did it."

"But you think he might have?"

He didn't answer, looking into the dark beyond the door.

"Poor Devon," she said, tucking a strand of hair behind his ear. "Do you think you could let him go?"

"I'd try," he said.

She nodded. "It wouldn't work. You know that, don't you? You could save him and he'd do it again. Pull you into his game and get you sent to prison too. You know what happens to cops in prison. Even that wouldn't satisfy him. He'd just keep right on till he was in there with you, then he'd watch it happening till one or both of you were dead. Do you believe that, Devon?"

"No."

"Of course not. If you did, his game wouldn't work. All he's ever wanted is to make you be like him."

"It won't happen," he said.

"If he's committed this murder you're investigating now, he's already won. Whatever you do, you've lost."

"Maybe he didn't."

She knelt by his chair. "Take yourself off the case, Devon. Don't let him be Abel to your Cain when it's the other way around."

"Maybe he didn't do it," he said again. "Another detective, looking at his record, might not try hard enough to clear him."

She stood up, turning her back to lean against the table and stare at the wall in front of her. Finally she asked, "Did Cain or Abel have a wife?"

"I don't know," he said.

"I'm sure they did," she said, " 'cause I know just how she felt."

In the kitchen, a man on the radio said, "A storm's moving in from the south, folks. If you're out after midnight, expect to get wet."

Devon drove Rim Road across the foot of the Franklins to the east side of town. Traversing the edge of the mountains, he looked down on the city spreading for miles into the desert. Development on the other side was cut off by New Mexico to the north and west, and Mexico to the south, but the east side of El Paso sprawled in an uncontained flat expanse of dark neighborhoods traversed with neon strips of commerce. He turned south on Alabama into Manhattan Heights, an older neighborhood snuggled up against the mountains, then turned left on Copper. In front of a modest bungalow, he parked at the curb behind an Impala with a mismatched front fender.

A low light burned in the living room of the bungalow as Devon walked up the cracked sidewalk. Knowing the doorbell didn't work, he knocked on the wooden frame of the torn screen door. The peephole opened and from the dim shadows a man grunted, then the door swung open. Devon could smell the fragrance of marijuana as he smiled at Tom Halprin.

Tom had slicked back dark hair and stoned black eyes. He was wearing a maroon T-shirt over jeans and huaraches. Squinting warily, he asked, "You here in your official capacity?"

Devon shook his head.

"Come on in, I guess," Tom said, unlatching the screen and turning away.

Devon followed him, letting the screen bounce against his fingertips then closing the heavy door behind himself. The living room was small with a high ceiling harboring a congestion of smoke. The TV was on to a boxing match with the blue MUTE in the corner, and the cushions were indented in the middle of the sofa as if Tom had been sitting in the same place for several hours. On the coffee table were half a dozen beer cans, an overflowing ashtray next to a pack of Marlboro's, a white pack of Zig-Zag rolling papers and a small yellow bowl of marijuana. As Tom sat down, he picked up the TV schedule and laid it on top of the bowl.

Devon pretended he hadn't seen Tom cover his stash. Choosing an overstuffed chair to the left of the sofa, he said, "I'm looking for Connie."

Tom watched him a minute. "Want a beer?"

"Sure."

Tom went into the kitchen and opened an old refrigerator just inside the door. The interior light illuminated the opposite counter and sink, cluttered with dirty dishes and the trash of take-out food. From the collection of pizza boxes and styrofoam cartons, it looked like a week's accumulation. Tom came back carrying two cans of Coors. He handed one to Devon, then opened the other and took a long drink, watching him.

Devon popped the top of the can, took a sip, and set the beer on the coffeetable. Absently watching the fight on TV—two Mexicans, the referee and spectators Mexican, a Juárez channel no doubt—Devon heard Tom sit down.

"He was here earlier," Tom said.

"What time?" Devon asked, dragging his eyes off the screen as if with regret.

"Middle of the afternoon."

"Was Eric with him?"

Tom nodded.

"Did he mention where he was going?"

"Said he was heading down to Cancun." Tom laughed, lighting a cigarette. "Was gonna stay in a fancy hotel, drink margaritas on the beach, and buy Eric his first whore."

Devon leaned back and watched the new smoke curl into the old.

"I figure that was bullshit, though," Tom said.

Devon looked at him.

"When Eric went to the can," Tom said, tapping his cigarette ash into the already full ashtray, "Connie asked if he could borrow a five-spot off me."

"Were you able to loan it to him?"

"Yeah, business has been good lately." He squinted through the smoke. "This is a social call, right? Anything I say won't be used against me?"

"I'm just a man trying to help his brother," Devon said.

Tom nodded. "Laura pissed off?"

"She's worried. Hasn't seen him since yesterday."

"Yeah, he told me he spent last night with Lucille."

"Didn't she marry Rick Ladrone?"

"He's a trucker, out of town a lot."

Devon looked at the screen and watched the fighter in white taking it hard. After a minute he looked back at Tom and asked, "Is Connie in trouble?"

Tom's eyes squinted shut even more. He took a hungry drag on his cigarette, exhaled through his nose, took another drag then stubbed the cigarette out in the smothering mountain of ashes and butts. "Lost his job," he muttered. "Did you know that?"

Devon nodded.

"Guess it's hard," Tom said with sympathy, "changing tires all day when he sees me, living soft without a boss."

Devon let his gaze wander the filthy room, suspecting Tom only left it to make a pickup; opening the door ten or fifteen times a day to let a customer in, sharing the taste, then pocketing tax-free cash before opening the door to let the customer out. Devon didn't know what Tom did with his money, but he wouldn't call spending all day inside this smoky room living soft. He heard Tom's lighter ignite, brightening the room in a brief flash, then turned to watch him sucking on a fresh cigarette. "Think he might be at Lucille's?"

Tom shook his head. "Rick was due back today."

"Laura thinks Connie's left her."

Tom nodded. "I figured the same, on account of Eric. Connie's never brought him here before."

Devon looked at the yellow bowl half-hidden under the newspaper, then met Tom's eyes.

"It wasn't the kid's first," Tom said. "He rolled it like a pro."

"Dealing to minors will double your sentence."

"I don't!" Tom said, his voice sharp. "Am I gonna regret letting you in?"

Devon looked at the screen in time to see the fighter in white knock the other guy down. "All I'm doing here," he said, not looking at Tom, "is trying to keep Connie out of jail."

Beneath his breath, Tom muttered, "He said he got caught in what he thought was a sweet deal turning sour."

Devon met his eyes.

"I don't know the details, man," Tom said. "But he was worried he'd stuck a toe under your door and had it slammed on his foot."

"Meaning?" Devon asked, though he caught the implications.

Tom shrugged. "I figure he was running a side bet that should've let him squeak through unnoticed, but someone in the game got knocked off the board." Tom exhaled a jet of smoke from his nostrils. "When he found out what he was into, he tried to slide the daddy checker your way but you pushed it back so he kept the kid with him."

Devon looked at the screen. The fighter in black was on his feet again, pummeling his opponent hard. The guy in white went down for the count. Tom clicked the TV off, darkening the room. Devon picked up his beer and swallowed half of what was left.

"He ain't going far on fifty bucks," Tom said.

Devon finished his beer, then crumpled the can in his fist.

Softly Tom asked, "If it falls that way, you gonna bust him?"

"I don't know," Devon said.

Tom snorted. "Life's a bitch, ain't she?"

Devon lay the crumpled can on the table next to the yellow bowl.

"Course I've seen this coming for years," Tom said. "Me

and Connie were cellmates in Huntsville when he got the news you'd graduated from the academy. Know what he said about it?"

Devon shook his head.

"The game's on." Tom snickered. "It took a while, but he finally got into your arena, didn't he."

"He's skirting the ropes," Devon said.

"You oughta take yourself off the case. Let someone else drop the axe."

"I'm afraid they'll drop it on the wrong man just 'cause he fits the profile."

"So you're gonna cut him slack even though it fits him like a birthday suit?"

"As long as I can."

"Then what? Tighten the noose when he walks into it, or keep it so loose he skates on through?"

"I'm hoping I don't have to do either one," Devon said.

"Yeah, well, I'm hoping for a Mazzaratti for Christmas. But I don't think I'll get it."

Lucille Ladrone lived in an old adobe on Fort Avenue. Inside the commodious structure, she ran a print shop specializing in the sort of flyers people found under their windshields when they parked at the mall. Her house had a portal along the front, its white-washed colonnade gleaming in the light from the streetlamps under a darkening sky. Devon parked at the curb and crossed the front yard to ring the bell. A man opened it, wearing only jeans. His belly, furred with a thick mat of dark hair, hung over his belt. Above his massive shoulders covered with tattoos, his face was benighted with a scowl.

Devon flashed his badge. "Is Lucille Ladrone here?"

She came into view behind her husband, her eyes widening as she recognized Devon. Quickly shaking her head in an entreaty that he not acknowledge their acquaintance, he complied by asking with polite formality, "Mrs. Ladrone?"

"Yeah," she said, the fear in her voice real.

"Can we talk privately?"

"What's this about?" her husband demanded.

Devon met his eyes. "Your wife did some work for a coin dealer we're investigating. I need to ask her some questions."

"At ten o'clock at night?" Ladrone growled. "Can't you come back tomorrow?"

"No, I can't," Devon said.

"I'll talk to him, Rick," she said, brushing past him to join Devon on the portal. She led him a few steps toward the street, then stopped with her back to her husband, who was watching from the door.

Softly Devon said, "I'm looking for Connie."

She nodded. "He told me you'd be around."

Devon studied her. She wore her curly black hair pulled back by a red ribbon tied in a floppy bow above her bangs, a young style that clashed with the deep creases in her fat cheeks, though given her natural unattractiveness the ribbon was a relief. "What'd he say?"

"That it was just a matter of time 'fore you connected him to those coins."

He watched her lick spit from the corner of her mouth, then he asked, "Did he tell you the deal?"

She shook her head. "But he told me he ain't going home till he finds out which way you're gonna fall."

"How deep is he?"

"Up to his neck, which he thinks you're gonna stretch." She licked her lips again. "Except they use lethal injection these days, don't they."

"Are you saying he pulled the trigger?"

"Connie's too smart to tell me that. Smarter'n you, is the joke of it. When he came asking your help, why'd you bellyache about how tough it is to be a cop? You don't know tough from shit, Devon. I've been in the slammer, you know that, but believe me, what women go through's nothing compared to what happens in men's units. The guards carry whips, and every single person in there's got a poker to make his point. Nobody comes out a better man, I don't care if they do call it the Department of Corrections. You pin this rap on Connie and you'll be doing him a favor to ask for the death penalty."

He watched her lick spit off her lips again. "Do you know where he is?"

"I wouldn't tell you if I did."

"I'm trying to help him, Lucille."

"Yeah? You gonna let him slide if you can prove he did it?"

"Maybe he didn't."

"Connie don't run scared from nothing."

"Is he scared?"

She nodded. "So's his kid. Jesus, Devon, when he asked you to take over with Eric, didn't it even cross your mind he was up a crick without a paddle?"

Devon shook his head.

She nodded again. When the screen door opened behind her, she raised her voice and asked with sarcasm, "Is there anything else you want to know, Detective Gray?"

He shook his head and walked back to his car, got in and drove around the corner, then parked again. Folding his arms on the steering wheel, he hid his face in their dark, trying to block the pain enough to let him think. If he could find Connie and get the story straight, it wouldn't be too hard to steer the investigation away from him. Devon was the only one pushing the connection. Teddy Truxal sure didn't want to talk about it.

So maybe he could concentrate on the family. Tell the lieutenant it looked like revenge against an abusive father but there wasn't enough evidence to ask the grand jury to indict. Close the case and bury it. Connie's name hadn't been written down yet. Officer Corbett had reported only that the man selling the coins had BORN TO LOSE tattooed on his arm. There must be a hundred men with that tattoo in El Paso. Without fingerprints, it was impossible to trace guilt through the shotgun, so the question of when Zane's gun had been returned was moot. The principal suspects all had an alibi. Anne's hadn't been verified but Devon was sure it would check out. If he didn't question the Baptists about when they first saw Elise prior to leaving for the retreat, he could accept Mrs. Truxal's word that her younger daughters were with her. He didn't quite believe Teddy's alibi, but all he had to write in his report was that both Tulles and Earl Carter backed it up. That left an unknown burglar as the next likely suspect, the same man who'd sold the coins.

Except burglars didn't carry shotguns. Why had Zane lied about when it had been returned? Why was it returned? If it'd been found with the corpse, no one would have questioned that the burglar grabbed it when he was surprised then left it behind. No thief would run through the streets carrying a murder weapon that couldn't be traced to him. The gun had been returned to implicate Zane, which meant whoever returned it was trying to protect someone else. If Elise used the gun to kill her father, it was conceivable Zane would lie to protect her, setting himself up in the name of love. But if that was how it happened, who used the coins to pay Connie to do what?

Maybe nothing. Maybe reporting the theft of the coins was only an afterthought. Teddy could have taken the coins at an earlier date and given them to Connie to sell with no inkling the old man was about to die. Connie sold the coins at eight o'clock that night, probably not knowing they were connected to a murder. If he had known, he would've got someone else to sell them. At least he would've hidden his tattoo. After the old man was killed, Teddy used the coins to divert Devon's attention away from the family. Elise had been the one to tell Devon they were missing, but from all indications, no one in that family made a move without consulting Teddy. So it all came back to the victim's children, and the coins were only camouflage.

Connie hadn't pulled the trigger, hadn't even been in the house. He was running scared for the same reason Devon was, because Connie was the obvious viper in the nest of a good, church-going family. But there was another snake in that nest, one that looked innocent though its fangs had struck the lethal blow. For the sake of his brother, Devon had to find the snake who didn't wear a rattle.

The storm hit as Devon parked in his empty driveway. Upstairs in his room, the wind belted the rain against the windows in gusts between quiet lulls that ended abruptly.

He lay in his bed staring at the shadows moving on the ceiling as the wind buffeted the trees between him and the streetlamp, trying to figure where Connie could be. Lucille was the only old girlfriend Devon knew of, Tom the friend Connie would most likely confide in. Among the other half million people in El Paso, he could be anywhere. Fifty dollars would go farther in Juárez, so it'd make sense if he scooted across the river, keeping himself close enough to buy the El Paso papers to stay abreast of the case.

Devon heard soft footsteps climbing the stairs, then a gentle knock and Misty's voice calling, "Uncle Devon?"

"Come on in, Misty," he answered, turning on his side to watch her slip through the door.

She closed it behind herself and stood in the dancing shadows, her white nightgown luminous in the dark. The flounced hem fell only to the middle of her thighs, and with her diminutive body just beginning to bud breasts and her cap of dark curls around her thirteen-year-old face, she looked like a waif.

Devon smiled. "What's up?"

"Can I get under the covers with you?" she asked, taking a few steps closer.

"I don't think you should," he said with regret.

"You used to let me," she argued.

"You were younger," he answered. "And I always knew when you were coming, so I wore pajamas."

"Only bottoms," she teased, moving to stand next to his bed.

"I'm not wearing anything now."

She lifted the covers and slid under them. "I'll stay over here," she said.

Deciding his best tactic would be to hurry her departure, he asked again, "What's up?"

"Do you know where Daddy is?"

"No, I don't."

"Is Eric with him?"

"Yeah."

"Mom was crying when I got home."

He nodded. "Where were you?"

"With Arnette."

"Doing what?"

"Just hanging out."

"At her house?"

She shook her head. "Is Daddy coming back?"

"Sure."

She watched him, her dark eyes sporadically catching light as the wind moved the trees. "Is he in trouble again?"

"Not that I know of."

"You'd know if he was, wouldn't you, being a cop?"

"Probably."

She sighed, looking at the ceiling. "It's nice up here, with the rain on the windows."

"You shouldn't be here, though," he said.

"I know," she said, meeting his eyes. "But I feel closer to you than anyone, Uncle Devon." She hesitated, then said, "Sometimes I think maybe I'm your daughter 'stead of his." She gave him a hopeful smile. "Am I?"

"No, but you're my favorite niece."

"I'm your only niece!"

He smiled. "That's true."

"How come you never got married?"

"Don't say never. I'm not too old to do it yet."

"You're thirty-three," she said. "Mom and Daddy were only eighteen when they got married."

He didn't say anything, waiting.

"Arnette said maybe you're gay, but I told her I'd never heard anything so dense. You're not, are you, Uncle Devon?"

"No," he said.

"Do you have a girlfriend?"

"Yeah."

"What's her name?"

He hesitated, then decided Misty wasn't likely to go into the library. "Samantha Sawyer."

"What's she look like?"

He closed his eyes, picturing Samantha naked, then shifted his image to when he'd last seen her coming out of the library. "She's five-five, weighs about one-twenty, has shoulder-length auburn hair, brown eyes, a straight nose and a dimple in her chin."

Misty laughed, rustling the covers. "That sounds like a description for a line-up."

He opened his eyes to see she'd moved closer. "What do you want to hear?"

"Does she have big boobs?"

"Average," he said.

"Do you like 'em?"

He studied her. "Where's this conversation going, Misty?"

"How come we've never met her?"

"I didn't realize you were so curious. Now that I know, I'll have to bring her around."

She looked away. "Do you have sex with her?"

"We're both of age," he said.

"How old is she?"

"Twenty-seven."

Watching the ceiling, she asked, "Do you wear a condom when you do it?"

"Sure," he lied.

She met his eyes. "I've been seeing a boy."

"What's his name?"

"Stone."

"That his first or last name?"

"His last name is Curtis."

"You meet him in school?"

She shook her head. "At the soccer field."

"Does he play soccer?"

"No, silly. That's where me and Arnette hang out."

"Watching the game?"

She looked at him. "For a cop, you sure don't know much."

"Why don't you enlighten me?"

She turned on her side to face him. "The soccer field isn't lit at night. Lots of kids hang out there."

"Doing what?"

"Just hang out."

"Drinking?"

"If I tell, will the kids get arrested?"

He shook his head. "That's not my beat."

"Some of 'em drink. And smoke."

"Marijuana?"

"Sometimes just cigarettes. Some of the kids go into the shadows under the trees and do it."

"Have sex?"

She nodded. "Stone wants me to go, but I tell him I'm not ready yet."

"That's a good answer."

"I don't want to do it in the grass with other kids listening. Not the first time. I'm afraid I'll scream or something and everybody'll make fun of me."

Devon racked his brain for something wise to say.

"The first time Arnette did it," Misty said, "she came back crying and everybody teased her. But now she says there's nothing to it."

"There oughta be," Devon said.

"You mean it should hurt every time?"

He shook his head. "It won't hurt much the first time, if you and the boy love each other."

She stared at him a long moment, then whispered, "I love you."

"I love you too, Misty," he said warily.

"Seems to me," she said, sidling closer, "it would be best if an older man helped a girl get started, a man she loves and who loves her. Since it's such a big deal, seems the first time oughta be a lesson by someone who knows how to do it."

"You make it sound like learning to drive a car."

"Isn't it kinda the same? Learning to step on the gas or the brake at just the right time, shift gears, pass another car or let him change lanes in front of you, pull off the freeway and park without hitting the curb?"

He laughed, rolling over to lie on his back and watch the shadows on the ceiling.

She laughed too, reaching out her small hand and laying it flat on his belly. "Can I touch you down there?" she whispered.

"No," he said, catching hold of her hand and moving it away from him before he let go of it.

"Why not?" she asked.

He sat up cross-legged, keeping the covers close around his hips. " 'Cause touching leads to the other and I'm not gonna do it with you, Misty. You may think you want me to, but in years to come you'd realize you missed out on one of the best things in life, and that's discovering it when you're both in love with each other. Don't let yourself settle for anything less."

She stared at him out of her huge, dark eyes, then she smiled. "Thanks, Uncle Devon."

"For what?" he half-laughed.

"The next time Stone wants me to touch him, I'll say the one leads to the other and I'm not gonna settle for anything less than love." She got up on her knees and leaned close to kiss his cheek, then with a giggle she scampered out the door and down the stairs.

Devon leaned over his knees holding his head in his hands, suspecting he'd escaped committing a terrible sin by the sheer luck of his answer. His body was primed, though, and the prospect of a lonely release was too pathetic to contemplate. He reached behind himself for the phone. Setting it on the bed still warm from Misty's body, he punched in Samantha's number. When she mumbled a hello, he asked, "Did I wake you?"

"Where are you, Devon?"

"On my way, if you'll let me in."

She laughed softly. "Did you lose your key?"

"No," he said. "I'll be there in fifteen minutes."

"I'll turn on the porch light."

"I can find your door in the dark."

"Ummm," she said. "That sounds like fun."

Driving through the rain, Devon chided himself for calling her because he felt needy. If Misty hadn't come to his room, he'd be asleep right now, not maneuvering wet streets to get to Samantha in a hurry. Then he realized if Misty had known about Samantha, she might not have come upstairs intent on propositioning him. When he asked himself why he'd never taken Samantha to the house, he didn't have an answer other than that he liked keeping her to himself. Which smacked of using her for sex.

He stopped at a red light, watching the rain slant onto the pavement in front of him, and suddenly he became intensely aware of himself as a man alone. Living like a shadow at home, comforting his brother's wife and instructing his brother's daughter on how to handle men, filling Connie's boots in relation to his women yet as cut off from his son as Devon had been from Connie when they were growing up. The light changed to green but Devon didn't move.

The street was empty behind and in front of him, only the rain catching light in the dark. Somewhere in this storm, Connie was hiding out, having so little faith in his brother that he'd taken Eric with him. And Devon couldn't blame Connie. He was surely aware that his wife and daughter considered Devon a man who stood head and shoulders above him. Equally aware that Eric considered Devon a traitor, wearing a badge when the kid's hero was an outlaw. Connie had *tried* to tuck Eric under Devon's wing. When Devon refused, Connie took his son with him, teaching him young how to run from the law.

It was happening all over again, only when they were kids it had been their father who kept Devon out from under Connie's influence. By doing that, the old man abandoned Connie. If he'd left his sons alone, their friendship might have been enough to pull Connie back. But the old man had killed any possibility of that with his constant catalog of Connie's failures. Now Devon had failed, and it was all too easy to imagine Connie using Devon's lack of initiative with Eric to keep the kid on the outlaw side of the family. The fact that Devon was trying to save his brother wouldn't count unless he succeeded.

He saw her blond hair first, falling long and wet to her waist. Then her thighs under short shorts, her halter top cut low and clinging to her breasts, which bounced as she ran toward him. Her uncannily beautiful face smirked with the come-on of a hooker until she recognized who he was.

Devon got out and stood in the rain as he gestured toward his open door. "Get in, Elise," he said. "I'll drive you home."

Chapter Seven

Devon slid in behind the wheel then studied the girl who looked trapped to be caught in his car. Elise Truxal's red spike heels were soaked, her naked legs shiny wet, her tight pink shorts and white halter top clinging to her skin, her long blond hair dripping with rain. Remnants of an elaborate makeup job, evidently contrived to hide her age, shone iridescent in the again red light of the traffic signal.

Giving her a regretful smile, he asked, "You always spend your Saturday nights hooking?"

She tossed her head in a gesture of feigned ignorance. "I don't know what you mean."

"Soliciting," Devon said. "The same crime you were arrested for in L.A."

She opened the door to get out, but he caught hold of her arm and leaned in front of her to close it again. With his face close to hers, he said, "I can take you home or to the station for booking. Where would you rather go?"

"Can't you take me to Zane's?"

He shook his head.

"I was only gonna ask you for a ride," she argued. "You can't pin soliciting on me."

He let his gaze slide down her naked legs, back up to tarry on the crevice of her breasts barely covered by her skimpy top, then met her eyes again. "If that outfit isn't illegal, it oughta be."

She smiled. "I'll give you a free taste if you take me where I want to go."

He smiled back. "That's soliciting."

She snarled and raised her hand to strike him. He grabbed her wrist as she twisted toward the door, jabbing the handle with her knee and drawing blood. The door swung open, illuminating them with light as she squirmed to escape. He yanked her down to lie on the seat as he swiveled around on his knees on the floor. Leaning his weight against her hips, he pinned her hands over her head, the dome light shining on the innocent lie of her face. She raised her knee up under his jacket and rubbed his back as she smiled an invitation. He could feel her blood soaking through his shirt.

Holding both her hands with one of his, he reached behind and opened the glovebox for his handcuffs. Her eyes widened when she saw the shiny steel, and she fell slack beneath him as he locked one onto her left wrist, the other onto his right. He closed the glovebox and stepped backward through the open door, dragging her with him. Slamming the door, he led her through the rain around the front of the car, through the beams of the headlights, to the driver's door. He opened it and pushed her in ahead of him, then they sat shackled together, watching each other warily.

"You cut my knee," she accused, looking at the bleeding gash. "I call that assault and battery."

"You can call it anything you want," he answered. "It doesn't change the truth."

"It's your word against mine," she retorted.

"There's blood on the door handle," he pointed out. "Probably some of your skin too."

"So what're you doing with a female minor in the front seat of your car? You're s'posed to put me in back."

He reached through the steering wheel to shift the transmission into drive, then slowly eased into the intersection.

Turning north on Oregon, he drove past the dark library, mentally wincing when he remembered Samantha was waiting at home. He drove up the hill and into the emergency entrance of Sun Towers Hospital, parked at the curb and shut off his engine. "Let's get you patched up," he said, opening the door and pulling her out after him. She followed, wobbly on her high heels.

They turned heads as they walked into the bright glare of the emergency waiting room. Patients lined benches on both sides of the corridor as he advanced to the desk. Clumsily he used his left hand to take his ID out of that side of his jacket and show his badge to the clerk. "Young lady cut her knee," he said. "Can someone see her right away?"

The woman looked at the handcuffs holding them together, then at the bleeding knee below the short shorts. A doctor walking by saw Devon's badge and stopped. "I'll take it," he told the clerk, then looked at Devon. "This way."

Devon followed him with Elise in tow. They walked into a small examining room that hadn't been cleaned yet. There was blood on the white paper covering the high bed. "Don't touch anything," the doctor advised. "Just sit her in that chair."

"If I catch AIDS," Elise threatened, "I'll sue the city."

"We're more likely to catch it from you," Devon answered, pushing her into the chair.

The doctor chuckled, pulling on a clean pair of gloves. He knelt in front of Elise and examined the wound, cleaning the blood away with a towel. "Only a deep abrasion," he said, then smiled up at her. "You won't need stitches."

"Will I have a scar?" she asked softly.

"Not on the outside," he answered, standing up. He peeled his gloves off as he looked at Devon. "I'll send a nurse in."

"Thanks," he said, watching the doctor toss the bloody towel on the bloody paper sheet and drop his gloves in a trash can then walk out the door. Devon looked down at Elise.

"You gonna book me?" she asked.

"Have to now."

"Can't you just say I tripped on the street, you saw it, brought me here then took me home?"

He shook his head.

"Why not?" she demanded.

"I don't cut slack to little girls who fight me," he answered.

The nurse came in, pursed her mouth in disapproval of Elise's attire, then set about cleaning her wound without saying a word. While she was swabbing it with antiseptic, the clerk came in with a clipboard. "I'll need some information," she said.

Devon gave her Elise's name, age, and address, then his own name and badge number.

"Is this a police charge?" the clerk asked.

"Yeah," Devon said.

"What was she arrested for?" the clerk asked.

"Solicitation," he said.

"You haven't read me my rights!" Elise accused.

Both women looked at her with pity, then at Devon with commiseration. The clerk left. The nurse asked, "What'd she cut herself on?"

"A door handle," he said.

"She'll need a tetanus, then. I'll have to drop her shorts to give it. You want to unhook her and leave us alone?"

"Can't you do it in the thigh?" Devon asked.

"All right." She shrugged. "Be right back."

"What's the matter, Detective?" Elise quipped as soon as they were alone. "You afraid if you see my ass you'll be sorry you didn't accept my offer?"

He studied her in silence, wondering where the vulnerable little girl he'd first seen in her mother's dining room had gone. Then he remembered Elise saying she wanted to be an actress, and he guessed she already was. "What if I *had* taken you to Zane's? You think he'd be happy to learn he's sharing his girlfriend with any stranger who's got twenty bucks?"

"You missed your chance on that one," she sassed.

"What about Teddy? Does he know how you spend your Saturday nights?"

Fear flashed on her face.

"Or does he think you're with Zane?"

Her eyes were ferocious but her voice a whisper when she said, "He knows I'm not."

"Where does he think you are?"

"I doubt that he's wasting his time worrying about me," she answered.

"I'm pretty sure you're wrong about that," he said.

The nurse came in with a hypodermic and squatted close to Elise. "This is gonna sting," she told her.

Elise shut her eyes tight, then whimpered when the needle pierced the muscle in her thigh.

"That's it," the nurse, standing up and walking out.

"Let's go," Devon said, tugging gently on the manacles.

When he booked her into juvenile detention, he left written instructions not to allow her any phone calls or visitors, intending to talk to Zane before she did to find out if either her boyfriend or her brother knew how she spent her

Saturday nights. Standard procedure meant the matron would call Mrs. Truxal to let her know where her daughter was, but being the next day was Sunday, Elise couldn't be released until she went before a judge on Monday morning. Devon figured she'd known that would happen. What he couldn't figure was why she'd kicked up such a ruckus rather than let him take her home.

From the patio of Samantha's apartments, he could see her living room light was on, and when he climbed the stairs, he saw the light of her television between the cracks in her drapes. He used his key to open the door, then stood on the threshold watching her look up from where she sat on the sofa. A box of Kleenex was on the coffee table in front of her, several wadded tissues evidence that she'd been crying. A music video was on the screen, Guns and Roses wailing about patience. "Sorry," he said, closing the door. "I got waylaid."

"It's three o'clock, Devon," she accused. "You called me at midnight!"

"I know," he said. "You want me to leave?"

She shook her head, then punched the button on the remote to turn off the TV. "What happened?" she asked with only slightly less anger. "Did you see a robbery in process on the way over here and feel impelled to stop it?"

"No, but if I had, I would be impelled to stop it."

She stared at him a long moment, then asked a little less stridently, "Well, what happened? Or don't I deserve an explanation?"

"I arrested a hooker," he said. "She put up a fight and I had to take her to the hospital before booking her."

Samantha stared at him. "Hookers are a dime a dozen, Devon. Couldn't you have just driven past her? Or were you so horny you thought a tussle with a whore would add to your evening?"

He winced. "If you think I get my kicks roughing up whores, maybe I should leave."

"No, I know you don't," she said. "I didn't mean that, but Jesus, Devon, couldn't you have passed her by? There must be dozens of prostitutes on the streets every Saturday night."

"She's involved in the case I'm working on," he said.

"And you're never off duty, are you."

He shook his head.

"Was she hurt bad?"

"Scraped her knee, is all. But it was bleeding."

"Did she scrape it on the pavement?" Samantha asked, obviously trying to imagine the scenario.

"Inside my car," he said. "She caught it on the door handle."

"You were wrestling with a hooker inside your car?"

He sighed, taking a step back and half-sitting on the edge of a stool in front of her breakfast bar. "She's underage and I offered to take her home. It was after that she started the fight."

"Is she pretty?" Samantha whimpered.

He nodded.

"How is she involved in your case?"

"I can't discuss that," he said gently.

She looked at the TV though the screen was dark.

"You want me to leave?" he asked again.

She shook her head, still staring at the blank screen. "Guess when you call and say you're coming, I don't want you to let anything stand in your way."

"I'd like that too," he said, "but things happen."

She sighed. "You want a beer?"

He shook his head. "I'd like to take a shower though, before I touch you."

She gave him a weak smile. "You know where it is."

He stood up and took off his jacket, then hung it on the back of the stool.

"You've got blood on your shirt," she said.

He turned around to face her again. "It's hers."

"How'd her knee get on your back?"

"Happened during the fight."

"Does she fight with her legs open?"

"What do you want me to say, Sam? Do you need to hear that I didn't fuck her?"

"Maybe," she whispered.

"I didn't fuck her. I haven't been with anyone but you since the first time we slept together."

She smiled. "That's been two years, Devon."

He laughed. "My niece was asking about you tonight."

"What'd you tell her?"

"That I'd been remiss in not bringing you around."

"You mean I'm finally going to meet your family?"

"Soon as my brother comes home."

"Where is he?"

"On the road," he said, pulling his shirttails out and unbuttoning the shirt. He took it off and folded it with the blood inside, then laid it across his jacket. "He'll be home soon."

When he faced her again, she let her admiring eyes linger on his chest as she said, "Hurry up with your shower."

At seven o'clock the next morning, he was in the shower again when Samantha joined him. He had the hot water running full blast, with only a dribble of cold, so he hadn't known she was there until the curtain opened and she stepped into the tub naked.

She smiled. "It's like a steambath in here."

He nodded then turned around to lift his face to the deluge one more time before stepping out. She leaned close against his back, sliding her arms around his waist, and he stood still, letting her caress him for a moment before he turned around again. She lowered herself onto her knees, taking him in her mouth while he stood watching her through the spiraling steam, not wanting to let her do that. She looked like a hooker servicing him on her knees, reminding him of the time Connie had taken him to Juárez to buy them both whores.

That had been just before Connie was arrested. When Devon realized that his first sexual experience had been paid for with the stolen money that sent Connie to jail, Devon hadn't had sex again until Connie was paroled. Even after that, Devon's love life had been limited to one-night stands with women he met in bars. One evening he'd been sitting in his car watching a murder suspect pick up a prostitute in San Jacinto Plaza when a call came over the radio about a flasher in the library. Seeing his suspect walk into the Plaza Hotel and knowing he'd be busy for a while, Devon answered the call. Samantha was the librarian in charge that night.

Devon hadn't been in the library since he was a kid researching reports for school. Librarians had changed in the interim. No longer stiffly proper spinsters and fuddy-dud old men, the profession had attracted a new breed of intellectuals who chose not to use their talents for a corporation's profits. When he asked Samantha Sawyer for a description of the flasher, she laughed and said he looked like John Wayne without any cavalry backing him up. Devon stared at her so long she laughed again and said, "You know, a loser with his flag at half-mast."

"Is that all you can tell me about him?" Devon asked.

"Well, it was the most pertinent part of his anatomy," she answered.

"Not one we usually look at in a lineup," he muttered, clicking his ballpoint.

She watched the point of his pen popping in and out of its plastic casing so long he stopped his thumb, suddenly aware of what he'd been doing.

"Don't quit," she whispered. "I was enjoying your rhythm."

He popped the point out again and held it over the blank in his report. "Is it Miss or Mrs. Sawyer?" he asked, not looking at her.

"Missing it," she said.

He met the honey brown of her eyes. "What time do you get off?"

She smiled. "We close at nine."

"Do you have a ride home?"

"My apartment's only a few blocks from here. I usually walk."

"With flashers in the neighborhood, maybe it'd be a good idea if I gave you a ride tonight."

"I'd like that," she said, her eyes following his pen as he put it back in his jacket pocket.

He looked at her jacket, how it curved over her breasts, then he met her eyes and smiled. "If you see this guy again, give us a call."

"Will you come if I call?" she asked.

He gave her his card, watching her read it. She looked up and whispered with a half-laugh, "A homicide detective?"

"I just happened to be in the neighborhood," he said.

"The only killers here," she said, "lurk between the pages of a book."

He laughed. "Sounds like a nice change."

She laughed too, the sound as melodious as a

meadowlark in the desert of his life.

He'd managed to keep her just that, a songbird sequestered from his days spent in the hot wind of murder. In the oasis of their Saturday nights, her whispered melodies and murmured cries of passion replenished the dry channels of his soul until they became flowing streams he could draw from all week. But now it was Sunday morning, the holy Sabbath, and she was servicing him on her knees like a whore. He pulled himself out of her mouth and pushed her to lie beneath him as he thrust himself between her thighs, knowing he was hurting her against the hard porcelain but suspecting she'd been trying to become the girl he'd fought in his car and needing to punish her for wanting that. He came with an explosion of anger, then withdrew to sit on his heels in the searing deluge of the shower as he said, "Don't ever do that again."

"Why not?" she whispered, blinking against the spray escaping from behind his back.

He pulled the curtain aside and left her behind.

She followed him without turning off the water. "Why not, Devon?" she cried. "Do you think my need of you isn't as real as a bloody prostitute's? You took *her* to the hospital. Are you just gonna leave me on my back?"

"From the hospital I took her to jail," he retorted. "Is that what you want?"

"Is that what you think love is?"

"From all the evidence, yes."

"Fuck your goddamned evidence!" she screamed. "Can't you give me a chance to make a difference in your life?"

"Not when you come on your knees, sucking me like a two-bit whore."

She slapped him, then stared with tears of bewilderment in her eyes, as if he had been the one to strike her.

He took hold of her shoulders and gently set her aside to reach into the shower and turn off the water. In the steamy confines of the room, he faced her again, knowing he feared marriage for the opposite reason she suspected: because it would open the door of the cage he kept her within and allow her to fly through the shadow and sun of his life at her whim rather than his. But remembering her cries of pain when he'd pinned her against the porcelain made him realize she couldn't thrive in a cage, and if he kept her there any longer he would become love's executioner. "All right, Sam," he said softly. "Get dressed and I'll take you home to meet my family."

Laura and Misty were sitting at the dining room table eating waffles when Devon brought Samantha in through the back door. As he introduced them, Laura looked struck with betrayal while Misty giggled and said, "It's about time, Uncle Devon."

Laura recovered herself, rising to offer them breakfast. "There's coffee hot," she said, watching Samantha, "and I could whip up some more batter real quick."

"Just coffee," Devon said, guiding Sam to his chair at the end of the table. He smiled down at her. "I'll go change." As he was climbing the stairs, he heard Laura say, "Devon never mentioned you."

"He told me," Misty piped up, then giggled again. "I knew you'd be pretty."

Devon closed his bedroom door, tossed his jacket on the bed and unbuttoned his shirt as he crossed the room to click on his answering machine. One call had come in at two-thirty, about the time he'd finished booking Elise into detention. There was a long pause, then Connie said softly, "*Ayudame,* bro." The light blinked to indicate no more messages. Devon backed the tape up and listened again. Connie was whispering, as if maybe Eric were asleep in the same room and he was trying not to wake him. That Connie had spoken Spanish as he petitioned his brother for help was probably a hint that he was in Juárez, someplace Devon couldn't legally go since the department had declared it off-limits after two El Paso officers raised a ruckus in a bar on the *Avenida*. Devon rewound the tape on the erase button. After dropping his laundry in the hamper, he changed into clean jeans and a blue shirt, then shrugged into his gray jacket as he walked back downstairs.

Misty was telling Samantha about the time Devon had saved Eric from drowning. They had gone fishing at Elephant Butte when Eric slipped off the front of the boat and fell into the water. Connie dove in and pulled him out, but it was Devon who pumped Eric's chest and got him breathing again. While Misty told the tale with excited triumph, Devon remembered how drunk Connie had gotten that night, and how he'd stared at Devon all weekend as if he were an alien mysteriously dropped into the family. Samantha watched him come into the room while Misty was still excitedly talking. He smiled at Samantha, then walked on into the kitchen where Laura was washing dishes.

Leaning against the counter beside her, he asked softly, "Have you heard from him?"

She shook her head, her eyes on her work.

"I had a message on my machine. I don't think he's left you, Laura."

"Where is he then?" she asked, setting a soapy plate in the empty sink.

Devon picked it up, rinsed it, and set it in the drainboard. "I think he's in Juárez."

She met his eyes. "What's he done?"

"I'm not sure." He took the next soapy plate from her hands, rinsed it and leaned it against the first.

She scrubbed the silverware with a vengeance, dropping each piece to clatter loudly in the sink. Devon took a cup from the cabinet and poured himself some coffee, then met her eyes, hurt with betrayal.

"Why didn't you tell me about her?" Laura whispered.

He shrugged. "Just hadn't gotten around to it."

"Bringing her home on Sunday morning must mean you've been seeing her a while, Devon."

"Two years," he said.

She turned away to snap the grills out of the waffle iron.

"I talked to Tom Halprin last night," Devon said, "and found out for sure Eric's with Connie."

"Why?" she asked, looking up from scrubbing a grill. "If he's hiding out in Juárez, why in high heaven did he take his son with him?"

"Maybe he wanted some company," Devon said softly.

"You expect me to believe," she hissed in a strident whisper, "that he's not using whores down there? He's prob'ly buying one for Eric too. Exposing him to AIDS and all sorts of filthy diseases. What kinda father would do that?"

"You don't know that he is, Laura."

"I'm pretty goddamned sure of it!" she cried. "He's not getting in my bed even if he does come back."

Misty fell silent in the dining room.

Laura wrung out the dishrag and turned away to wipe off the stove, though it was clean. Devon put his cup down and pulled her close in a hug, letting her cry against his chest.

"Why is this happening, Devon?" she whimpered.

He had no answer, so kept quiet.

"Go on," she said, pushing him away. "I'm sure you have

plans for the day with your girlfriend."

He watched her dump the dregs of the coffee and immerse the pot in her dishpan, then he walked into the dining room and met Samantha's eyes. "You ready to go?"

She rose as he walked over to Misty and gave her a hug. She looked up at him with scared eyes. "Take care of your mom today," he said softly. "Stay with her. Can you do that?"

Misty nodded and he gave her a smile.

Laura came to the door drying her hands on a towel. "It was nice meeting you, Samantha," she said, studiously not looking at Devon. "I hope we see you again."

"Thank you," Samantha answered.

Devon held out his hand and led her from the house. As he turned the key in the ignition of his car, he gave her a wry smile and said, "Your typical happy family."

Her smile was sad. "Misty thinks the world of you."

He didn't answer, watching the rearview as he backed down the driveway into the street. When he stopped to change gears, Samantha asked, "Am I right in thinking Laura does too?"

He accelerated up the hill to Piedmont, then turned left down Morrow. "She's going through a rough time," he said. "You want to go to Mass with me?"

She looked startled. "I didn't bring a scarf."

He laughed. "They got rid of that rule a few years ago."

"Then yes, I'd be pleased, Devon, to go to church with you."

Our Lady of the Angels was a small mission built for Smeltertown at the turn of the century. A pathetic cemetery of wooden crosses leaning above the parched desert sand held the graves of Devon's parents as well as many of the men who had worked at Asarco before Smeltertown was closed in the Seventies. Now the church and cemetery were the only remnants of the company town. The congregation was composed of elderly widows whose husbands were buried under the lead and zinc drifting from the eight-hundred-foot smokestack which dominated the western sky-line of town.

Devon liked the church because he never saw anyone he knew, other than the priest and the old ladies who recognized but didn't speak to him. At the door, he crossed himself with holy water, then led Samantha to a middle row. The interior of the church was humble, the pews and prayer benches worn, the altar graced with a peeling painting of the Virgin of Guadalupe. Devon knelt on the prayer bench, leaning on the pew in front of him as he held his forehead in his hand and silently recited a rosary for his mother. He never prayed for his father, maybe only because he'd begun the ritual when the old man was still alive.

Devon had been twelve when his mother died of leukemia, probably caused by inhaling the lead and zinc of Smeltertown before they moved to the house high enough up the mountain to escape the worst of the smog. Devon couldn't remember living in the company town, but the town didn't forget his mother, pulling her back into the dust of its graveyard. Every Sunday he and his father had celebrated Mass in this church, and after his father's death Devon continued the ritual exactly as he always had, the only change a gentle relief to think of his father now buried beside his mother, the long lament of his bitterness removed from Devon's life.

Today, however, there *was* a change. A woman sat on the bench behind him as he prayed, and before he rose off his knees to sit beside her, he petitioned God for the wisdom to help his brother. When he met Samantha's eyes as he took her hand, he saw that the simple act of sharing his family and religion with her had already deepened their love enough to dissolve the cage he'd fashioned around her. The sweetness of sharing her freedom made their two years of compartmentalized togetherness feel like starvation when merely the day before he had considered it his only sustenance.

Responding to the Mass, he listened to her reading words he knew by heart, felt her follow him when they knelt or stood in obedience to the rules, and suddenly he understood what it all meant. Unity of the congregation, consecration of togetherness, worship not of God but of His love incarnate in people. Hearing the altar boy ring the bell of sacrifice, Devon remembered a time his father had denied his mother something she dearly wanted. She capitulated silently without a fuss, and when Devon demanded to know why, she said, "Our togetherness is of more value than what I want."

That hadn't made sense to Devon then, but he thought he understood it now. Now he couldn't even remember what his mother had wanted, but he remembered the strength of his parents' unity. It was ironic that his father, working inside the smelter, had been protected from the fumes falling on his home and infecting his wife with the price of earning a living. It was a tragedy that she had died when her sons were still young, leaving them with only their father who had never recovered from her loss enough to give them even a small part of the love she'd taken with her.

Devon had come of age striving to counteract his father's bitterness. Connie had rejected it, spewing it back at the world with violence. He'd ridden high for a few years, flaunting his rebellion while Devon shouldered the weight.

Connie's freedom had been the euphoria of youthful defiance, while Devon's obedience was rote duty. Now Connie was trapped across the border, his only solace a son he'd stolen from the patriarch's realm, while Devon's duty demanded he conjure a miracle or destroy his brother in the name of justice.

When he led Samantha to the door at the finish of Mass, the priest greeted him with a hope for matrimony shining from his eyes. Devon introduced Samantha, realizing that if he hadn't kept her sequestered from his life, his consequent severance from his brother's family might have allowed Connie to become the patriarch in their father's house.

Samantha held his hand as they walked past the bleak cemetery to his car parked on the street. When he opened the door, she didn't get in but stood facing him, her full acceptance of who he was evidenced by the grace of her acquiescence to his religion. Her intellectual independence and financial autonomy magnified her love into an homage Devon felt unworthy to accept. It humbled him with the conviction that only by saving his brother would he deserve her. The two were disparate, without connection except through his self-respect.

As he turned the key in the ignition, he tore his gaze from the forlorn patch of a cemetery to look at the vibrant woman beside him. "I have to talk to Zane Kalinsky," he said. "If you don't mind waiting in the car, we could go to lunch afterwards."

She smiled. "I don't mind."

He took Sunland Park Drive past the new mall to Mesa, then turned north. Cruising by the carports first, he saw the Dakota parked in its space. With a name like Kalinsky, Devon had suspected Zane might be Catholic, and being a conscientious kid with a well-developed sense of duty, if he was Catholic he'd go to Mass on Sunday. But if he had, he'd gone early. Devon parked in a visitor's space that was shaded by a desert willow, gave Samantha a smile, then walked toward the manager's apartment.The door was ajar. It was a warm day so the suggestion that Zane had cracked his door to catch the breeze didn't alarm Devon. Something else did. Maybe it was his cop's instinct, or maybe his sensitivity to the smell of fresh blood that came from being in its vicinity more often than most. He took his pen from his pocket and pushed the door all the way open, his eyes searching for anything amiss.

The room was empty, as neat and impersonal as he remembered. Anyone else would have called a greeting, but feeling certain he wouldn't receive an answer, Devon walked through the living room into the bedroom. Zane was naked in bed, lying sideways with one leg on top of the sheet, his foot almost reaching the floor, his elbow bent so his hand had fallen against his face, his fingers wrapped around the grip of a pistol, its barrel sunk into the congealed pulp of his exposed brain.

Devon let his gaze wander the room, fighting denial as he saw the kid's clothes dropped on a chair in the corner, his sneakers and socks on the floor underneath, the golden curtain lifting in the breeze coming in the open window, the short stack of *Popular Mechanics* on the far bedstand, a radio clock on the near one, the kid's watch on the floor by the bed. Lying next to the watch was a coin. Devon leaned over to look at it more closely. Seeing it was an 1888 silver dollar, he winced. Then without letting himself think about what he was doing, he picked up the coin and dropped it into his shirt pocket.

Devon retraced his steps, making sure the door didn't quite close when he pulled it to with his pen. Watching the back of Samantha's head as he walked toward his car, he decided he'd made the wrong choice in her apartment that morning. Rather than drawing her into his life, he should have excised her from it. Then he wouldn't now have to watch her face when he told her how he'd be spending the rest of his Sunday.

He hunkered down outside the driver's door, folding his arms on the open window, needing that barrier between them. Softly he said, "I'm afraid I have to send you home, Sam."

She studied him a long moment before she whispered, "What's wrong?"

"The boy's dead," he answered, watching the news register with the horror it merited.

"Murdered?" she whimpered forlornly.

Devon nodded, then reached for his radio. When the dispatcher came on the line, he said, "This is Detective Gray. I have a 409 at the Sunset Apartments, 7800 Mesa, unit one. Need a coroner and lab team stat."

The radio crackled then the woman's voice asked, "Was that a 409 at Sunset Apartments, 7800 Mesa, unit one, Detective Gray?"

"Roger," he said, watching Samantha wipe tears from her cheeks. "I have a civilian with me. Will you send a taxi to take her home?"

"Will do," the dispatcher said, her voice teasing with humor.

Samantha met his eyes with anger. "Is this a joke?"

He shook his head. "Murder's my business, Sam. Are you gonna cry every time I get a new assignment?"

She looked away, blinking back tears. "No," she said. "Only every time it makes you miss lunch."

Chapter Eight

Darryl Brent was the first officer on the scene. Sauntering into the apartment, he grinned and said, "We have to stop meeting like this."

Devon chuckled, standing in front of the refrigerator where Zane had stood the last time they talked, drinking a cup of coffee out of the pot that had come on when the automatic timer told it to.

"Where's our guest?" Brent asked.

"Bedroom," Devon answered, nodding toward the door.

Brent went as far as the threshold and whispered, "Jesus." He turned around to face Devon again. "Looks like a 410. Didn't you call in a 409?"

Devon nodded.

"What makes you think he didn't do himself?"

"He was getting up. Probably throwing a punch with the hand the killer planted the gun in."

Brent turned around and looked again. "Knocked his watch off the table," he said, accepting Devon's scenario. "Did it stop?"

"No such luck," Devon said.

Brent turned back with a weak smile. "You want me to call the next detective on rotation since you're still on the Truxal case?"

"Same case," Devon said. "He was the daughter's boyfriend."

"Shit," Brent muttered with surprise. "Think she did it?"

Devon shook his head. "I booked her into juvenile detention last night for soliciting."

"Nice family," Brent said.

Devon nodded. "They ought to be getting home from church right about now. Think I'll go talk to them."

"What do you want done here?"

"The whole place dusted for prints. From the toilet handle to the front door and everything in between. A check run on the gun, everybody in the building questioned about the last time they saw Zane, if they heard the shot or saw anyone coming or going last night."

"His name was Zane?" Brent asked.

"Yeah. Kalinsky. His parents live in Fabens. Instruct whoever tells them to watch their reaction on the off-chance the two killings aren't related."

"Anything else?"

"Have the lab compare the prints they get here with the ones they took from the Truxal house." Devon set his empty cup in the sink. "Tell them not to bother with this cup." He gave Brent a smile. "And turn the coffee off on your way out."

Teddy Truxal lived in one of the new neighborhoods sprawling into the desert northeast of the city. The developer was obviously a baseball fan because he'd named all the streets after famous players. Driving west on Micky Mantle, Devon passed Roger Hornsby, Yogi Berra, Casey Stengel, Duke Snider, and Babe Ruth before he came to Dizzy Dean. Knowing he'd never buy a house on a street named Dizzy Dean, Devon wondered about people who could see their lives as a joke. None of the Truxals had impressed him with their sense of humor, but surely a person would have to laugh with the world every time he gave out such an address.

Wanda Truxal opened the door. Her short brown hair

looked as if it hadn't been combed yet, and her face without makeup had an unappealing lack of sheen. Though her eyes flared with recognition, her smile was tentative until he showed her his badge and reminded her they'd met.

"I remember," she said. "Teddy's not home."

"Do you know where he is?"

"At his mother's."

Devon nodded. "Do you mind if I come in?"

She hesitated, then said, "Guess it's all right."

She unhooked the screen and led him through a short foyer into the living room. Petey sat in a playpen chewing on a pink plastic doughnut, apparently wearing a clean diaper because an odorous one lay on the rug beside his pen. A church service was on television, the sound barely audible. It was a small black and white, and Devon remembered Earl Carter saying Teddy's wife wanted a new TV they couldn't afford. The furniture was a hodge-podge of styles, probably hand-me-downs from relatives, the only new piece a maple guncase in the corner.

"Would you like coffee?" Wanda asked, picking up the dirty diaper and hiding it behind herself.

Devon smiled at her gesture toward delicacy. "No thanks," he said.

"Have a seat," she said. "I'll be right back."

He nodded though he didn't sit down. He walked over to the guncase and tried the door. It was locked, as he'd hoped it would be with a toddler in the house, but through the glass he could see the .22 Remington and the .44 Winchester Teddy had said he owned. The top drawer wasn't locked. Inside it were several boxes of bullets and a .357 magnum Ruger nestled in a holster without a belt. Devon slid the pistol far enough out to read the serial number on the barrel, wrote it down in his notebook, replaced the gun and closed the drawer, then put his notebook away as he turned around to smile at Petey watching him.

Wanda came back. She'd combed her hair and put on lipstick, but its red gloss only accentuated the unhealthy tinge of her complexion. "Please sit down, Mr. Gray," she said, choosing an overstuffed maple rocker for herself.

He sat at the end of the sofa farthest away from her, then took his pen and notebook from his pocket and laid them on the table in front of him. "Was your husband home last night?" he asked.

She blinked in surprise. "Last night?"

He nodded.

"He went out with some friends," she said.

"Do you know their names?"

She shrugged. "Men from work."

"You don't know who?"

She shook her head.

"What time did he get home?"

"I'm not sure. I was asleep."

"What time did you go to bed?"

"Not till late," she said. "I fell asleep on the couch first."

He smiled as if in camaraderie. "In front of the TV?"

"Yeah," she answered with a laugh.

"What was on when you woke up?"

She looked at the TV, trying to remember. "Some western with Jimmy Stewart," she said, then laughed again. "I opened my eyes just in time to see him kiss the girl, then it was over."

Devon laughed softly with her. "But Teddy was home when you woke up this morning?"

She nodded.

"Sleeping pretty heavy, I guess, after a night out drinking with the boys."

"No, he was up," she said. "Rummaging through the garage for something."

"Did he find it?"

"I guess. He never told me what he was looking for. If he hadn't found it, he would've."

Devon gave her a sympathetic smile. "You were alone Friday night, too, weren't you?"

She nodded. "Teddy hadn't been home but fifteen minutes when Anne called about his father."

"How'd he take the news?"

"Not like I'd expect," she said, "but . . ."

"But what?" Devon coaxed.

She shook her head. "His family's weird. Not like mine. If my dad died suddenly, I'd be heartbroken. But then we're a close family. Oh, Teddy's family's close too, but different."

"In what way?"

"They're wild," she said. "When I first married Teddy, I couldn't believe it. His sisters were almost always fighting. Slapping each other! If you can believe that. Nobody in my family ever hit anyone. We had our fights, but they were just words, you know?"

He nodded. "Sunny and Elise fought a lot?"

"Anne, too. She only moved out a coupla months ago."

"What prompted that?"

"Teddy's father threw a potato at her." Wanda giggled, then looked chastened. "It sounds funny, but I can understand how Anne took offense at getting hit in the head by a baked potato." She giggled again, then forced her mouth into a frown. "It really isn't funny."

Devon smiled. "No, it isn't."

They both laughed. Petey did too, watching from inside his playpen.

"I'm glad he can't understand us," Wanda said. "I know

it isn't right, but I'm glad Teddy's father won't be around when Petey's growing up. Mr. Truxal was an awful role model for Teddy. Maybe now he's gone, Elise will settle down and Teddy can get on with his life."

Devon said, "She's often in trouble, isn't she."

"You don't know the half of it," Wanda scoffed.

"I know she was arrested in California," he said.

She stared at him, then said, "Teddy's father went on a rampage about that. It was an ugly scene when she came home."

"What happened?" Devon asked sympathetically.

"I saw her the next day, and I swear to God, I thought she'd have scars from his belt."

"From what I understand, he used it on her pretty often."

Wanda looked at the preacher on the television screen. "Trying to beat the devil out of her." She sighed. "That's what the Baptists call it."

"You're not a Baptist?"

"Methodist," she said. "First thing I did when we got married was get Teddy out of that church and into mine. I'm not saying all Baptists are bad people, but if you take their teaching to heart, what they're really saying is children are born evil and you have to bend the twig when it's young." She looked at Petey. "Does that boy look evil, Mr. Gray?"

"No," he said.

She beamed. "What church do you attend?"

"I'm Catholic," he said.

She frowned, then said magnanimously, "I try to keep an open mind toward every religion. How to be a good person is what they're all trying to teach us, don't you think?"

He nodded. "I know this is a painful question, Mrs.

Truxal, but did you ever have any suspicion Teddy's father was sexually abusing Elise?"

"I thought so at first," she said forthrightly. "When I found out how promiscuous she is, I thought, well someone must've taught her that. But I've talked to her about it quite a bit and I don't think so anymore."

"What changed your mind?"

"She told me she's been doing it to herself since before she started school. Can you imagine that? She said when she was a toddler not much older'n Petey, she'd look forward to her naps 'cause she'd do it. And she told me about her first lover. He was a transient her father picked up hitchhiking, let him stay in the room in their basement, you know there's a room down there with a bath and all, and Teddy's father let that man stay there in exchange for doing the yard work. Elise was only eleven when she started going to that man's bed. She just flat-out likes sex. Makes me think some girls oughta marry young. She was ready at twelve, in my opinion. Now she's got this boyfriend, Zane, and I think she'd marry him just to get out of the house."

Devon looked away, thinking of Zane Kalinsky, who would never marry anyone now. The television screen showed a choir in white robes. He could faintly hear them singing, but he didn't know the song.

"He's not really a kid any more'n she is," Wanda went on, "the way his folks saddled him with responsibility so young. But they have money, his folks do, and in my opinion Elise and Zane oughta get married. He'd settle her down. Give her a coupla kids lickety-split and that'd take the wind out of her sails. She'd be too busy to get in trouble. But they're both underage and his parents won't allow it. That's what Elise told me."

Devon looked at Petey, trying to imagine the child Elise

and Zane might have had. With his red hair and her beauty, their daughter would've been a knockout. He looked back at Wanda. "How does Teddy feel about Zane?"

"He agrees with me," Wanda said, nodding emphatically. "With three sisters, you know, and a father who hasn't lived at home for as long as I've known them, Teddy's had it rough being the man of the family. After we got married, he wanted us to move into that room in the basement, but I refused. You've done your best for 'em, Teddy, I said, and now you gotta think of me and Petey. You can't be forever looking after your sisters."

"Does he like Zane?" Devon asked.

"Sure. They went hunting together last winter, and Teddy said he had a real good time."

"Was that when he borrowed Zane's shotgun?"

"After they got back, yeah," she said guardedly.

"Why'd he borrow it after they got back?"

"Teddy wanted to practice with it, said it'd be a good thing to know how to use a shotgun. They're different, I guess, from regular rifles."

Devon nodded. "Do you know when he gave the gun back?"

"About a week later he took it home and asked Elise to give it back for him, but she didn't for a while. She kept it there in the house. I saw it behind the door in her closet and I asked why she hadn't given it back to Zane yet. She told me the next time her father came at her with his belt, she was gonna let him have it both barrels." She paused, looking chastened. "I didn't give her the best advice."

"What'd you say?" Devon asked softly.

Wanda sighed. "I told her she'd prob'ly get off if she did. That the courts are coming around to believing women when they defend themselves. Used to be, you know, a man could do anything to his wife or daughters but if they retaliated there wasn't a justifiable defense. With this battered wife syndrome they got now, women are getting off, and I told Elise she prob'ly would too, if she shot him."

Petey babbled in the silence between them. Faintly from the TV the chorus could be heard singing, "Come by here, my Lord, come by here. Oh Lord, come by here."

Finally Devon asked, "Do you think that's what happened?"

Wanda shook her head. "I told Teddy Elise still had the gun and he took it back himself. Made a joke about not wanting to tempt her. But it wasn't nothing to joke about with that family. Teddy's father didn't have any morals to speak of. We all knew he was sleeping with his housekeeper down at that rat trap hotel he owned. I don't think Helen, that's Teddy's mom, I don't think she knew 'cause she never went down there, but the rest of us did and it was obvious. The woman lived in his room. And Teddy's father couldn't pay his bills half the time, so he used Teddy's credit cards. Ran 'em up so high it was taking food out of our mouths to meet the payments. What kind of man would ruin the credit of his own son?" She paused, as if suddenly aware of what she was saying. "Still in all, I don't want you thinking Teddy killed his father. He'd thought about it, though. I guess we all had, the way Mr. Truxal would get so ornery drunk sometimes. But even that Connie Gray told Teddy not to do it."

"Who's Connie Gray?" Devon asked.

She frowned, then looked embarrassed when she asked, "Is he a relative of yours?"

"Gray's a common name," Devon said.

She nodded. "I didn't like him one bit. Oh, he came on free and easy, complimenting me and playing nice with

Petey, but the first time Teddy brought him here, soon as the door closed behind him, I said to Teddy, what're you doing with a man like that? Connie flat-out told me he'd been in prison, dropped it into the conversation the way anyone else would say they'd been to Florida or Hawaii, you know, and I said to Teddy, don't you know a man like that's trouble?"

"What did Teddy say back?" Devon asked.

"He said when trouble comes, a man like that's good to know. Hah! That sort of man never got nobody out of trouble, he just gets everybody in deeper. I told Teddy, don't ever bring that man home again. And Teddy said okay, and he didn't. But one time we ran into Connie at the flea market. You know the one way out on Dyer? Teddy was fixing to buy a silver dollar for his sister. You know Elise had a collection of silver dollars going back to 1840? Well, Teddy found one from 1888. Elise was missing that year, and he was fixing to buy it for her, but just then that Connie Gray happened along. I could tell by the way they said hello they'd been seeing each other away from the house, you know? Connie told Teddy the man was asking too much for that dollar. That it was minted in New Orleans, and for that price, he oughta get one minted in San Francisco 'cause they didn't make so many and the ones from San Francisco are worth more." She snorted with disdain. "Teddy believed him and didn't buy the dollar. But last week Connie showed up at the house with an 1888 silver dollar minted in San Francisco. After he left, I said to Teddy, what's he doing giving you a present worth that much money? What're you doing for *him?* I asked. And Teddy, he said he's throwing a little business his way. What kind of business? I asked. A man like Connie, I said, don't do any business you'd stand up in church and talk about. Teddy laughed and said

Connie works in a place that sells tires, and he gets a commission on the ones he sells and Teddy has been sending him business. Well, I wasn't sure I believed that." She paused again, as if suddenly remembering who she was talking to. "I'm not saying Teddy was doing anything illegal. It's not like what Connie gave him was an awful big deal. That coin was only worth about twenty dollars, but still in all, a man doesn't give someone twenty dollars for nothing, you know? And I was worried that maybe Teddy owed Connie just 'cause of that coin. But when it comes to Elise, Teddy throws caution to the wind." She paused to shake her head. "There's something about her that drives men to cross a line they wouldn't ordinarily cross. You know what I mean?"

Devon nodded.

"One time Teddy got real mad at Connie 'cause of Elise. He'd taken her to the Target store out by the Sunland Park Mall, and they'd run into Connie there. Teddy said he turned his back just for a second, and when he turned around again, Connie had his hands all over Elise. She was prob'ly lapping it up, but Teddy was fit to be tied. He was still so mad about it when they got home, I thought he was gonna have a heart attack or something. Elise thought it was funny, which didn't improve Teddy's mood none. But she's like that. She drove her father over the brink of control lots of times, the way she'd taunt and sass him so he'd see red like a bull, you know?

"Well, the reason I got off on Connie Gray was 'cause I overheard him and Teddy talking in the garage the day he brought that silver dollar, and I heard Connie say a man killing his father is something he doesn't ever get over. Made me feel Connie knew what he was talking about, that maybe he'd killed his father, you know? Gave me the creeps."

"When was it you overheard this conversation, Mrs. Truxal?"

She stared at the ceiling, calculating. "Oh, it must've been about a month ago."

"I thought you said it was last week."

"Did I?" She giggled nervously. "Well, I don't really remember exactly when it was."

"But Connie Gray did come to your house after that first time?"

"He didn't come *in,*" she protested. "They were just talking in the garage. Teddy's still got the dollar. He was saving it for Elise's birthday present. Her birthday's next week. She'll be sixteen, but not exactly sweet and never been kissed. And that dollar'll be the start of a whole new collection now that Teddy's father sold the old one."

"Sold it?" Devon asked.

Wanda nodded. "To pay his fine for drunk driving. Said it came from *his* father so it was rightfully his before it was hers. That wasn't right, though. Her grandpa gave it to her, not him."

"When did he sell it, Mrs. Truxal?"

"Must've been about two or three weeks ago. I thought Teddy was gonna cry when he told me. He tried to get it back, but of course the dealer wouldn't sell it for what he paid for it. Teddy tried to trade his best gun for it, but the dealer just laughed in his face, said the collection was worth more'n *all* his guns. So Teddy went to his father and made an awful scene and Mr. Truxal said he'd get the coins back himself, being as Teddy was so upset. When Teddy asked where he meant to get the money, Mr. Truxal said he'd sell his housekeeper's car, which he bought for her. But I don't think he did, 'cause the next night Teddy told me Connie offered to get the coins back. I said, what're you doing,

Teddy, paying a criminal to steal for you? When I put it like that, Teddy said he guessed he wouldn't. I know it hurt him to see Elise grieving over those coins, but I said better the coins than having to visit her brother in jail, and he said he guessed I was right. I hope to shout. I can just see me and Petey trying to live off welfare while Teddy spent a coupla years in prison. Texas isn't exactly a welfare state."

"No, it isn't," Devon said.

"And the world isn't kind to ex-cons either," she said. "Connie told us he couldn't make ends meet if his brother hadn't let him move his family into the brother's house. Any man worth his salt provides for his family. So if you ask me, Connie was doomed when he accepted his brother's help. His brother should've known that and made him make it on his own. Don't you think so?"

Softly, Devon said, "There's nothing wrong with family helping each other through hard times."

"You ever hear of tough love?" she asked.

He nodded.

She said anyway, "It's when you deny someone you love something they think they want 'cause you know they won't be better off if they get it. That's what I believe in: tough love."

Devon closed his notebook and put it away. "Well, thanks, Mrs. Truxal," he said, trying to give her a smile that didn't make it to his mouth. "You've been a big help."

"Teddy's at his mother's," she said, following him through the foyer to the door. "You can find him there if you need to talk to him."

"Thanks," he said again, pushing through the screen without looking back.

His mind whirling with the complications Wanda Truxal had introduced, he caught Gateway South to Interstate 10 and drove all the way to the Porfirio Diaz exit before he realized where he was. Parking on Santa Fe Street in front of Samantha's apartment, he hesitated with his hand on the key in his ignition, trying to decide whether to seek solace or continue the fight without respite. Making up his mind, he pulled away from the curb, knowing he had to see Teddy and watch his reaction to the news of Zane's death. But numbing Devon's mind was the image of Connie with his hands all over Elise.

Chapter Nine

Teddy Truxal was a devastated man. Devon saw it as soon as Teddy opened the door to his mother's kitchen. His cheeks were marked with several tiny slants of scabs from where he'd cut himself shaving, and his light brown hair was disheveled, as if he'd been running his hand through it all morning. Devon gave him a friendly smile and said, "Even though I don't have a warrant, I'm hoping you'll let me in."

Teddy frowned remembering his former threat, but he took a step back and let go of the door.

Devon walked in and closed it behind himself, watching Teddy watch him in a long moment of mutual assessment.

Finally Teddy said in a husky voice, "Elise is in jail."

Devon nodded. "I put her there."

"You?" Teddy whispered.

Devon nodded again. "I picked her up soliciting on a street corner downtown."

Teddy stared in angry silence.

"As it turned out," Devon said, "jail was a fortunate place for her to be."

"What do you mean?" Teddy asked belligerently.

Carefully, Devon said, "Zane Kalinsky died last night."

Teddy pulled a chair out from under the table and sat down hard. "What do you mean he died?"

Softly Devon said, "Looks like suicide. We won't know till we get the autopsy report."

Teddy began to cry, hiding his face with his hands. Devon pulled out the opposite chair and sat down, watching

Teddy's head jerk with his sobs, a muffled lament that sounded like fatigue more than guilt. Finally Teddy was quiet. He raised his head, took a green paper napkin from the yellow plastic holder on the gray formica table and blew his nose. He crumpled the napkin into a ball and closed it inside his fist as he met Devon's eyes.

"Where were you last night?" Devon asked.

"In Juárez," he said.

"Alone?"

"I was supposed to meet a friend, but he wasn't there."

"What's his name?" Devon asked, suspecting he knew.

"Connie Gray."

"He called you and arranged the meeting?"

Teddy nodded.

"What was it about?"

"I don't know."

"Cut the crap, Teddy."

"I don't know!" he shouted. "He just said to meet him at the Kentucky Club at eight!"

"You always do what he tells you?"

"He said he needed help."

"With what?"

"He didn't say."

"Why'd he call you?"

He shrugged. "We're friends."

"So you went to Juárez the night after your father was killed to help a friend?"

"That's right," Teddy said, sitting up straighter as if he liked the sound of the way Devon had phrased it.

"Think the bartender could verify you were there?"

"I don't know," Teddy said. "Maybe the cocktail waitress."

"Did you get her name?"

Teddy shook his head.

"Was the place crowded?"

"It was Saturday night."

Devon nodded. "How long were you there?"

"I waited till ten."

"Then what?"

"I went home."

"What time did you get there?"

"Must've been about ten-thirty," Teddy said, running a hand through his hair.

"Can your wife verify that?"

He shook his head. "She was asleep and I was careful not to wake her."

"Was she asleep in bed?"

"Sure."

"When was the last time you saw Zane Kalinsky?"

Teddy's eyes blurred with tears again. "Jesus," he whispered. "Did Zane really kill himself?"

"He's dead," Devon said.

Teddy looked at the napkin in his fist. "Last Saturday night," he said in a weak voice, "I brought my family here for supper. Zane came to pick up Elise. They had a date."

Devon listened to the silence of the house. "Where's your mother and Sunny?"

"Still at church," Teddy said, then his eyes hardened on Devon. "I don't have to tell you where Elise is."

"Did you know she was hooking?"

"I still don't know it," Teddy retorted. "Didn't it occur to you she might not've been doing what it looked like but maybe just wanted to talk to you?"

Devon shook his head. "She wasn't in a conversational mood."

Teddy seemed relieved to hear that, but his voice was

just as belligerent when he asked, "Couldn't you have made allowances for her being grief-stricken and brought her home?"

Devon hadn't seen much grief in this family, but all he said was, "When I offered to do that, she tried to get out of my car."

Teddy stared at him.

"Didn't make sense to me either," Devon said, "but she cut her knee on the door handle so I took her to the hospital to get the cut bandaged. After that, I had to book her."

"Why?"

"Because she'd been hurt resisting arrest and I had to file a report."

Again Teddy stared in silence.

"Why do you think," Devon asked, "she chose to go to jail rather than come home?"

"I don't know that she did," Teddy said. "All I know is what you're telling me. I think you were seeing your own dirty mind in the body of a confused little girl. She must've put up quite a fight to get cut so bad you took her to the hospital."

"What are you implying?" Devon asked dryly.

"Contributing to the delinquency of a minor," Teddy accused. "Isn't that what they call it? Or is it using a minor for immoral purposes? You must've had a reason not to allow Elise any visitors. Is it 'cause you're afraid she's not gonna tell the same story you're telling about what happened last night?"

Devon shook his head. "You're in the middle of two murders, Teddy. If I were you, I wouldn't be antagonizing the investigating officer."

Teddy worked his mouth like a fish on a dock. Finally he said, "I thought you said Zane committed suicide."

"I said it looked like suicide."

"You're trying to scare me."

"What're you afraid of?"

"You," Teddy said. "I don't like your methods. And I sure as hell think it's suspicious you were the one to arrest my sister."

"At least she has an alibi for last night," Devon said. "You don't."

"I told you where I was!"

"Drinking alone in a bar in Juárez, two miles from where I picked up your sister soliciting in the rain. Did she go out by herself last night, Teddy? Or did you tell her which corner to work?"

"You sonofabitch! You've got no right to make accusations like that!"

"Zane was found with a .357 Ruger in his hand. Didn't you tell me you own a .357?"

"So did Zane, and prob'ly a coupla hundred other people in El Paso. My gun's at home. And you know something else? I've never fired it, so you can't pin his murder on me."

"Was he murdered?"

Teddy paled. "Didn't you just say so?"

Devon shook his head.

Teddy stood up, his closed fist making him look threatening. "Get out of here."

"All right, Teddy," Devon said, standing too. "But if you try to leave town, I'll have you arrested."

"What for?"

"Murder," Devon said.

Teddy blanched. "If you had any proof, you'd arrest me right now."

Devon nodded. "It's a funny thing about murder, though. No matter how perfectly the crime was executed, it tends to snowball until it becomes an avalanche out of control. I figure Zane got caught in the slide."

"Maybe you're wrong."

Devon smiled. "It's happened before."

Teddy didn't smile back.

Elise came into the interrogation room wearing one of the orange smocks issued to county inmates. The color was wrong for her, making her complexion look sallow, but unlike the last time he'd seen her, she wasn't wearing makeup and the length of her long blond hair was dry. She met Devon's eyes with hostility and stayed near the door as he stood up.

"How's your knee?" he asked.

"It hurts," she sassed.

Devon made a clucking sound of sympathy. "Why don't we sit down?"

She walked around the table and pulled the white plastic chair out. Keeping it a distance removed, she sat down and crossed her legs, hiking the hem of her smock up high enough to reveal her bandaged knee.

Devon sat down across from her, leaning on his elbows to be closer. "I'm afraid I have bad news."

She stared at him, her blue eyes chiseled sapphires.

Softly he said, "Zane was killed in his apartment last night."

She jerked back, brimming with tears as if he'd slapped her. But she surprised him when she asked in a whisper, "What time?"

"We won't know until the coroner's report, but I estimate it happened around when I picked you up downtown."

"If you'd taken me there," she accused, "maybe we could have saved him."

"Or maybe you'd be dead too."

Her eyes flared with surprise. "Who'd want to kill me?"

"Who'd want to kill Zane?"

She shook her head, then stared at the tabletop.

Gently he said, "It looked like you were hooking last night, Elise, but I'm having trouble believing you'd work in the rain without someone pushing you." When she didn't respond, he asked even more softly, "Do you have a pimp?"

"I wasn't hooking!" she shouted angrily.

"Okay," he said, conceding her the benefit of doubt. "How'd you get downtown?"

She didn't answer.

"Did you walk?"

"I had a ride," she whispered.

"With who?"

"Just someone."

"A man?"

She nodded.

"Was it your brother?"

Tears fell across her cheeks as she met his eyes. "Do you think he killed Zane?"

"Do you?"

She shook her head, then mumbled, "I don't know."

"Zane died because he loved you," Devon coaxed. "Don't you think you owe it to him to help catch his killer?"

"It's not my fault that he loved me," she whimpered.

Devon leaned back and studied her from a greater distance. "Are you in love with someone else?"

She nodded, her eyes entreating for mercy.

"Who?"

"He doesn't have anything to do with this."

"If that's true, it won't hurt if you tell me his name."

"Yes, it will."

"How?"

"It's complicated," she said.

"Were you with him last night?"

"Yes," she whispered.

"Downtown?"

She nodded, hiding her eyes.

"Is he an older man, Elise? Is that why you're trying to protect him?"

She didn't answer.

"There've been two murders committed," he said. "As of right now, your brother's strongly implicated. How do you feel about that?"

She shrugged, not raising her eyes.

"What if I arrested him for the murders of your father and Zane? What would you do?"

After a long moment she whispered, "Nothing."

"Does that mean you think he's guilty?"

She shrugged.

"Do you know he isn't guilty?"

She tossed her head, her eyes dry with defiance. "Don't expect me to do your job, Detective Gray."

He smiled. "Let me run through the scenario of what I think happened last night, and you tell me when I'm wrong. Will you do that?"

She shrugged.

"Your brother told me he went to Juárez last night. On his way, he gave you a ride downtown." He watched her slant her head, her eyes brightening with an appreciation he read as meaning he was at least partly right. "Teddy dropped you off someplace close to where you were supposed to meet your boyfriend. You were dressed the way you were, not because you were hooking, but because it's how your boyfriend likes to see you. Am I right about that?"

She nodded.

"Didn't Teddy object to you going out barely dressed?"

"I wore a coat," she said.

Devon smiled. "What kind of coat?"

"A khaki raincoat."

"What happened to it?"

"I left it somewhere."

"At your boyfriend's?"

"Maybe."

"And Teddy was angry when he picked you up and saw how you were dressed?"

"I walked back," she said.

"From where?"

"My boyfriend's."

"To downtown?"

She nodded.

"What time was that?"

"Just before I saw you."

"And you really came over to my car simply hoping to get a ride?"

She nodded, her eyes bright with vindication.

"I'm sorry I didn't believe you," he said.

For the first time, she smiled.

"Why didn't you want me to take you home?"

Her smiled vanished. "I thought you'd tell my mother I'd been hooking again."

"But by going to jail, you guaranteed that."

"I wanted you to take me to Zane's," she reminded him.

"Why?"

"Teddy likes Zane."

"But not your boyfriend?"

She shook her head.

"Why not?"

"Zane's family has money."

"And your boyfriend doesn't?"

She shook her head.

"How does your boyfriend feel about Zane?"

"He doesn't know about him."

"You sure?"

She nodded.

"So you wanted me to take you to Zane's so Teddy wouldn't know you'd been with your boyfriend?"

She nodded.

"Sounds innocent enough, except that someone killed Zane last night."

A quiver of sorrow slid across her face.

Gently he asked, "Do you think it was the same person who killed your father?"

She shook her head.

"Why not?"

She shrugged.

"Do you know who killed your father?"

She shook her head emphatically.

"So how do you know it wasn't the same person who killed Zane?"

"I just know," she answered.

"Because you know who killed Zane and you don't believe he killed your father?"

"I don't know who killed either one of them," she said.

He nodded. "If your boyfriend is innocent, Elise, why don't you tell me his name so I can clear him?"

"You can't arrest him if you don't know his name," she said.

"I'm on the verge of arresting your brother. Doesn't that bother you?"

She met his eyes without replying.

"Okay, Elise. You can go now."

She didn't move.

He watched her a moment, then asked, "What?"

"How long are you gonna keep me here?"

"Till you see the judge in the morning."

"Since you know I wasn't hooking, can't you drop the charges and let me go now?"

"Not until you go before the judge." He watched her carefully. "But I'll make a trade, Elise. I'll drop the charges if you tell me your boyfriend's name."

"I can't," she whimpered.

"Why not?"

"He was there," she whispered.

"When your father was killed?"

She nodded.

"If you tell me his name and where I can find him, I promise you, Elise, I'll listen to what he has to say. If he truly didn't do it, maybe I can keep him out of my report."

She just stared at him.

Gently, Devon asked, "Is it because he's over twenty-one and you're trying to protect him from being charged with statutory rape?"

She didn't answer.

"Or does he have a prison record? Is that why you think it'll look like he did it?"

She kept quiet.

"Elise, did you kill your father?"

She stood up, ran across the room, and banged on the door for the matron. When the door opened, Elise turned back with tears in her eyes. *"Ayudame,"* she begged, echoing

Connie's plea for help. Then she disappeared and the door softly thudded shut behind her.

Anne Truxal didn't smile when she opened the door of her apartment. She looked pained to find Devon on her doorstep, and the rash beneath her lower lip was worse than the last time they'd talked. Behind her, he could see the small kitchen table covered with books and papers.

"Still studying?" he asked with a sympathetic smile.

She nodded.

"I'm sorry to interrupt you, Miss Truxal, but I need to ask a few more questions."

"My last final is tomorrow morning," she said. "Can't you talk to me after that?"

"I'd rather speak to you now," he said. When she still hesitated, he said again, "I won't keep you long."

She opened the door wider and gestured for him to come in. Her apartment was a cubicle of a living room with a daybed, the kitchen an extension of the living room. She nodded at the one overstuffed chair under a reading lamp, then settled herself in the middle of the daybed, watching him expectantly.

He took his notebook from his pocket and pretended to scan his notes, aware when she fidgeted nervously. Still he kept quiet.

Finally she asked, "Would you like some coffee?"

"No, thanks," he said, looking up from his notebook. "Why did your mother change the lock on the back door?"

She blinked in surprise.

He smiled. "You told me you went in through the kitchen because you didn't have a key for the back since your mother changed the lock. Was it recently she did that?"

Anne nodded.

"What prompted the change?"

"The lock quit working."

"Just wore out?"

She shrugged. "I guess."

"I thought maybe someone had a key she couldn't get back."

"I don't think so," Anne said.

He smiled. "It was just a thought. Wanda told me you moved out after a fight with your father."

"That wasn't the reason," she said.

"What was?"

"Why don't you quit beating around the bush, Mr. Gray, and tell me what you want to know?"

"All right. Who killed your father?"

"I don't know."

He smiled. "I don't either, Miss Truxal. Until I do, I ask questions that might lead me in the right direction. The purpose of beating around the bush is to see what runs out from under it."

She laughed. "I'm afraid I can't help you."

"Will you let me be the judge of that?"

She studied him a long moment. "What do you want to know?"

"How'd you feel about Elise's boyfriend?"

"I haven't met him."

"I thought they'd been dating a while."

She shook her head. "She was going with Zane till she met this new one. We all liked Zane."

"What's the new one's name?"

"I don't remember having heard it."

"Your family just called him Elise's new boyfriend?"

"I don't think he merited being called that. She snuck

out and met him places, he never picked her up at the house."

"Why?"

She shrugged.

"Is he an older man?"

"I really don't know."

"Has anyone in your family met him?"

"Teddy has. He's the one discovered she was seeing him."

"Does Teddy like him?"

"He doesn't like Elise seeing him, that's all I know."

"What'd he say about him?"

"That he wouldn't do the right thing if he got Elise pregnant." She bit her lip, then said angrily, "I'm not letting out any secrets by telling you Elise is sexually active. So was Teddy. He was only eighteen when he got married, saying it was the honorable thing to do. He said this new guy won't do that for Elise, and I guess Teddy's worried he'll get stuck supporting her child if she has one. He probably will. Teddy's always taken care of the family. Our father, you know, didn't contribute much financially."

"He seems to have been the head of your family despite that."

"Mom let him pretend he was. Let him punish us when as far as we were concerned he didn't have any rights in the house. She gave him rights he hadn't earned."

"Why do you think she did that?"

"She loved him," Anne said with disgust. "Lots of women choose loyalty to a man they love over the well-being of their children. It's not how it should be. You know, the maternal instinct and all that. But sometimes a bond between a man and a woman is stronger. It seems wrong to me, but I've never been in love. Maybe when I am it'll make more sense."

Devon nodded. "So your brother took up the slack as far as the paternal role was concerned?"

"From an early age," Anne agreed. "That was Mom's doing too. Even though he was younger than me, his word always carried more weight just because he's a man. I tried to tell Mom there wasn't anything we could do about Elise's promiscuity except get her on the pill. Punishing that kind of behavior always makes it worse. But she wouldn't listen to me."

"What was your brother's approach to the problem?"

"He wanted her to marry Zane. I guess Teddy thought, once she was married, she wouldn't be his responsibility anymore. He was fit to be tied when she started seeing this other guy, blamed himself because he'd been the one to introduce them, but he said it never occurred to him that she'd find him attractive. You know what I really think though? I think this guy, whoever he is, stuck up for Elise in a way Zane wouldn't and that's why she warmed up to him so fast. Zane, you know, didn't like what Daddy did to Elise but he never did anything about it. I suspect this other guy would have. Teddy told me he was violent."

"Do you think this other guy might have killed your father?"

"I think he might have if he'd had the opportunity, but Teddy put a stop to Elise seeing him."

"How'd he do that?"

"He told me he threatened the guy, that he had something on him and if he didn't stay away from Elise he'd use it."

"What was it?"

"Something illegal, I think that's pretty obvious because Teddy said the guy was scared enough that he agreed he wouldn't see her anymore."

"In all this conversation, Teddy never used the guy's name?"

Anne shook her head. "I got the impression he was deliberately not using it, because even though Teddy said he threatened him, I felt he was afraid of this guy, that Teddy didn't want this man's name connected to us." She stopped, biting her lip with worry. "If you tell Teddy I told you this, he'll probably deny it."

"Why are you telling me, Anne?"

"I don't think it's right what he's doing."

"What isn't right?"

"The way he tries to control Elise. Teddy's not our father, and I don't think he has an exceptionally high degree of wisdom. Like I said, Mom's from the old school and thinks just because he's a man he deserves more respect than we do."

"The night your father was killed," he gently pointed out, "you seemed to defer to Teddy, even calling him before you called the police."

"I was scared," she said, "and in times of crisis you fall back on old habits just 'cause they're familiar. But you know something? I think I was set up."

"What do you mean?" he asked softly.

"I think they all knew Daddy was dead, and they left him there knowing I was coming." Her voice broke with tears she bit back. "They let me walk into all that thinking my ignorance would be the best front to present to the police."

"Do you realize what you're saying?"

"Yeah, I do," she asserted. "But I'm tired of getting the short end of the stick."

"What makes you think they knew he was dead?"

"When my mother and sisters got home that night? All they talked about was what you'd asked and what Teddy and I said. They didn't ask a single question about how Daddy died or who might've done it. Like I said, I was scared, and I didn't put it together till the next day. Then it hit me. They knew, and they let me walk into that dark house with him lying there dead. Would you feel any loyalty to people who did that to you?"

"No, I don't think I would," Devon said. "Are you saying your father was dead before your mother and sisters left for the retreat?"

"I'm not sure about that, but I'm sure they knew before they left for Cloudcroft."

"So you think Teddy killed him, then let them know before they left the church?"

"I don't know who killed him," she said. "And frankly I don't care. I moved out because I didn't want anything to do with them anymore. I only went over there that night because my neighbors were having a party. They invited me that afternoon, but I told them I had to study for finals. I called Mom and asked, since the house would be empty, would it be all right if I studied there? I really called to make sure Daddy wouldn't be home. She knew that. Then she left him there dead, knowing I was coming."

"But if she loved him as much as you say she did, Anne, do you think she would do that?"

"Teddy convinced her. That's what I think. Convinced her it would be best if they all went on with their plans like nothing had happened. She never thinks for herself. With Daddy gone, who else has she got to follow?"

"It sounds as if you think Teddy killed him."

She shook her head. "I don't think he's capable of doing that. He's an honorable man, you know, and an honorable man doesn't kill his father for any reason."

"Do you think maybe Elise did it?"

Again she shook her head. "Elise sneaks around. She's not one for bold confrontation. Oh, she'd sass him when he was giving her a hard time, but as soon as he got physical, she just lay down and took it."

"So who does that leave? Your mother?"

"No way."

"Sunny?"

"I guess you noticed Sunny's not real bright. I don't think she could figure out how to use a shotgun."

"That leaves Elise's boyfriend."

"Teddy wouldn't protect him. Not in a million years." She smiled with commiseration. "You see, Detective Gray, I really can't help you."

Chapter Ten

The shadows were long when he parked outside Samantha's building and walked up to her apartment. Her door was open, a CD playing softly, Vince Gill singing, "I Still Believe In You." Samantha came out of the bedroom carrying a small stack of newspapers and the wicker trash basket from her bathroom. Her face had been placid in the banal preoccupation of housework, but seeing him, she shone with love. He smiled as she walked on through to the kitchen where she dropped the newspapers beside a black plastic garbage bag, dumped the trash into the bag, then turned around and faced him with the empty basket.

"How you doing?" he asked.

"I'm hungry," she said.

"Let's go to dinner."

She studied him a moment before she asked, "Do you promise not to find any dead bodies in the restaurant?"

He walked over and took the basket from her hands, dropped it on the floor, and pulled her close in a hug. "I'm sorry, Sam," he murmured into the spicy silk of her hair.

She shook her head, her face against his shirt, her body pressing into his chest the silver dollar he'd picked up off the floor in Zane's bedroom. "I'll learn to handle it," Samantha said.

On the floor behind her, he saw last week's TV schedule on the stack of newspapers. He pulled his mind away from work, looked down and lifted her face to gently kiss her mouth, surprised to taste spearmint gum.

She smiled, then said, "I'll go change."

As soon as she was gone, he picked up the TV schedule and opened it to Saturday night. Searching through the late movies, he found a Jimmy Stewart western on Channel 21. The movie had ended at two-thirty in the morning. Devon dropped the schedule back on the stack, made a note in his notebook, then walked to the phone and punched in his home number.

The first message began with a long pause before his brother whispered, "*No me mata,* bro." The beep sounded and Laura said, "Devon? Are you coming home today? Will you call me if you're not?" Then the beep signaled the end of the messages. Devon cut the connection and hit the redial button. He listened again to Connie say in Spanish, "Don't kill me, bro." Then he sank onto the sofa and punched in Laura's number. When she answered on the first ring, he said, "Hi, Laura. What's up?"

"Have you heard from him?" she asked frantically.

"No," he said.

"What am I s'posed to do about Eric's school tomorrow? If he doesn't go, I don't think they'll pass him this year. He's already missed so much, playing hooky half the time."

"Just call them," Devon said calmly, "and say he's on a business trip with his father."

"In Juárez?" she mocked. "Yeah, they'll believe that, won't they."

"You don't have to say where. You're his mother. As long as you've taken him out of school, he isn't truant."

"But I haven't taken him out. Connie has."

"Same thing," he said.

"This is Eric's senior year, Devon. If he fails, he won't go back, you know that as well as I do. What's he gonna do without a high school diploma?"

"He'll have to deal with it, Laura. At this point it's out of your hands."

She sobbed. "I feel like a total failure as a mother."

"Is Misty there?"

"Yeah," she whimpered. "She even helped with the dinner dishes. Did you tell her to do that?"

"No," he said.

"She's walking around on eggshells, treating me like someone died or something. Oh God, Devon," she sobbed. "Is Eric all right?"

"Sure. Connie's taking care of him."

"Who's taking care of Connie?"

"I am," he said.

"Are you?" she whispered.

"Try not to worry. They'll both be home in a couple of days."

"Do you know that for sure? Or are you hoping it's true?"

"I'm pretty sure," he said.

"Are you coming home tonight?"

"I don't know."

"Please," she whimpered. "I need you."

"You just think you do, but what we all need right now is not to muddy the situation any more than it is."

"Do you think he'd feel any loyalty to you if things were reversed?"

"That kind of thinking only leads to bad decisions."

She laughed pathetically. "Oh, you're so wise, Devon."

"Let me talk to Misty," he said.

She sighed. "All right."

He heard Laura put down the phone, then looked up and saw Samantha watching from her bedroom door.

"Uncle Devon?" Misty asked, her voice buoyant.

"I'm glad you stayed home, Misty."

"I'd do anything for you, Uncle Devon. Guess I proved that the other night."

He laughed softly. "How's Stone?"

"I won't know till I see him in school tomorrow. I liked Samantha. You gonna bring her around again?"

"Probably."

"You with her now?"

"No, I'm working."

"On Sunday? Give me a break!"

"Happens that way sometimes."

"Good Uncle Devon," she teased, "catching the bad guys."

"When I'm lucky," he said. "Stay with your mother tonight, will you? She's pretty upset."

"Yeah, I know," Misty said. "She's worried Daddy's getting Eric in trouble." She whispered, "He called me."

"Your father did?"

"No. Eric. It was real weird."

"What'd he say?"

"He just asked what you'd said about him and Daddy being gone."

"What'd you tell him?"

"That you told Mom they were in Juárez. He asked how you knew that and I said I didn't know. Then he cursed and said it was just their luck to have such a good detective in the family."

After a minute, Devon asked, "Did he say anything else?"

"Uh-uh," she said, still whispering. "I asked when they were coming home and he said that was up to you, Uncle Devon. Then he told me not to tell you he'd called and I promised I wouldn't, but it's just too scary with Mom crying all the time. I haven't told her but I figure, if Daddy's in trouble, I should tell you so you can help. Can you help him, Uncle Devon?"

"You did the right thing, Misty. Stick close to your mom. Will you do that for me?"

"Sure," she said in a normal tone of voice. "Are you coming home soon?"

"I'll call later and make sure you're all right."

"You mean you'll call and make sure I stayed with Mom." She laughed. "Don't worry. I'll be here."

"Good girl," Devon said. "Talk to you later."

He hung up and met Samantha's eyes where she still stood in the door.

"Don't tell me you're leaving," she said sadly.

He shook his head, then gave her a smile. "Yeah, we're going to dinner, remember?"

Samantha preferred taking her car, saying Devon wasn't really with her when he was at the beck and call of the police radio. This time he conceded without hesitation. Once they were inside, he opened the ashtray she never used and dropped the silver dollar to clink in the metallic chamber.

"What's that?" Samantha asked.

"Don't ask," Devon said. "And don't touch it."

Her eyes widened with apprehension. "All right," she said.

As soon as they returned to Samantha's apartment, Devon called his home phone and listened to Connie's message again. "*No me mata,* bro," Connie whispered with desperation. Devon hung up, hit the redial button and listened again, though there was no more information to be gleaned from Connie's plea. Devon called Laura, noting she'd been drinking from the slurred way she said hello.

"Have you heard from him?" Devon asked.

"If you're referring to my husband," she said, "the answer's no."

"Is Misty home?"

"Asleep. You told her to stay with me, didn't you, Devon."

"I asked her to."

She laughed. "It's amazing how all you have to do is hint at something and she does it, while I can beg on my knees and she still won't do it."

"Kids feel obligated to rebel against their parents."

"I think there's a little more to it. What was she whispering to you on the phone?"

"Just that she's worried about you," Devon said.

"But you're more worried about Connie, aren't you."

"Laura, do you have any idea where he might be in Juárez?"

"You can't go over there, Devon. It'll be your job if you do, so don't even consider it."

"Without some idea of where to look, it'd be pretty pointless."

"If I knew, I'd go myself."

"You should stay home in case he calls. I'll check back with you in the morning."

"Are you staying with Samantha tonight?"

"Yeah."

"Does she know this sudden deepening of your relationship has more to do with being afraid of your lonely sister-in-law than your feelings for her?"

"It doesn't," he said.

"Oh. Forgive me if I think it's odd your abrupt decision to bring her into the family coincides with Connie's leaving me."

"I don't think he's done that."

"He's gone. And as soon as I threw myself in your face, you conjured up a girlfriend to spend the night with. Don't you think that's odd, Devon?"

"I'll see you tomorrow, Laura. Try'n get some sleep."

"I'll have to finish the bottle before I can manage that. Oh by the way, I noticed blood on the lining of your tan jacket. You want me to send it to the cleaners?"

"I'll take care of it," he said.

"Uh-huh. You gonna start changing your sheets, too? Or is Samantha gonna do it?"

He didn't say anything.

"How'd you get blood on the inside of your jacket, Devon? Did she scratch you? Is that the problem? That you like rough sex and you don't want Connie to find the evidence? He won't, you know, 'cause he's not coming home. And I'll tell you what, I can be as rough as that little priss you waltzed into the dining room this morning. Why don't you give me a chance?"

Gently he said, "You're drunk, Laura. Go to bed."

"Yeah, I'm drunk. But I'm not going to bed." She sobbed. "I don't like sleeping alone. It reminds me of when Connie was in prison. He's gonna be there again, isn't he? Eric too in another few years. You'll marry Samantha and Misty'll leave home and where'll I be? Living alone in your father's house. Is that fair, Devon?"

"Get hold of yourself, Laura. None of that's happened yet."

"You're not gonna marry Samantha?"

"I'll call you in the morning," he said, then hung up before she could say more. Devon held his head in his hands, remembering the scritch of the rocking chair accompanying his father's litany of complaints about Connie. If the old man had ever believed Connie could amount to something, he might have. But their father had pitted them against each other from the beginning, and now it seemed the gears he'd set in motion were meshing with his predicted destruction: Connie had finally managed to get Devon into the position of breaking the law to save his brother.

With the mournful lilt of a nightingale, Samantha's voice broke into Devon's thoughts. "Now are you leaving?" she asked.

He looked up at her standing in her bedroom door wearing her green velvet robe, her auburn hair like the silky thistle atop a stalk of wild wheat. "Do you want me to leave?" he asked, thinking she should.

She shook her head. "I want you to stay the night so we can wake up together in the morning. We've never done that, you know."

"Maybe you won't like me in the morning," he said.

"Is that what you're afraid of?" she teased. "That if I see you with whiskers, I won't like you anymore?"

"I don't know why you like me now. Being a hippie pacifist, what do you see in a man who never leaves home without a gun in his belt?"

"A man who uses his gun for justice," she said.

"Sometimes justice is a damn hard call."

"I love you because you know that."

He nodded. "What would you think, Sam, if I let justice slide for the sake of my brother? Would you still like me?"

She considered her answer, and he loved her more for taking the time to understand what he was asking. "You wouldn't side with your brother if justice wasn't with him," she finally said, "no matter what's in the law books."

In the morning, he watched her wake up and open her

eyes to meet his. Her smile in the golden light convinced him he never wanted to start another day without her. The love in her eyes made it clear he would never have to if he simply asked a question, the answer to which he knew, but he didn't ask it. He declined everything she offered, including a shower and breakfast, and drove home in yesterday's clothes.

Laura was asleep on the sofa, the bottle she'd promised to finish lying empty on the floor. Devon threw it away, started a pot of coffee, then went upstairs to shower and change. When he came back down, Misty was standing in the kitchen eating a bowl of cereal. They smiled at each other but didn't speak, neither of them wanting to wake her mother. He poured himself a cup of coffee while Misty quietly set her bowl in the sink. She came close and stood on tiptoe to kiss his cheek, then took her books off the dining room table and left for school through the back door.

Devon took his cup upstairs and stood looking out the window as he sipped his coffee. The sky was blue without a hint of haze. Across the green canopy of trees in his neighborhood, he could see far into the desert of New Mexico, the two round humps of Mount Cox and Mount Riley like gumdrops in the distance. Cox and Riley had both been minor principals in the Lincoln County War, a conflagration of violence between opposing mercantile firms in the 1870's. Their descendants were now lawyers and gentlemen ranchers in the Rio Grande Valley, respectable citizens despite the bloody avarice of their ancestors. Devon rewound the tape on his answering machine and listened to his brother say again, "*No me mata,* bro."

If not guilty of murder, why would Connie think Devon, as an extension of the law, could kill him? Maybe the plea was simply a metaphor suggesting his return to prison would be a living death. Fencing the coin collection would be a third degree felony but only Connie's second offense. Unless the prosecution proved Truxal had been murdered in conjunction with the theft of the coins, Connie's sentence would be two to ten. Even given the maximum, he'd be out in seven. Eric would be twenty-four, Misty twenty, both on their own. Connie would probably be a grandfather, maybe an uncle. Laura would be a lush, living alone in their father's house. Even if Connie wasn't convicted of murder, his imprisonment would be a death sentence for her.

Devon opened his closet door and reached high on a shelf for a shoebox of photographs, then sat down on the bed and opened the box. At the front were old snapshots of his parents when they were first married, baby pictures of Connie and Devon, and one of their sister, Rosemary, who'd died as an infant. Devon paused a moment, looking at her newborn face, feeling the ancient wound of her loss like a memory of fear. After that came a couple dozen school portraits of Devon and Connie, photos of their few family outings and the obligatory pictures of the family in front of the Christmas tree, always taken by their mother. Intermixed and out of sequence were pictures of Connie and Laura after he'd come home from prison, and of their children growing up. Rifling through for the one he wanted, Devon found one he'd forgotten.

His mother had taken it two years before she died. Devon had been ten, Connie almost twelve. They were standing on the front porch with their father behind them, one heavy hand on Devon's right shoulder. Connie stood alone. Even then his face wore the cocky sneer of a kid who'd trained himself not to care. What had he done, as young as eleven and with their mother still alive, to earn their father's disfavor?

Flipping through a few more photos, Devon stopped at one taken by Laura of the three of them in the same pose. They were standing in almost the same place on the porch and their father's hand, clawed by then with age, was again on Devon's shoulder. Connie stood a good foot away from them, the emptiness between like a crevice slowly expanding through time. It had been taken a month before his arrest, a week before he took Devon to Juárez and bought him a whore. At eighteen, Connie had looked almost exactly like Eric did now. Devon pulled the photo out and laid it on the bed, then kept flipping through the passage of years until he found the one he wanted.

He had taken it himself only last August, on Eric's seventeenth birthday. Again on the front porch, aglow with the rosy light of sunset, Connie stood up straight and proud, his right hand on his son's shoulder. It was Eric who sneered at the camera. Devon set the box aside and compared the two images. Connie at eighteen, Eric only a year younger. Their right hands, held stiffly by their thighs, were clenched into fists as if they were ready to strike out at the sentimental family ritual of recording a moment so quickly gone.

The night after Laura took that photo of Devon and Connie with their father on the porch, Connie walked into a 7-11 with a gun in his hand and walked out with three hundred dollars and a six-pack of beer. He drank that beer alone in the back yard. Finding him drunk flaunting his gun and his pocket full of stolen money, their father screamed under the stars, "You've killed me, Connie!" Devon was watching from the door. Under the weight of their father's curse, Connie met Devon's eyes and laughed at the absurdity that anything he did could touch the old man. Looking into the photo of Eric's face, Devon heard Connie say again, "*No me mata,* bro."

Devon took the photo and drove to Sun City Coins. It wasn't open yet but Devon could see the shadow of someone moving around the back room. He pounded on the door until a man peered out. He was small and squat, his black hair slicked away from his face, his dark eyes as hostile as a fighting cock's. When Devon flattened his badge against the glass, the man reluctantly crossed the room and opened the door.

"Elvis Short?" Devon asked.

"Yeah," he grumbled. "Whaddaya want?"

Devon smiled, returning his badge to his pocket. "The silver dollar collection you fenced last Friday night."

"I didn't fence it," he scoffed. "I bought it off a dude who said he owned it."

Devon pulled the photo of Connie and Eric from the pocket of his jacket and showed it to Short. "The older guy. Does he look familiar?"

Short scowled at the photo. "Maybe," he said.

Devon slid the picture back inside his pocket, then grabbed Short's shirtfront and threw him against the wall. He hit with a thud, sliding to the floor. "You need to see it again?" Devon asked.

Short shook his head.

"Is he the one you bought the coins from?"

"Yeah," Short said.

"I want to see 'em," Devon said.

"You got any papers?" Short asked.

Devon reached under his jacket and brought out his gun. "Will this do?"

Short stared at the snub-nosed .38, then nodded, pulling himself to his feet. "In here," he mumbled, trundling toward the back room.

Devon followed him into a small office and watched him turn the combination lock to open the safe. Short stood up and offered him a black leather notebook.

"Put it on the desk," Devon said.

Short did, then backed away as Devon moved closer, opened the notebook and saw the first plastic sheet of silver dollars nestled in circular windows to show front and back as Elise had said. Devon flipped through the pages, seeing they were all full, then closed the book and met the man's eyes. "What's this worth?"

"I paid twenty-four hundred."

"What're you gonna sell it for?"

"Maybe three grand."

"Maybe five?"

"Maybe."

"Did you know it was stolen?"

Short shook his head.

"Tell me about Theodore Truxal," Devon said.

"Never heard of him," Short answered.

Devon took a step closer and hit him across the mouth with the barrel of his gun. Short staggered backwards, spitting blood. "Try again," Devon said.

"I met him in jail," Short mumbled.

"And?"

"He told me he had a coin collection, asked what it was worth and if I'd be interested in buying it. I said I would."

"Did you buy it twice?"

Short nodded, warily watching Devon's gun. "Screwiest deal I've ever been involved in."

"Who sold it to you the first time?"

"Truxal, then he bought it back."

"For the same price?"

"I'd only had it a few days. Being as he was a friend," Short shrugged, "I traded back even-steven."

"Then what happened?"

"Truxal's son, Teddy, called and said they wanted to sell it again."

"When was that?"

"Last Friday."

"Were you surprised when this other guy came in to sell it?"

Short shook his head. "Teddy told me he was coming."

"Did he tell you his name?"

"Said he'd have BORN TO LOSE tattooed on his arm. That's how I'd know he was the one."

"You talk to Teddy after the deal?"

Short nodded.

"Was he happy with it?"

"Yeah," Short said with a sleazy smile. "My customers are always happy with my deals."

"Did you know Teddy's father was murdered?"

Short blanched, then shook his head.

"Don't you read the papers, Elvis?" Devon mocked.

Short spit more blood on the floor. "Didn't have nothing to do with my deal."

"These coins were reported stolen at the time of the murder."

Short watched Devon's gun as he said, "I bought 'em on good faith."

"When?"

" 'Bout eight o'clock last Friday night."

"Theodore Truxal had been dead two hours at eight o'clock last Friday night."

Short stared at him for a long moment of heavy silence, then said with a quiver in his voice, "I didn't know they was stolen. A collection like that don't come with proof of ownership."

Devon hesitated, then asked, "How soon can you sell 'em?"

Short's eyes lit with hope. "I got a buyer already lined up."

"A cop was here yesterday asking about 'em. What're you gonna say if he comes back?"

"That I was wrong. I misunderstood what he was asking."

"And the photo I showed you?"

"I never saw that guy in my life."

"If you cross me, Elvis, the next time you're walking down a dark alley, you won't get to the other end."

Elvis smiled. "This buyer lives in Phoenix. I like that city. Think I'll deliver the coins personal and stay there."

"It's hotter'n hell in Phoenix," Devon said, "so might be the right place for you."

Elvis laughed. "You know what they say: if you pay your dues in Phoenix, you get an air-conditioned suite in hell."

Devon smiled. "We understand each other then."

Elvis smiled back. "Perfectly."

Devon nodded, put his gun away and walked out. He drove to the courthouse, flashed his badge at Records, and was shown the receipt book for the day Theodore Truxal was released from jail. Truxal paid his fine with a Visa card. Devon wrote down the number, drove to headquarters, and walked into the detective's bullpen. At his desk, he turned on his computer and requested the status of the Visa account. It belonged to Theodore Truxal, Jr., had a credit limit of fifteen hundred, but was overdrawn to the tune of two thousand, declared delinquent and rescinded. He requested a full credit report on Teddy. While he waited, he ran a check on the .357 Ruger he'd seen at Teddy's house. The screen flashed PLEASE WAIT, then ran an updated list. The Ruger had been purchased at 5 p.m. on Saturday, May 22, 1993, by Theodore Truxal, Jr., from Frontier Sporting Goods at 9873 Dyer, El Paso, Texas.

Devon called up Officer Brent's investigative report on Zane Kalinsky's murder. He wrote down the weapon's serial number, cleared the screen and ran a check on that .357. It was registered to Theodore Truxal, Sr., but had been reported stolen on April 4th. Devon cleared his screen and called up the Crime Report on the theft of the gun. The complaint had been taken at the Cristo Rey Hotel. Nothing else was reported missing. There was a notation under Comments that because of the lack of forcible entry, Truxal suspected the gun had been taken by someone living or working in the hotel. The credit report came through Devon's printer. Besides the rescinded VISA, Teddy'd had two other credit cards canceled within the last month, and his mortgage was in the process of foreclosure.

Devon shut off his computer and walked out before Lieutenant Dreyfus could catch him. Checking out another sedan with a full gas tank and no dried blood on its door handle, he drove to the courthouse to make his appearance at Elise's arraignment.

Chapter Eleven

The city-county building was a new glass skyscraper on San Antonio Street. Devon drove to the parking garage behind it on Overland, left his sedan in a space reserved for police, and took the elevator to the skywalk across to the courthouse. He went to the juvenile court and walked into the plushly-carpeted, wood-paneled chamber. In the front row of seats, Teddy Truxal sat alone in the spectators gallery. Devon walked down the aisle and through the swinging half-door to the bench. He flashed his badge at the clerk and said he wanted to see his prisoner. The clerk waved him through a back door to the holding room.

Half a dozen kids sat in the two rows of white plastic chairs facing each other across the room. Five of them were male, three Mexicans and two Anglos, wearing identical hostile sneers that crossed all lines of ethnicity as they sat beneath the watchful eye of a deputy sheriff. On the other side of the room, Elise was the sole prisoner of a female deputy. Devon showed the female officer his badge. "Give me a minute with her?"

The officer nodded and moved across the room to stand chatting softly with her fellow deputy as Devon sat down beside Elise. "How're you feeling?" he asked softly.

She shrugged with an attitude, still wearing the orange smock of an inmate, the innocence of her face without makeup belied by her defensive smirk.

"Teddy's outside," Devon said.

Her eyes softened with fear. "You gonna let him take me home?"

"I'll give you a ride, if you like."

"Home?" she whispered.

"To your boyfriend's," he said.

She studied him warily. "You're not doing this for me."

"No I'm not," he agreed.

"How soon?"

"When your case is called, I'll explain to the judge it was a misunderstanding and he'll drop the charges, then I'll walk your release papers to detention myself and take you out as soon as you've changed clothes. Do we have a deal?"

Elise nodded.

Devon stood up and walked back into the courtroom. Teddy watched him come through the door. There were a few more people in the gallery now, worried parents of the boys in the holding room. Devon stopped at the clerk's desk and read the calendar upside down. Elise was first on the roster. He turned around and met Teddy's eyes for a moment before he walked over and extended his hand.

Teddy stood up to shake hands. "Morning," he said guardedly.

Devon smiled. "You here to take your sister home?"

"Yeah," Teddy said. "How long do you think it'll be? The funeral's at two."

"Once they're finished here, it'll take about an hour to get her release papers over to detention, then maybe another hour to get her out, depending on how busy the matrons are, so you're looking at eleven o'clock, maybe noon."

"Can't you hurry it up?" Teddy asked peevishly.

Devon shook his head. "The wheels of justice are famous for their slow turning."

"Justice," Teddy scoffed.

Devon smiled. "I wouldn't expect you to like that word."

Teddy frowned. "You trying to scare me, Detective?"

"When I am, you won't have any doubts."

Teddy's frown deepened. "That sounds like a threat."

Devon smiled again. "Why don't we sit down?"

Teddy took a step back and sank heavily into the chair behind him. Devon left an empty seat between them, leaning forward with his elbows on his knees as he watched the clerk arranging papers on the bench for the judge. Turning his head to look sideways at Teddy, Devon said, "In my six years as a detective, this is my third case of patricide."

Teddy's eyes flared with fear.

"In both prior cases," Devon said softly, "if anyone had asked my opinion, I would've said the murder was justified."

"I didn't kill my father," Teddy whispered between clenched teeth.

"No, probably not," Devon said. "But the way I've got it figured, you killed Zane to protect whoever did."

Teddy stared in a long moment of silence, then muttered, "If you could prove anything, you wouldn't be sitting here telling me this."

"I can prove Zane was killed," Devon said softly, "with the gun reported stolen from your father's hotel."

"It could've been taken by anyone," Teddy argued.

"Anyone with access to the hotel," Devon agreed. "But it was reported missing on April 4th. On the 3rd, you had an argument with your father over the kind of hitch you had on your truck. Remember that?"

Teddy just stared at him.

Devon smiled. "It could be that when you went into his hotel right after that argument, you didn't take the gun but something else. And stretching possibilities, Zane could have stolen the gun or even bought it from whoever did. But it's at least a coincidence that he used your father's gun to commit suicide. If it *was* suicide. I won't know until I read the coroner's report."

"What'll it tell you?" Teddy asked with a glimmer of hope.

"How far away from his head the gun was fired."

"So if it was close," Teddy asked, his hope brightening, "that'll mean it was suicide?"

"There's also angle of entry," Devon said. "If a man shoots himself, he generally holds the gun lower than his head. But if someone else fired the gun, since Zane was in bed the angle of entry most likely came from above."

"Couldn't you tell that by looking?" Teddy sneered.

"The skull was pretty well shattered," Devon said, watching him closely.

Teddy stared hard, then gave him a sick smile. "You're fishing again. But I'm not gonna bite this time."

Devon shrugged. "What I can't figure is why Zane was a threat to whoever killed your father." He sighed. "Unless it was just the shotgun."

"What shotgun?" Teddy asked.

"The one you borrowed from Zane."

"I returned it a long time ago. I told you that."

"Yeah, Zane said the same thing. But when I looked at it in his apartment Saturday morning, I could smell that it had been recently fired."

"So maybe Zane killed my father, then felt so bad about it he killed himself."

"I hadn't thought of that," Devon said. "It's a feasible theory for suicide. Or maybe, if it turns out it was homicide, that's what the killer's hoping I'll think. Course, it would've helped it he'd left us a note, something along the line of 'I can't live with what I've done' or, even better, 'I killed Theodore Truxal and have decided to throw myself on the mercy of the Highest Court.' " Devon smiled. "Zane was Catholic, wasn't he?"

"Yeah, he was," Teddy said eagerly.

"Too bad," Devon said. "If done for altruistic reasons, murder can be atoned, but according to the priests, suicide's a one-way ticket to hell."

Hearing the holding room door open, Devon smiled at Teddy and said, "Here comes the cause of all your grief." He watched Teddy look at Elise, and the hurt and love mingled in her brother's eyes made Devon wince with sympathy.

An hour later, Devon escorted Elise through the halls of juvenile detention toward the back door into the employees' parking lot. Wearing her red spike heels, pink short shorts and skimpy white halter, she turned heads even in the jaded environs of cops accustomed to working with underage hookers. Outside, Devon opened the door to his car and watched her slide in.

"If you try to give me the slip," he warned, "I'll arrest and cuff you again."

She gave him a secretive smile of mutual conspiracy, so he closed the door and walked around to the driver's side. As he turned the ignition, he said, "I have a stop to make on the way."

"All right," she said, lifting her face to bask in the sunlight coming through her window.

Impressed again with her flawless beauty, Devon found himself thinking her looks should be registered as a lethal weapon. Two men had died because of Elise Truxal's attributes, and the game wasn't over. Someone would stand before the bench of justice to be held accountable for the mayhem she'd inspired. If committed in the passion of the moment, the maximum sentence for her father's murder would have been life imprisonment, but by entangling the motive with burglary, she had upped the maximum sentence to death, and the degree of her apparent lack of concern sent a chill down Devon's spine.

From San Antonio, he turned right on Santa Fe, again on Franklin, then left into the parking lot behind the library. Nosing his car into the only empty space, probably vacated by some hapless civil servant who'd taken an early lunch, Devon locked his door getting out, then locked Elise's behind her, knowing the car wouldn't be towed because it was a city vehicle. He held her elbow as they walked around to the front of the building. When she saw where they were, Elise laughed and asked, "What're we doing here?"

"Trading cars," Devon said, opening the door and guiding her through.

Samantha wasn't at the desk, so Devon led Elise upstairs to administration. As head of reference, Samantha had a small office with a window overlooking the street. The door was open and she was sitting behind her desk, talking on the phone. She was wearing red. Her expression didn't change when she saw Devon and Elise come in, but he could see her gaze move down the girl's long bare legs before she met Devon's eyes. He gave her a smile.

"Can I call you back, Tom?" Samantha asked into the phone. She hung up, gave Elise a small smile, then looked at Devon.

"I was wondering if I could borrow your car," he said.

She flicked her gaze at the girl again, opened a low drawer on her desk, took out her purse and set it on her lap as she zipped it open, then extracted her keys and extended them toward him.

"Thanks," he said, taking them. "Is it at your apartment?"

She shook her head. "I drove today because the radio said we might have rain this afternoon."

"I'll have it back before you get off," he said.

She looked at the girl again, then said with a hint of sarcasm but no trace of a smile. "Have a good time."

He laughed, steering Elise out the door. They walked back downstairs and around the building to the parking lot.

As Elise fastened her seatbelt, she asked, "Is she your girlfriend?"

Devon nodded, turning the key.

Elise smiled. "She's pretty."

He made no reply, backing out of the space and turning left on Franklin, right on Oregon and again on Main, then south on Santa Fe toward the border.

As they crested the arch of the bridge, Elise looked at the river in its concrete channel emblazoned with rebel graffiti, then she asked, "Do you really expect me to take you to see him?"

"Yeah I do," he said. After smiling at the Mexican border guard waving them through, Devon coasted to a stop at the first red light on the Avenida. "Now where?"

"I don't want to do this," she argued.

"I don't give a fuck, Elise," he said. "As a cop, it's against policy for me to even be here, and it's a federal offense for anyone to transport a minor across the border for illicit purposes. That means I'm looking at five to twenty right now. A charge of assault wouldn't make it much worse."

Her eyes flared with alarm, catching green from the light as it changed.

He eased into the intersection. "Where're we going?"

"The market," she said.

He drove another few blocks through the tourist zone,

passing the Kentucky Club set amid other brazen bars attracting soldiers off Fort Bliss, curio shops offering indigenous folk art, and liquor stores selling duty-free alcohol. The tourist zone quickly faded into nondescript stores and bakeries catering to Mexicans. At *Avenida 16 de Septiembre,* he turned right, drove another few blocks and stopped at another red light in front of the Cathedral. The street was crowded with city buses, their propane engines filling the air with a sickly sweet smell, the plaza congested with loiterers and beggars. The loiterers were mostly unemployed men, the beggars were old Indian women with rebozos hiding their faces. The market was straight ahead.

"Now where?" Devon asked.

"We have to park," she said.

He drove another two blocks and found an empty space at the curb in front of the governmental palace. Its adobe walls were still pocked with bullet holes from the 1910 Revolution, and a plaque by the door proclaimed the building had been the headquarters of General Francisco Villa. Devon said a silent prayer for Samantha's car as they left it behind, walking south on *Calle Mariscal.*

Closed to vehicles, the market was crowded with native shoppers and noisy with the cries of vendors. The center of the street was jammed with permanent wooden stalls selling food: bins of bright red tomatoes, vibrant green chiles, orange mangos, purple grapes, red and yellow and white onions, dried herbs, cobs of corn, ripe bananas, yams and red and white potatoes, red chiles, yellow chiles, oranges, lemons, limes, and apples polished like rubies. Peppered among the stalls were stand-up cafes offering sugared fruit drinks or tacos made of pork cut from sizzling spits, tortilla factories clacking their rhythmic machines, and stalls selling cassette tapes, each with its own speakers blaring the voices of ranchero singers, Mexico's complement to American country music.

On both sides were the original buildings of Juárez, second stories stacked on ancient adobes with low portals running the length of the street paved with cobblestones. El Paso had once looked like this. So had every city in the Southwest, before the Anglos came with their Victorian gingerbread which gave way to glass skyscrapers. Here in the birthplace of Juárez, the portalled adobes remained, plastered countless times and painted decades ago with primary colors now peeling from the sun and rain. Just past a green facade advertising baths and rooms, Elise turned into a courtyard. Immediately the noise of the street was subdued behind high adobe walls.

The white stone floor of the patio sparkled with mica as she led Devon to a flight of rickety wooden stairs at the far end. They climbed to an upper story veranda, turned left and walked past three rooms to a door painted blue. She knocked, then bit her lip as she turned around to look at Devon.

Connie opened the door wearing only Levi's. He stared a moment in stunned surprise, then grinned. "I'll be goddamned. Come on in."

The apartment had two rooms, the front one furnished with a red plastic couch and a glass coffee table on wrought-iron legs. The walls were pink, their only decoration a vivid print of an Aztec warrior carrying a dead princess in his arms. Devon stepped inside and closed the door, surprised Connie had made no move to touch Elise.

"Hey Eric!" Connie called through the door open to the other room. "Come see who's here."

Eric appeared on the threshold, his face brightening with pleasure when he saw Elise, then falling into a frown when he saw his uncle. Elise ran to Eric. He took her in his arms, burying his face in the flaxen cascade of her hair for a long moment before he looked up at the men watching them.

"Go on," Connie said. "Me and Devon'll work things out."

Eric stepped backward into the room, taking Elise with him, and closed the door.

Devon looked at his brother.

Connie laughed. "Did you think I was balling her?"

Devon nodded.

"I take that as a high compliment," Connie snickered. "Have a seat, bro. You want a drink?"

"Yeah," Devon said, sitting down on the sofa and hearing its plastic crinkle under his weight.

"I guess!" Connie said with another laugh as he opened a metal cabinet and took out two glasses and a bottle of tequila. He set them all on the table, filled each glass, nudged one toward Devon and lifted the other. "Salud," Connie said.

"Salud," Devon murmured, downing the shot.

Connie's face fell solemn. "You're in deep, Devon, coming here at all, to say nothing of bringing her. No matter what happens here on out, I want you to know I appreciate it."

Devon looked down at an overflowing ashtray with a crumpled, nearly empty pack of Vantage cigarettes beside it. Knowing his brother didn't smoke, Devon met his eyes. "I thought I had it figured," Devon said.

Connie smiled with sympathy. "How's Laura?"

"Crying a lot."

Connie picked up the bottle of tequila. "Want another?"

Devon shook his head. "Why don't we start at the beginning?"

"Where's that?" Connie asked, filling one of the glasses. He threw his head back and drank the shot down, then smiled.

"Let's start with the coins," Devon said.

"That's closer to the end," Connie said, pouring himself another shot, "but if you want to start there it's okay with me."

"What was the beginning?" Devon asked.

Connie toyed with the full shot, not lifting it off the table, merely turning it in his fingers. *"No me mata,"* he said, smiling sadly. Then he met Devon's eyes. "You remember when the old man said I'd killed him, that night in the back yard after my first heist?"

Devon nodded. "But it wasn't your first."

"It was the first one I'd done alone," Connie said. "Didn't you ever wonder why I didn't celebrate with friends who would've thought I was hot shit for pulling it off?"

Softly Devon said, "I figured you thought the old man's wrath would be more fun."

Connie downed the shot, then met his eyes. "I came home that night to be with you, Devon."

Devon remembered walking into the back yard to see Connie drinking in the shadows of the pomegranate trees, and how at first he'd wanted to join the party. He'd gone halfway across the yard in answer to his brother's summons, then just stood there without accepting the proffered beer because laying beside the empties on the grass he could see the dark silhouette of a gun.

"You'd just come from band practice," Connie smiled, "and you had your clarinet case in your hand. You remember that?"

Devon shrugged.

"I'd had a few beers before I got up the nerve to walk

into that 7-11," Connie paused to smile, "and I'd had three from the six pack I lifted on my way out, so I was pretty drunk. Lying on the grass looking up at you against the stars with your clarinet in your hand, I felt like shit. A minute before you walked through that gate, I was high on the hog. Three hundred dollars in my pocket, that's a lot of money to a kid. Then you walked in with your damn clarinet and I felt like dirt."

Connie reached for the tequila again, but Devon beat him to it, recapped the bottle and set it on the floor, then met his brother's eyes.

Connie laughed. "You're just like the old man."

"No," Devon said. "I just want to hear your story before you get drunk."

"All right," Connie said. "Here it is in a nutshell: I killed our sister."

Devon stared at him, then slowly said, "She died in her crib when the old house burnt down."

"I set the fire," Connie said.

For another long moment, Devon stared at his brother. Finally he asked, "Accidentally, right?"

Connie shook his head. "But I didn't know Rosemary was in there. It was Sunday morning and she'd kept us awake all night crying 'cause she was sick. It wasn't anything serious, just one of those baby sicknesses. When she finally quit crying, I fell asleep and Mom took you to Mass before I woke up. 'Cause the house was quiet, I figured she'd taken Rosemary too. I went into the kitchen to fix myself a bowl of cereal, but when I was getting the milk out of the refrigerator, I dropped the bottle and it broke. Dad came in, and I guess he was at the end of his rope after being up all night. He whipped me, told me to clean up the milk, then went out and sat on the front porch." Connie squeezed his eyes shut, remembering. "I stood there in the middle of the kitchen with my jeans down around my ankles and welts all over my legs from his belt. I stood there a long time, hating him." Connie opened his eyes, but there was no remnant of that hatred in them, only a boy's sorrow and fear. "I left the milk where it was, and I took the matches off the stove and went out on the back porch and set a pile of newspapers on fire. You probably don't remember, but their bedroom was right next to that porch, and that house was a shack. The fire caught real fast. I ran into the yard and laughed, watching the smoke curl out of the porch, then the flames lick up through the open windows toward the roof. Dad had fallen asleep in the front. By the time he woke up, the bedroom was burning. Rosemary must've died from the smoke. I never heard her cry."

Devon closed his eyes, remembering that moment on the walk home from church when his mother saw the smoke. She began running, leaving him behind. He was only four, hadn't started school yet, and that was the first time his mother had left him anywhere. He ran after her, crying from fear at being alone on the road, but when he got home, his mother's screams filled him with terror. That encompassing terror was all he remembered of his sister. Soon after that, they moved to the house on the hill and nobody mentioned the baby girl who had once been part of their family. Meeting his brother's eyes, Devon whispered, "Why didn't you tell me?"

Connie shrugged, blinking back tears. "I never even told Laura. Guess I figured, once anyone knew, they'd hate me like Dad did. I'm surprised he never told you."

Devon shook his head. "Those nights he sat in his rocker talking about you, he never mentioned that." Belatedly he said, "He didn't hate you, Connie."

"Yeah, he did. And I hated him back. All the time we were growing up, I watched the difference in the way he treated us, all the beatings I took while you waltzed through unmarked, and I wanted to be you so bad. But I wasn't and all my wishing didn't do any good. When I got out of prison, I made up my mind never to hit Eric, and I never have, but that didn't do any good either."

Devon looked at the crumpled pack of cigarettes beside the full ashtray, then at his brother. "Did Eric shoot Truxal?"

Connie nodded, his eyes blurring with tears. "If you arrest him, you'll kill me, Devon." He hid his eyes behind his hand a moment, then wiped his tears and looked at Devon again. "The Bible says a father's sins are always laid on his children, but you skated free. I took Dad's hatred so he had nothing but love for you. That wasn't your doing, I know that, but what happens now is. Can you see your way clear to letting Eric skate?"

Devon reached for the tequila, opened it and took a swig straight from the bottle, then passed it to his brother. "Tell me about the coins," Devon said, feeling the liquor burn all the way down.

Connie took a long drink and set the bottle on the table between them. Hitching his chair closer, he said, "Teddy Truxal was a friend of mine. When he first asked me to sell the coins, I was surprised 'cause he'd already told me how his old man had sold 'em and how much trouble Teddy went to getting 'em back. But he hadn't given 'em to Elise yet when he got hit with the foreclosure on his house. Teddy said he'd explained the whole deal to her, and that she'd offered the coins to keep him from losing his house. I've found out since that was a lie. He never told her he got 'em back. But I didn't know that then. I told Teddy I'd take him down there and he could sell 'em himself, but he said I knew more about coins and I'd get a better price. When I got down there, though, the guy wouldn't budge on the price. I called Teddy and said I thought he'd do better with another dealer, but he said to go ahead and take what the man was offering, so I did. The guy threw an 1888 silver dollar into the deal, saying the little girl could start a new collection with that. I took the money and that dollar up to Teddy's place. Wanda doesn't like me much, so me and Teddy talked in the garage. Then I went out drinking, trying to figure how I could cut myself loose from that shit job I had.

"When I went up to your room the next night, I had no idea you'd just come from the Truxal house or that the old man had been murdered. I went into the back yard to talk to Eric and he told me what happened. As soon as I heard it, I knew Teddy had set me up, that he'd say Eric stole the coins and I fenced 'em. I should've seen that when Teddy told me to go in there flashing my tattoo. He said the man would know I'd come from him 'cause of it, but I should've seen he was setting me up. I couldn't figure what to do but run. The newspaper story the next day said you were on the case, and I thought maybe if I gave you a coupla days to get all the details straight, you'd find a way to keep Eric out of it." Connie leaned even closer. "He's been with me since Friday night, Devon. Can't you pin both raps on whoever knocked off Kalinsky?"

Devon picked over Connie's story, knowing it had flaws. But his mind was still reeling from the impact of the fire, so all he said was, "It's probably Teddy. You think he'll go down and keep his mouth shut?"

Connie nodded. "He thinks Elise killed their old man. Right after it happened, Elise called Teddy and said she'd done it, that the old man was coming at her again and she couldn't take it anymore. Teddy'll do anything to protect her. Hell, look at her. Who wouldn't?"

"Me," Devon said. "And maybe that's exactly what I'd be doing."

Connie frowned, leaning back in his chair. "You think Eric lied about who pulled the trigger?"

"Hasn't it ever crossed your mind?"

Connie shook his head. "But maybe it should've," he said.

Devon looked at the closed bedroom door. "Get her out of there," he said. "Let me hear it from him."

Devon sat on the bed while Eric paced the room. It was long and narrow, furnished only with an iron double bed opposite the door. There were small windows at both ends, one overlooking the patio leading to the market, the other an ally. The bed was unmade, its white sheets fragrant with the fresh scent of sex.

Eric hadn't changed clothes since leaving home. He wore sneakers and jeans and a yellow T-shirt that smelled sweaty even from a distance. His dark hair was dirty, falling to his shoulders, and his face, so reminiscent of his father's as a teenager, was set in the hard lines of defense. Finally he stopped pacing and met Devon's eyes from the end of the room farthest from the door.

"Elise and I were having sex when her father came home," Eric began. "We heard him coming out of the garage, so we were dressed by the time he got inside."

"Which door did he use?" Devon asked.

"There's an outside hall between Elise's room and the family room," Eric said. "That hall leads from the yard to the back door."

Devon nodded. "I've been there."

Eric watched his uncle a moment, obviously uncomfortable with Devon's knowledge of the house. "We heard him coming up those steps," Eric said. "I tried to go out the window, but I couldn't get the screen open, so I hid in the closet. It was dark in there and I had to push shoes out of my way to find a place to stand. That closet's real small so I was kinda leaning forward against the door 'cause I couldn't stand up straight under her dresses and stuff."

Devon nodded, remembering the disarray of Elise's shoes on the closet floor. At the time he'd thought it was simply the sloppiness of a teenager but now, remembering how neat the rest of the room was, he realized he should have noticed the disparity. "Go on," he said.

"When I was trying to catch my balance so I could hold still for what might be more'n a few minutes," Eric said, "I touched something metal, cold and hard, and it seemed real stable, like maybe I could lean on it. When I did, I discovered it was a shotgun. I could feel the two round holes of the double barrel, and I crouched down and held onto the gun to keep me steady." He stopped, watching his uncle.

"Go on," Devon said again.

"I heard Elise's father come in. He didn't knock or nothing, just opened the door, and I could hear him breathing hard, like maybe climbing those stairs had cut his wind. He asked her if she wasn't going with her mother, and Elise said she had to stay home and write a report for school." Eric smiled. "I kinda laughed at that. I didn't make any noise, but I knew it was a flat-out lie. Her father, he said he didn't think it was a good idea for her to be home alone, that she wasn't trustworthy and he wanted her to come spend the weekend at his hotel. Elise said she didn't want to go to his dump hotel, and he said he guessed she'd rather stay here and smoke cigarettes." Eric shrugged. "I'd had a cigarette when we'd first gone into her room, and I guess he could smell the smoke. Elise said *he* smoked cigarettes so she couldn't see why he cared if she did. He got mad then and said adults could do what they wanted but she was a child and was s'posed to do what he told her. Then he left the room. I knew that 'cause when he yelled at her again, his voice was farther away. He said he was gonna call the church and make sure her mother knew she was home alone, that he didn't believe her mother would let her do that. Elise yelled back that Anne was coming to stay with her, and if he didn't have such a dirty mind he'd trust his kids not to do what he did. 'Like smoking cigarettes?' he yelled, and I could hear he'd come closer again but he was still in the hall. 'Like fucking your maid,' Elise said. Then I heard a little clinking sound. I didn't know what it was till later, but it was his buckle and he was coming back, taking his belt off to whip her. She screamed she wouldn't let him do that again and he laughed." Eric stopped, his face no longer set in the hard sneer of a punk but appalled now with what he was remembering. He shook his head then said, "The way he laughed was the ugliest thing I'd ever heard. It was like he was playing with her and having a good time doing it. When he asked how she was gonna stop him, she yanked open the closet door."

Eric turned around and looked out the window. Devon watched him, wondering what he was hiding in that gesture of avoidance, his shoulders rigid, his hands limp at his sides. Gently, Devon said, "Look at me, Eric."

Eric swung back around, the motion abrupt with anger, his eyes squinting either with camouflage or the mimicking of memory. "Like I said, I was leaning on the gun, so I had it in my hands when she opened the door. I couldn't see much 'cause it'd been dark in that closet and it was daylight in the room, but I turned toward the hall and heard the gun fire twice, real quick, boom-BOOM." He shuddered. "I acted on instinct, Uncle Devon. It wasn't till I saw the blood that I realized I'd shot him."

"Do you remember cocking the gun?"

Eric thought a minute, then shook his head.

"It takes two motions," Devon said. "You have to slide the magazine forward and back to get the shells into position. Probably takes a second each way, enough time for your vision to clear."

"I don't remember that," Eric said.

"Did you see Truxal fall?" Devon asked.

Eric shook his head. "The first I saw him, he was on the floor, his shirt all bloody."

"What did you do?" Devon asked.

"I went into the hall and crouched down beside him and watched the blood bubbling with his heartbeat till it stopped."

"Did you still have the gun?"

Eric frowned, then shook his head. "I guess I'd left it in the room. I don't remember putting it down, but I guess I did."

"Then what?"

"Elise came to stand beside me, and she asked if I thought we should call an ambulance, but I told her it was too late. Can I get a cigarette now, Uncle Devon?"

"In a minute," he said. "What happened after you decided he was dead?"

Eric shrugged. "We went back into her room and closed the door and sat down on her bed and I had a cigarette. I kept staring at the gun leaning just inside the door, and I told her I'd get rid of it and that she should go to the church with her mother and pretend nothing had happened, that she'd just changed her mind about going on the retreat, and that if we left right then she'd get there before they left for Cloudcroft. So that's what we did."

"What'd you do with the gun?"

Eric thought, as if trying to remember. "She put it in her father's car, under the front seat. She said her brother had borrowed the gun and she'd return it and nobody'd think to look for it there. She packed a little suitcase real fast and we left."

"In your car?"

"Yeah. I'd parked it around the corner so her brother wouldn't see it." He smiled sheepishly. "He doesn't like me much, and if he saw my car outside her house, he would've come in."

"So you drove her to the church?"

"Within half a block. We could see the parking lot and that the people hadn't left yet. So she got out and walked into the crowd like nothing had happened."

"Then what did you do?"

"I drove around for a long time, with the radio real loud so I wouldn't have to think. It didn't help though, I couldn't stop thinking about it. I didn't want to go home 'cause I felt . . . ," he stopped, looked at the floor, then met Devon's eyes, "I felt you'd know just by looking that I was different. Like I had the mark of Cain on me now, like it says in the Bible. So even when I finally went home, I sat in the yard, watching the light in your room. I thought I was afraid of you, Uncle Devon, but I guess I was really afraid of going to jail for something I didn't mean to do. It was like an accident, and I thought I should've called you from Elise's house, that maybe somehow you could've got me out of the whole situation, but since I'd run, I'd lost that chance and I just had to deal with it. Then, too, Elise and I had got our story together, and I thought if I backed out it'd look bad for her, so I decided I couldn't. When Dad came out to the yard, I lost it." He tossed his head to throw his hair back out of his eyes. "I cried like a baby, said I'd done something that'd put me in jail for life. Dad was cool. He didn't even ask what I'd done, he just took me out to his truck so we could get away from you while we worked it out. I told him all about it when we were driving around, and he said we wouldn't go home till we saw how you were gonna fall, and if you fell wrong, we just wouldn't go back."

Devon studied Eric, picking over his story for flaws. It was tight, but he'd expect that from someone who'd had days to rehearse it. The thing that bothered Devon most was Eric putting down the gun so fast. It didn't seem a scared kid who'd just shot a man would do that until he was sure the man wasn't getting back up. When Devon put himself in Eric's place at that moment, the first thing he'd do is reload the gun and keep it in his hands when he walked over to assess the damage. But then Devon was experienced with guns and no stranger to murder, while Eric must have been scared out of his wits.

With a tremble of feigned defiance in his voice, Eric asked, "You gonna arrest me, Uncle Devon?"

"Mexico's outside my jurisdiction." Devon smiled, watching the kid relax.

Eric actually laughed. "What're you gonna do?"

"Take Elise home," he said, standing up.

"Thanks for bringing her." Eric grinned. "It was cool seeing her."

Devon hesitated then said, "This may sound silly in the light of everything else, but do you use a condom?"

"She's on the pill," Eric boasted.

"You're not the only one she sleeps with. Did you know that?"

Eric's smile vanished in a flash of honest surprise, then his habitual sneer returned and he said, "She's not the only one I sleep with either."

Devon nodded. "I just wanted you to know that if you're lying to protect her, you're not the only man who is."

"Who else?" Eric scoffed. "Teddy?"

"Is he sleeping with her?"

"I meant lying to protect her."

"Are you doing that?"

Eric snorted. "You're a cop all right, twisting people's answers into what you want to hear."

"Why would I do that with you, Eric?"

The kid shrugged, hiding his eyes.

Devon sighed. "Why don't you get Elise's raincoat and I'll take her home."

Eric looked up. "Her raincoat?"

"Didn't she leave it here last time she came?"

Eric shook his head.

For a long moment, they held each other's eyes across the room, and in Eric's Devon thought he saw a lessening of faith. Devon asked, "Do you know who Zane Kalinsky was?"

Again, Eric shook his head.

"Haven't you been reading the newspapers?"

"Dad won't let me. Says it could muddy my story."

Devon had to admire the wiliness of his brother, though he didn't think Connie had helped Eric much. "Zane was Elise's front door boyfriend," Devon told the kid. "The one she didn't have to sneak into her house or hide in her closet. Somebody killed him."

Eric paled.

Softly Devon asked, "Do you want to change your story?"

For the third time, Eric shook his head, though now Devon could see fear in his eyes.

Devon smiled. "Wherever your thoughts lead you in the next few days, don't make a move without talking to me first. Okay?"

"I won't," Eric promised.

"And don't call Elise no matter what. It may seem like a local call, but an international connection sticks out like a sore thumb in the phone company's records. Remember that."

"Yes, sir," Eric said.

Devon chuckled. "You haven't called me sir for years."

Eric shrugged, embarrassed.

"Don't be too hard on yourself," Devon said. "You aren't the first man taken in by a pretty girl, and you sure as hell won't be the last."

In a near whisper, Eric asked, "Does that mean you don't believe me?"

"I don't know," Devon said. "But either way, I think she used you."

"Maybe you're wrong," Eric said, regaining his sneer.

"Maybe," Devon said. "I'm gonna open the door now. When you go out there, watch her eyes. If I'm right, she'll look scared that you changed your story."

Devon opened the door and let Eric go first. Elise was sitting on the couch, her long smooth legs gracefully arranged. She gave Eric such a dazzling smile, the kid blushed when he laughed and looked at Devon. Devon didn't smile. He thought she was the best actress he'd ever seen. "Let's go," he told her.

She stood up and walked over to give Eric a parting kiss. Connie stood up too and met Devon at the door. "What do you think?" Connie whispered.

Devon took his notebook out and wrote Samantha's number on a page he tore free and gave to Connie. "Call me there at nine o'clock tonight."

Connie nodded, looking solemn, then asked, "Can't you tell me anything now?"

"Stay here," Devon said. "And make sure he does too."

"It's bad then."

"Lethal," Devon said.

"Shit," Connie whispered. "There's something else, Devon. I sold the coins to a man named Elvis Short at Sun City Pawn. 'Cause of the way I flashed my tattoo, he won't have any trouble picking me out of a line up."

"Don't worry about him," Devon said. "He had an irresistible urge to move to Phoenix."

Connie stared at him, then slowly smiled. "Sonofabitch. For the first time in my life, I'm glad you're a cop."

"I wasn't a cop when I did that," Devon said. "Just a brother."

"You're the best brother a man could have," Connie said.

Devon turned away, wondering if it were possible to be a good cop and the best brother Connie could have. Watching the kids still sharing their goodbye kiss, he said, "Let's go, Elise, or you'll miss your father's funeral."

Chapter Twelve

Samantha's car was still parked in front of Pancho Villa's Revolutionary headquarters. Devon unlocked the door and opened it for Elise, then walked around and got in behind the wheel. They didn't speak until he was stopped in the traffic backed up across the bridge. "Why don't you tell me, Elise," Devon suggested with a friendly smile, "what happened the night your father died."

"Here?" she asked, looking around at the lines of cars surrounding them.

"We've probably got about twenty minutes," Devon said. "Seems like enough time."

She reached down and took off her shoes, then put one bare foot on the dashboard and hugged her bandaged knee. "Eric and I were in bed when my father came home," she said, staring through the windshield at the long line of cars ahead of them. "We heard him come out of the garage, so we got dressed real fast and Eric hid in the closet." She looked at Devon, her blue eyes as innocent as a baby's butt. "Isn't that what Eric told you?"

Devon nodded.

She sighed, looking away again. "Daddy was drunk, as usual, and yelling about one thing after another. Coming off so high and mighty, accusing me of things he does all the time." She shrugged. "Maybe just 'cause I knew Eric was listening, I told Daddy he was full of shit." She picked up one lock of her hair close to her head, pulled it out taut and ran her hand down its length, twisting it around her finger as she went, then let it fall. As she continued, her voice was flat with what Devon heard as anger that had been mashed down for years. "Daddy was on his way out when I said that, but he turned around and unbuckled his belt. I knew what he meant to do with it. When I started crying, begging him not to, he laughed at me." She swiveled her head and met Devon's eyes, hers burning, though her face remained a chiseled perfection of beauty, cold as stone, her voice coyly pleading as she said, "I just wanted Eric to help me. I'd forgotten that gun was even in the closet, and when I opened the door, I sure didn't expect him to come out of there like Arnold Schwarzenegger in *The Terminator*. But that's what he did, both barrels blazing. When he killed that mean sonofabitch, I felt glad." She looked away and shrugged, her hair rippling all the way down.

"Who put the gun in your closet?" Devon asked.

"Teddy."

"Why?"

"He was gonna have a scope or something put on it to surprise Zane as a present, and he asked if he could leave it in my closet just till the weekend when he'd have it done."

"Did he leave it there cocked?"

She turned around and met his eyes, hers puzzled. "I wouldn't know how to tell if it was or not."

"A shotgun makes a loud noise being cocked. Did you hear Eric cock it before you opened the door?"

She shook her head.

"After?"

"I don't remember."

"Okay," Devon said. "What'd you do then?"

"We sat on my bed while Eric smoked a cigarette." She smiled wistfully. "It felt cool, sitting there with him, both of us kinda shocked by what we'd done but feeling important too, you know? I mean, we'd just killed a man. There's a power in knowing that." She studied him a moment. "Have you ever killed anyone?"

He shook his head. "After this moment of epiphany, then what'd you do?"

"We decided I'd go on the church retreat like nothing happened. Eric drove me down there, and I found Mom and told her I'd changed my mind. Then I went and sat in the car with Sunny. Neither of us wanted to go on that stupid retreat. If I'd had my license, I think I would've taken the car and split, but I figured, you know, after just killing my father, I shouldn't be caught driving without a license."

Devon eased forward in the line of traffic, then stopped again. "What'd you do with the gun?"

"First I told Eric to go start his car," she said, twisting a lock of her hair again as she stared through the windshield. "I packed a bag and made the bed—that was the weirdest part: making my bed real neat, the way Daddy was always yelling at me to do, while he lay dead in the hall. I picked up the gun and my overnight bag, and I stood there a minute and stared at him. I was glad he was dead. That's what gave me the idea to put the gun in his car, it seemed like a good joke. So I stepped over him and went to the garage and slid the gun under the front seat. Then I went back through the house and out the kitchen door and around the corner to where Eric was waiting."

For Eric's sake, Devon tried to latch onto something redeemable in her story. "Have you felt sorry since?"

"No," she said. "We're all better off without him."

Except Eric, Devon thought. "When did you call Teddy?" he asked.

She looked at him as he eased forward in the traffic again. "What makes you think I did?"

"The gun wasn't in your father's car when we searched it."

"You searched it?" she whispered.

He nodded. "Did you think we wouldn't?"

"Why would you?"

"When a murder's committed," he said, "finding the weapon is first priority."

"It wasn't murder," she argued. "It was self-defense."

"Not quite," he said. "Was Teddy home when you called him?"

She nodded. "He'd just walked in. Wanda and Petey were out in the back yard and he caught the phone on the first ring. He told me later he left so fast she never knew he'd been there."

"Did you call him before you left with Eric?"

She shook her head, then laughed. "I called him from the church. It felt cool standing there in the pastor's office telling Teddy I'd just shot our father."

"I thought Eric shot him."

"I didn't tell Teddy that," she said with disdain. "Eric'd be in jail right now if I had."

The car behind him honked, and Devon moved forward again. "So what else did you tell Teddy?"

"Where I was and what I was doing, where I'd put the gun, that was all. He said he'd take care of it."

"Meaning what?"

"That he'd get rid of the gun, I guess, since you say it was gone."

"Do you know what he did with it?"

"He had it in his truck the next day, and we took it back to Zane. See, Teddy had asked me to borrow the gun without Zane knowing 'cause he wanted to surprise him when he brought it back with the new scope or whatever it was. So Saturday morning, after you left, me and Teddy went up there and I talked to Zane out by the pool while Teddy put the gun back where Zane kept it in the other bedroom of his apartment, the one he hardly ever went into."

"Didn't you think possession of the gun might make Zane look guilty?"

"Nobody knew we'd had his gun. Not even Zane. Teddy said there was no way the police could connect it to what happened."

"He was wrong," Devon said. "Did Teddy know Eric was in your room when you supposedly killed your father?"

"He knew someone was."

"How?"

"I had to tell him something, didn't I, about why Daddy was mad at me?"

"What did you tell him?"

"That his friend who knew so much about old coins had come to see me, and I'd taken him back to my room to show him my collection, and that was when Daddy came home. I said Connie went out the window, but Daddy saw him and threw a fit. The first thing I did when I got home from Cloudcroft was go into my room before Teddy could. I cut the screen out so it'd look like it was true, then I thought I'd get my coin collection and lay it on the bed. That's when I discovered it was gone."

"So you lied to Teddy about everything," Devon said.

"To protect Eric!" she protested.

He shook his head. "Nobody but you knew Eric was there, and I can't see how you'd think bringing Connie into the picture would help Eric."

" 'Cause it made Teddy feel guilty! He's the one first brought Connie around, and I guess you know your brother can't keep his hands off a pretty girl. Teddy saw him put his arm around me once and went into overdrive. You would've thought we were doing it right there in public. So I figured, if Teddy thought Daddy got mad 'cause of Connie, he'd help me."

"Help you help Eric?"

"That's right."

Devon moved forward again. They were only two cars away from the border when he said, "You're lying, Elise."

She turned on him. "I'm not!"

"I think you're using everyone involved to save yourself."

"I didn't do it!" she retorted. "Eric did. I didn't think about the gun being in the closet when I told him to hide there, and I sure didn't think he'd come out shooting when I opened the door. But that's what happened. It was over before I could stop him."

"Doesn't sound like you wanted to stop him," Devon said, taking his foot off the brake and letting the car move again.

"Doesn't sound to me like you want to know the truth," she accused.

Devon watched the border guard lean into the car ahead, then glanced at Elise. "I do want to know the truth. I'm just not sure I'm hearing it any more than Teddy did."

The man in the car got out and walked around to open his trunk for the guard.

Elise got Devon's attention by twisting to sit cross-legged on the seat, her shorts so skimpy it was obvious she wasn't wearing panties. "You've already broken the law just by bringing me here. If I screamed rape right now, you couldn't keep yourself out of jail, let alone Eric, so maybe you oughta start giving me a little respect."

"Threats won't get you anywhere, Elise," he said.

"Oh yeah? You said you could go to prison just for taking a minor across the border for immoral purposes, and you threatened to assault me if I didn't cooperate. I've got Eric's sperm inside me right now, so throw in kidnapping and rape, and you're looking at life, Detective Gray. If you don't apologize for calling me a liar, I'll make a scene with that border guard that'll put you and your brother both on death row."

Devon watched the man close his trunk and walk back toward his open door. "I'm sorry," Devon said.

"Look at me and use my name when you say it," she commanded.

Devon watched the man get back in his car and drive through, leaving the guard motioning Devon forward with impatience. "I'm sorry, Elise," Devon said, meeting her eyes.

She smiled, swiveling her legs down in front of her and crossing them demurely.

Devon took his foot off the brake and moved up to stop in front of the scowling guard.

"Country of origin?" the guard asked, leaning down to look at Elise's long, naked legs.

"United States," Devon said.

"You, miss?" the guard asked.

"United States, sir," she answered sweetly.

"Are you bringing anything back from Mexico?" the guard asked, still looking at her.

She looked at Devon and smiled with mischief, then said to the guard, "Nothing we didn't take with us."

"All right," the guard said, waving them through.

Devon kept glancing into his rearview mirror until the guard was busy with the next car, then he looked at Elise.

She laughed. "I'll bet no other woman has heard you apologize to her twice in one breath, Devon. Maybe we oughta do this again. I thought it was fun."

Devon drove up Santa Fe and turned east on Texas, then north again on Stanton. Passing the plaza, he remembered Elise running through the rain not wearing any more than she was now, and he wondered where she'd left her coat. She had said she left it with her boyfriend but Eric didn't have it, and Devon couldn't picture her walking over the bridge dressed the way she was. The Mexican boys always loitering on the sidewalk would have shown her no mercy, to say nothing of the border guard letting a half-naked minor waltz through his turnstile unimpeded.

As they left downtown and drove up the hill into the gentrified neighborhood of Kern Place, Devon watched Elise as much as the road. Her bravado was fast disappearing with every spin of the tires carrying her closer to home. Softly he asked, "What're you gonna tell Teddy about where you've been?"

She sighed. "I'll think of something."

All of a sudden she looked like a little girl caught in a situation out of control. Devon decided she was, though she was manipulating the hell out of everyone to keep as much control as she could. Despite her underhanded methods, he couldn't help admiring her ability to always land on her feet. "Tell him I kept you for questioning and brought you home," he said.

She met his eyes with a grateful smile. "We could be friends in all this, couldn't we, Devon."

"If you'd tell me the truth," he said.

"I have told you the truth."

"All of it?"

"Yes," she whispered, then looked away as he turned off Stanton and drove up her street toward the mountain.

"I'm gonna find out, Elise. If you've lied, you've only hurt yourself."

"I don't even care anymore," she said with a weariness beyond her age. "All I want is to get Eric out of this mess I got him into."

Devon believed her. "If I manage to do that," he asked, downshifting up the hill, "will you promise not to see him again?"

She jerked around to meet his eyes, hers brimming with tears. "That isn't fair!"

"It's what I'm asking," he said. "And I want your answer before you get out of this car."

She looked up at her house as he stopped at the curb. "I promise," she whimpered. Then she opened the door and left it that way as she ran up the steps without looking back.

He waited until she was inside the kitchen before he leaned across and closed the door.

Samantha was at the reference desk when he walked into the library. He smiled as he handed over her keys and said, "Thanks."

She stood up, sliding the keys into the pocket of her red paisley dress. With her auburn hair, she looked like a slender flame in the wind as she called across to a man helping a patron with the on-line catalog, "I'll be right back."

The man nodded, looked at Devon with curiosity, then returned his attention to the middle-aged woman frowning at the computer screen.

Samantha held Devon's arm as they walked through the double-wide doors to the street. They were at the corner before she asked, "Was she the girl on your case?"

"Yes," Devon said.

"She certainly is pretty," Samantha said. "And she doesn't leave anything to doubt, does she?"

Devon smiled as they entered the parking lot. "That's what she was wearing when I arrested her. We came here straight from jail."

"Where'd you go?"

"Juárez," he said.

She stopped. "You took my car to Mexico?"

He nodded.

"What're you doing, Devon?" she asked. "You're not supposed to go there at all, and she sure didn't look eighteen."

He guided her to the passenger door of his car, unlocked and opened it, then met her eyes.

With an angry flounce of her full skirt, she got in and let him close the door. He walked around and got in the driver's side, then stared at the rock wall of the back of the library a moment before he looked at her again. "She's fifteen," he said.

"For heaven's sake, Devon. Why'd you take her to Juárez?"

"To see her boyfriend."

"Who is he? Some kingpin in the Mexican mafia?"

Devon shook his head. "He's my nephew."

"Eric?" she whispered.

He nodded. "Their story is, he killed her father."

Samantha stared at him a moment, then pleaded, "Take yourself off the case, Devon. You can't fairly investigate a murder when your own family's involved."

"I'm trying to keep them uninvolved," he said.

"By breaking laws to protect them? All you're doing is implicating yourself. Do you realize what you're risking?"

"My badge," he said.

"How about joining your nephew in prison for being an accomplice after the fact? Isn't that what they call it?"

He nodded, touched by the depth of her concern.

"Devon, you're a good cop," she argued. "More than that, you're a good man. If you help your nephew escape the consequences of murder, the blood will be on your hands as much as his. Is that what you want?"

"It's more complicated than that, Sam," he said.

"No, it isn't. You're letting it become complicated. Take yourself off the case and let justice work. Help Eric all you can from a stance of being right. What you're doing now is joining him in being wrong."

"It's not just Eric. It's my brother."

"Who's never done anything but give you grief for being an honorable man while he went to prison. No, I won't be quiet, Devon. I've held my tongue for two years now. Every time you mention your brother your face is full of pain. Do you know that? What he's done with his life isn't your fault. The fact that your father liked you more than him means your father saw the truth from the beginning. You're a detective, Devon. You make your living by seeing through people, but you close your eyes when you look at your brother. You see through your heart, and what you see is your own sense of failure for not being able to help him. He doesn't want help. He wants to drag you into the dirt where he lives. If you don't take yourself off this case, he'll do that."

Painfully he said, "I can't not help him, Sam."

"If you don't help him within the law, what you'll do is destroy yourself."

"It's a sharp edge to walk," he admitted.

"Oh, Devon," she moaned, sliding across the seat and holding him close. "I don't want him to hurt you anymore."

He buried his face in the soothing perfume of her hair, then lifted her chin and kissed her mouth. Meeting her eyes, he said, "I asked him to call me tonight at your place. If that's not okay with you, just tell him he has the wrong number."

She gave him a sad smile. "At least I'll get to see you three nights in a row. That's a first for us, Devon."

"As soon as this case is over," he said, then hesitated to finish, realizing what he wanted was unfair to her.

"You'll take some time for us," she sighed. "Yes, I know."

"That isn't what I was gonna say," he smiled, brushing her hair away from her face.

"Say it, Devon," she pleaded.

He shook his head. "Not now. Soon."

She nodded, blinking back tears.

"Go on back to work," he said. "I'll see you tonight."

She nodded again, then slid across to the door and got out. Leaning back in, she blew him a kiss off her fingers, and he managed to laugh before she closed the door.

He drove up Mesa to a 7-11 that had a phone he could use from his car. Calling his home number, he listened to his messages. First was Lieutenant Dreyfus. "Where the hell are you, Devon? I've got two murders and a missing detective. The press is crucifying both me and the mayor. I want you and your report in my office now."

Then came Laura's voice. "Devon? I just got a call from Ace Wrecking and Towing. They've got Connie's truck. Do you think you could drive out there and give them a deposit to hold it?" She paused then said, "They want fifty dollars for the tow and twenty-five a day storage, otherwise they'll declare it abandoned and sell it at auction, but they said they'd hold it if I paid them the fifty. They won't take a check, though." She laughed, embarrassed. "Course I don't have any cash, but I'll pay you back soon as Connie's last check . . . ." The beep cut her off, then the second, lower beep indicating there were no more messages.

Devon drove home. Laura was sitting at the dining room table reading the newspaper. As he came in through the kitchen, she gave him a tentative smile. Leaning down to kiss her cheek, he saw she had the paper open to the classifieds. She'd circled in red several ads for cocktail waitresses. He stood up straight and met her eyes.

"I'm looking for a job," she said.

"I'd hate to see you working in a bar again, Laura."

"Yeah, well, there's not much else I know how to do."

"If you want to go to one of those technical schools, I'll pay your tuition."

"Do they take people my age?"

He laughed. "Sure. You got the address of this wrecking company?"

"It's by the phone," she said.

He walked into the living room and across to the phone on an end table next to the sofa. "Did they say where they'd picked up the truck?"

"A parking lot by the Santa Fe Bridge," she called from behind him. "Guess it makes sense, if Connie's in Juárez."

Devon looked down at the notepad, the top sheet covered with her hastily scrawled numbers, half of them with dollar signs in front. He tore the sheet off and slid it into his pocket as he walked back into the dining room. "I saw Connie," he said.

She tossed her hair out of her face. "Did he ask about me?"

Devon nodded.

"What'd you tell him?"

"That you're doing fine."

She stared at him. "What the hell, if I can get a job, I will be doing fine without him. It's about time, isn't it, Devon?"

"It beats drinking in front of soap operas all day," he said.

"Shit," she said. "You think I'll have to cut my hair to get a job?"

He shook his head, reached for his wallet, and took out half of what he had. "Payday's Friday," he said. "Let me know if you need more."

She stared down at the five twenties on the table, then met his eyes. "Did you see Eric?"

He nodded.

"Is he okay?"

"He needs a bath. Other than that, he's all right."

She studied him a moment, then asked, "Did you see them in Juárez?"

He nodded again.

"Shit, Devon. What the fuck're you doing?"

"I was in and out 'fore the Rangers caught wind I was there," he quipped, using a line from her favorite western novel, a story about an outlaw who kept trying to go straight but was foiled by helping people in a world where the lawmen were crooked. The last time Devon had been home sick with the flu, Laura read him the whole book in an effort to lift his spirits, but the story hadn't done that.

She smiled now, remembering those days she lay beside him in bed reading that paperback novel. "The last I heard," she said, her smile turning sad, "you are the Rangers. Has that changed?"

"I've still got my badge," Devon said, going into the kitchen and opening the junk drawer. He rummaged through the clutter of coupons, take-out menus, ball-point pens, matchbooks, odd screws and bottle openers until he found the extra keys for Connie's truck. Closing the drawer and already moving toward the door, he told Laura,

"I'll see you tomorrow."

"You're not coming home tonight?" she called after him.

"No," he said, walking out without looking back.

Ace Wrecking and Towing was in the twenty-seven thousand block of Montana, so far out the street had turned into the highway to Carlsbad. Devon drove through the gate in the eight-foot chain link fence and parked in front of a shack, the only edifice among acres of rusting vehicles. He could see Connie's truck, an '86 chocolate brown Ram that Devon helped pay for, backed into a line of Chevy's and Fords. Devon had suggested Connie buy a Dodge because most of the car thieves in El Paso sold their take across the border and Mexicans had trouble getting parts for Chrysler products. Devon didn't know why Chrysler didn't do business in Mexico, but he knew the vast majority of stolen vehicles were Chevys and Fords because they were easy to sell there. He walked across to the Ram and looked in the window, noting the doors were locked.

A man came out of the shack and scowled. "Can I help ya?" he shouted, not sounding like he wanted to.

Devon studied him: a big-bellied man in greasy overalls and a face stubbled with graying whiskers, one cheek bulging with chewing tobacco. "Want to pay the fees on this truck," Devon said.

"Is it yours?"

"My brother's."

"Cost ya a hundred dollars to take it."

"How much to leave it here a while?"

"Twenty-five a day storage. Fifty towing. Pay the fifty cash and I'll hold it a week." He turned to spit tobacco juice off to the side, then said, "Pay the week's storage and I'll hold it another."

Devon took his wallet out as he walked toward him, then handed the man two twenties and a ten.

"Come inside," the man said, taking the money and trundling toward the shack.

Devon followed him. The office held a gray metal desk, a lopsided secretary chair, and one steel file cabinet with a lock. The man sat down behind the desk and wrote out a receipt. Handing it to Devon, he said, "That gives you one week."

"When did you bring it in?"

"Yesterday afternoon."

"From where?"

"Parking lot at the foot of Santa Fe Street."

"How long had it been there?"

The man shrugged. "Longer'n the guy paid for."

Devon nodded. "Any objection to my looking inside?"

"It's locked. You want me to jimmie it?"

"No, I've got a key." Devon walked out and across the oily dirt of the yard to the truck. Smelling perfume when he opened the driver's door, he looked at the empty bench seat and floor, then shifted the seat forward and saw a khaki raincoat lying full-length along the ledge. He took the coat out and looked at the label to see it was size seven, then dropped the coat onto the seat, got in and leaned across to open the glove box. A flashlight, matchbooks from bars and restaurants Connie had never taken Laura to, a small, yellow piece of paper. Devon unfolded it and saw it was a receipt from Frontier Sporting Goods for a box of .357 cartridges.

Still holding the receipt, he crossed his arms on the steering wheel and hid his face in their shadow, feeling the cheap paper prick the skin on his forehead.

"Ya all right?" the man shouted.

Devon looked at him standing in the door of the shack. "Yeah," he called across the distance. He slid the receipt into his shirt pocket and took the coat as he got out and locked the door. "Thanks," he called to the man still watching him. He kept watching until Devon drove through the gate and turned east on Montana. At George Dieter he turned south and drove another five miles to the crime lab office within the Department of Safety, which was the new name for the umbrella bureaucracy of the Texas Rangers.

Devon didn't feel like one of them when he walked into the lab office. The female clerk was young, Hispanic, pretty. He showed her his badge and asked to see the forensic reports on the Truxal and Kalinsky murders, asking for them by the numbers he himself had assigned. When she brought the reports, she opened the daily activity log on the counter and asked again to see his badge, then wrote his name and number on the roster.

Taking the reports to a cubicle reserved for investigating officers, Devon opened the two manila folders side by side on the table in front of him. Theodore Truxal's death had occurred between five and six p.m. on Friday, May 21, 1993. Which meant Teddy's alibi had been fixed. Tulles had remembered only that it was still light outside when Teddy and Earl Carter arrived, but Carter had said they'd gone to Rosa's straight from work. Carter had lied. Teddy had gone home, caught Elise's call and driven to their mother's house to retrieve the shotgun, then met Carter at Rosa's, probably closer to six o'clock than five. Since Tulles remembered them arriving together, Teddy must have called Carter and arranged the alibi. None of this surprised Devon. He'd suspected when he questioned Carter that the man was lying.

The forensic report said the cause of Theodore Truxal's death was the combined effect of eighteen buckshot fired from a shotgun at a distance of not more than six feet, causing extensive damage to the heart and lungs which resulted in death within three minutes. Fingerprints taken from the house matched those of the family, with two exceptions: one complete set of unidentified prints taken from the interior of the closet door in the small, back bedroom, another incomplete set found on the interior of the kitchen door leading outside matching the prints taken from the corpse of Zane Kalinsky.

Zane had died between ten and eleven on the night of Saturday, May 22, 1993. Cause of death was a bullet fired from a .357 magnum handgun into the right temple, destroying the brain and the left hemisphere of the skull. Angle of entry had been determined as coming from approximately two feet above the skull and not more than a foot away. For the wound to be self-inflicted, the report noted, the position of the weapon was extremely unusual, and the position of the body indicated the subject was possibly in the process of getting up to defend himself when the fatal shot was fired. Cordite residue had been found on the subject's palm, indicating the gun had been fired while in his hand, but the presence of a second bullet found in the mattress could have resulted from the perpetrator placing the gun in the hand of his victim and firing it again. Conclusion: inconclusive homicide/suicide.

The fingerprint report said there were so many prints in Zane's living room it was impossible to identify all of them. That made sense, being Zane was the manager of the apartment complex. The rest of the apartment yielded only Zane's prints. None of the neighbors remembered hearing shots that night, and nobody had seen anyone entering or leaving Zane's apartment.

Devon looked again at the time of death. One, maybe

two hours before he picked up Elise near the plaza. Her raincoat in Connie's truck along with a receipt for bullets fitting the murder weapon. The murder weapon stolen from Theodore Truxal's hotel, probably taken by Teddy after arguing with his father. Teddy purchasing a new gun after telling Devon he owned a .357, which meant the one he had when he made that statement had since become undesirable property.

Teddy, believing Elise had killed their father after he interrupted her with Connie, could have given the stolen .357 to Connie to use against Zane. Connie, acting to protect his son, and Teddy, acting to protect his sister, conspiring to kill Zane in such a way that the police would think he'd committed suicide in remorse for killing Truxal. After all, it was Zane's shotgun.

The irony was, if Devon hadn't been trying so hard to protect Connie, the ploy might have worked. Sergeant Brent was ready to call Zane's death a suicide until Devon objected. If it hadn't been Devon's case, another detective might have closed it after learning of Zane's connection to Elise. It all could have worked if Devon had taken himself off the case.

Why hadn't he? Because Connie sold the coins. But when Elvis Short was questioned by the patrolman, Short hadn't mentioned Connie by name; he'd merely said he bought the coins from a man with BORN TO LOSE tattooed on his arm. Maybe Teddy hadn't originally intended to set Connie up with the coins; maybe it was only after Elise told him Connie had been in her bedroom that Teddy decided to implicate him in the first murder by pressuring him to commit the second. Being as Teddy didn't know Eric was involved, how had he pressured Connie to kill Zane? By threatening him with statutory rape? Had Connie pretended to buckle under that threat because of Eric, or had he been another recipient of Elise's favors? If not, what was she doing in Connie's truck the night Zane was killed?

Maybe Connie had given her a ride back across the border after she'd visited Eric. But if he'd taken his truck to Juárez the first time, why did he leave it in the parking lot that night? Why had she taken her coat off? If Connie had given her a ride, had he demanded payment? Despite her history as a hooker, had she been unable to service her boyfriend's father? She'd offered Devon a taste only a short time later. Had she panicked with Connie for some other reason, jumping out and running through the rain to where Devon picked her up? Why was she afraid to go home when he offered to take her? Was it before or after she'd been in Connie's truck that Zane was killed? If Connie was wily enough to put the gun in Zane's dead hand and fire it again, he wouldn't leave the receipt in his truck, knowing that when it was towed Devon would be the one to get it out of hock. Maybe he was toying with Devon, knowing whichever way it fell he'd come out on top; because whether or not Devon fell with him, Connie would have saved Eric and proved himself a better man.

But if Connie was that wily, he wouldn't have dropped the silver dollar on the floor of Zane's bedroom. Teddy could have put it there in an effort to frame Connie, hoping the police would think Connie and Zane were in cahoots to sell the coins. Could Teddy also have put Elise's raincoat and the receipt in Connie's truck? Or was Devon twisting everything beyond credence in his effort to clear Connie? Was that what he truly wanted to do? Even if it was, could he get anyone else to believe Teddy had framed Connie? The odds were against it, because as soon as Connie's name came into the case, it would be assigned to another detective.

Almost absently, Devon turned to the last page of the Truxal file. It was the report on the shotgun. The ballistics results he'd already heard on the phone, that the gun had been recently fired but it was impossible to trace a pellet from a shotgun. In the interim, the gun had been dusted for prints. Devon's were on it, and Zane's, and the one thing Devon needed: a single print from the right forefinger of Teddy Truxal.

Devon closed the reports and returned them to the desk. "Have these been sent to Five Points?" he asked the clerk.

"Let me check," she answered, opening the daily activity log on the counter. "Yes," she said. "They went by special courier this morning and should be on your desk now, Detective Gray."

"Thanks." He gave her a smile, then walked out to his car. It was parked facing the sunset, golden mauve in the sky. He sat staring for a long time at the smoky silhouette of the Franklin Mountains intersecting El Paso, a city renown in the Old West as a haven for outlaws.

Chapter Thirteen

Connie called exactly at nine. Devon was sitting on Samantha's sofa listening to the CD of Miles Davis called *Kind of Blue* playing softly while she took a shower. Devon picked up the phone on the first ring. Before he could even say hello, Connie asked, "Devon?"

"Yeah," he said.

Connie chuckled with camaraderie. "Where are you, bro? In some girl's apartment you've been keeping a secret?"

"No, just a friend who's out of town," Devon said. He already regretted giving out Sam's number, but at the time he'd been feeling close to Connie. Now he felt there was more than a border marked by a river between them.

"So, what've you got?" Connie asked in a more guarded tone, indicating he'd picked up on the distance Devon was feeling.

"A lot of questions," Devon said.

"Let's hear 'em. Maybe I've got the answers."

"Okay. Let's start with your truck. Where is it?"

"I left it in the lot on Santa Fe. You know the one behind that big red building with *ropa usada* plastered all over it?"

"When?"

"Friday 'bout midnight. You think it's still there?"

"No," Devon said. "It was towed."

"Sonofabitch. You know where?"

"Ace Wrecking way out on Montana. I was there today and the truck's all right. I paid the guy to hold it."

"Thanks," Connie said, his voice warmer again.

"Somebody was in it on Saturday night, though."

"Did they bust a window?"

"No," Devon said.

"How'd they get in?"

"There're ways."

Connie laughed. "You cops know the same shit we do. If they didn't bust in, how'd you know they were there?"

"They left some souvenirs."

"What'd they leave?" Connie asked, his voice tightening so Devon could picture his eyes narrowing with suspicion.

"Elise's raincoat, for one."

"Her coat?"

"Yeah, behind the seat."

"The one she wore down here that night?"

"I guess. What time was she there?"

"She sailed in 'bout eight."

"What time did she leave?"

"Eleven, eleven-thirty."

"Was she wearing the coat when she left?"

"Sure."

"Did she walk back?"

"Yeah, Eric went with her as far as the bridge."

"You didn't go with them?"

"No."

"How long was Eric gone?"

"Half an hour. I told him to come right back and he did."

Devon nodded, calculating it was about a fifteen-minute walk from their rooms to the border. "And he was with you the rest of the night?"

" 'Cept for that half-hour, we've been together since we came down here." Connie chuckled. "Course, part of that time he was behind a closed door with Elise, but I could hear 'em plain. What else did you find in my truck?"

"A receipt for a box of .357 bullets."

Connie was quiet a long time before he said, "I don't own a .357, Devon."

Devon wasn't aware Connie owned any guns, but all he said was, "Zane Kalinsky was killed with a .357."

"Shit," Connie said. "I didn't buy 'em, Devon."

"Who did?"

"Teddy Truxal."

"Why would he put the receipt in your truck?"

"Ain't it obvious?" Connie asked with disgust.

"I was you to tell me."

"He's setting me up."

"For what?"

"What else happened that night?"

"You tell me."

"Zane Kalinsky was murdered."

"Was he?"

"What the hell, Devon? It was in the papers."

"They reported it as a possible suicide. We haven't been able to prove otherwise."

"He was murdered," Connie said.

"How do you know that?"

"Stands to reason."

"Explain it to me, Connie."

"You're fishing, aren't you, Devon?"

"What I am is way the hell out on a limb for you, bro. If you want to keep Eric out of jail, give me some help."

"Don't get your hackles up. All I know is Kalinsky owned the shotgun in question. Elise told Eric she and Teddy put it back in Kalinsky's closet without him knowing. I figure they was maybe afraid he'd jinx the deal."

Devon thought a moment, then asked, "That's it?"

"What's wrong with it?"

"Seems like a flimsy reason for murder."

"Yeah, well, amateurs panic, you know."

"Whoever killed Zane didn't act like an amateur. He put the gun in Zane's hand and fired it into the mattress so we'd pick up residue off his palm."

"But it didn't work, did it? You found the bullet in the mattress, didn't you?"

"Yeah. But that alone doesn't rule out suicide. Maybe he wanted to test the gun and make sure it worked. Or maybe he lost his nerve and had to make a second try."

"With a name like Kalinsky," Connie scoffed, "he must've been Catholic. You know a Catholic boy wouldn't kill himself to skate from murder. Why trade execution out of this world for eternity in hell?"

Devon smiled, "When did you last see Teddy?"

"Friday night."

"At Rosa's?"

"Yeah."

"When I asked if you'd seen Tulles recently," Devon queried sharply, "why did you lie?"

Again, Connie was quiet a while. "I knew Teddy didn't have any right to sell those coins. He offered too big a piece of the action to be clean, but I didn't know the deal was so dirty."

"How much did he pay you?"

"A quarter of the take."

"Why'd you borrow fifty from Tom Halprin?"

"You've been making the rounds, haven't you, bro?"

"Just answer the question, Connie."

"Teddy never paid me. I was supposed to meet him but he didn't show."

"When was that?"

"Saturday night."

"Did you arrange the meeting?"

"Yeah, I called him and asked for my goddamned money!"

"Was that before or after Elise's visit?"

"Before. She came into the Kentucky Club and said Teddy had dropped her off downtown on his way somewhere else." Connie snickered. "She told him she was going to the library to study. So I came back here with her and Eric."

"I though you said she sailed into your room at eight o'clock."

"I said she sailed in, I didn't say where."

Devon stifled his anger so he could concentrate on the nuances of Connie's answers. "Why didn't you take your cut of the money before giving what you got to Teddy?"

"He asked me not to. Said he needed the full amount to make his mortgage payment so the bank wouldn't take his house. That he had to have the money in the bank that day, but he had some more coming on Saturday morning and he'd pay me out of that."

"More from where?"

"I didn't ask."

"When did you give him the money?"

"Thursday night. I took it to his house and gave it to him in the garage. I told you that."

"Elvis Short said you sold him the coins on Friday night."

"It was Thursday."

"Why would he lie?"

"There's a time limit on how long you got to report receipt of stolen property. Maybe he was thinking of that."

"When did you get the coins?"

"Thursday afternoon. I met Teddy at the Tampico just before five and he gave 'em to me then."

Devon remembered he'd been there drinking a beer on Saturday. "Is that the deal you were closing with your phony bet in Rosa's?"

Connie laughed. "You don't miss much, do you?"

"Sounded like a bogus bet to me. Carter thought so, too."

"It was code," Connie laughed. "Sixers meant I wanted my six hundred, and Bullets meant I'd get it on Saturday as planned."

"Teddy's wife said she overheard a conversation between the two of you in their garage and you were telling Teddy not to kill his father."

"I was talking about Eric, how I was worried about him, and I told Teddy what Dad said that night, how I'd killed him by robbing that 7-11 and how I understood now what he meant. Wanda got it wrong. Or maybe she was lying. I wouldn't blame her for that. Laura'd lie for me if I asked her to. How's she doing?"

"She misses you, Connie."

"I miss her too. Juárez ain't what it used to be. Was a time when the whores were sweet young things just in from the country. Now they're so far past ripe you can smell their rot from across the room. Remember that time we came down here and I bought your first piece?"

"Yeah," Devon said.

"She was pretty enough to be Miss Mexico, 'cept she was prob'ly too young to compete."

"About the same age as Elise," Devon agreed.

Connie chuckled. "You weren't much older."

"As old as Eric," Devon said.

Connie was quiet, then said, "I'm keeping myself clean down here, Devon. But it sure wasn't easy listening to Eric and that creampuff going at it in the bedroom. What happened to Juárez?"

"Guess it got tired of being El Paso's brothel."

"Huh," Connie said.

The wire stretching across the river was a heavy weight of connection. Then Devon said, "There's something about Eric's story that bothers me."

"What?"

"He doesn't remember cocking the gun."

Connie thought a minute. "Takes some effort to cock a shotgun."

"Elise said Teddy put the gun in her closet, that he meant to get a scope put on it as a surprise for Zane."

"I never heard of a scope on a shotgun."

"Neither have I. But what I'm wondering is why he'd leave it primed in his sister's closet."

"Sounds like he meant to use it in a hurry," Connie said.

"Did you know Elise told Teddy it was you in her bedroom when her father came home?"

"No," Connie said.

"Have you fucked her?"

"No!"

"Did Teddy have reason to think otherwise?"

Connie thought a minute. "Maybe," he finally said.

"Looks to me," Devon said, "that Teddy wanted the old man gunned down in front of Elise's door, knowing when she reported the missing coins we'd suspect a burglar, which left whoever sold those coins walking around wearing a noose."

"Sonofabitch," Connie said.

"What I can't figure is why he killed Zane. Except for his

shotgun, Zane was outside the circle, and I'd already questioned him and believed everything he said. He willingly let me take the gun so obviously didn't know it'd been used in the murder. What made Teddy afraid of him?"

"Maybe you're expecting it to make too much sense, Devon. If Teddy had his father's murder planned and suddenly the unexpected happened and he's faced with protecting his baby sister, I could see him losing his grip and making a bad decision. Now he's trying to make amends for his mistake by planting stuff in my truck so it'll look like I knocked off Zane too. But why would I? If I supposedly killed Truxal while robbing the coins, how would I know Zane from Moses? There's no link. But Teddy can't see that."

Devon nodded, seeing it for the first time himself. "He planted something else, though," he said.

"What?" Connie asked warily.

"The silver dollar Elvis Short gave you as part of the deal. I found it on the floor in Zane's bedroom."

Connie was quiet.

"You sure you gave it to Teddy?"

"Yeah, I'm sure," Connie answered testily.

"In the garage?"

"Yeah."

"Did you put it in his hand?"

"He was working on his car and had grease on his hands, so I laid it on this worktable he's got. The money, too."

"That probably means the coin only has your prints on it."

"Have you had it dusted?"

"No," Devon said.

"Where is it?"

"Someplace safe."

"Shit, Devon. Are you thinking I knocked off Zane?"

Devon sighed. "No, it looks like a frame to me."

"I hope to shout," Connie said. "I can't figure why Teddy would turn on me like this, though."

"Probably because he jumped to the same conclusion I did: that you were the one balling Elise. Which might explain something else that's had me stumped."

"What?" Connie asked with hope.

"When I picked up Elise downtown on Saturday night, I thought she was hooking, but when I offered to take her home, she kicked up such a ruckus I had to book her. I couldn't figure why she'd choose jail over home. But if Teddy finds out it was Eric instead of Elise who pulled the trigger, that means Teddy killed Zane for nothing, which could explain why Elise is so afraid of him."

"Yeah, it could," Connie said.

"It also means," Devon said, "she knew Teddy meant to kill Zane. The coroner said Zane died between ten and eleven. You told me she sailed into the Kentucky Club at eight saying Teddy had dropped her off on his way somewhere else. So all the time she was with Eric, she knew what Teddy was doing."

"Damn cold," Connie whispered.

"Except that she was giving Eric an alibi. And maybe something else to her credit: when I offered to take her home, she asked me to take her to Zane's instead."

"Hoping you could save him?"

"That's what I'm thinking. But you know, her alibi only holds for Eric. Neither one of them could testify to what you were doing while they were in the bedroom."

"Listen, Devon. Maybe Eric should turn himself in and tell the truth. It would blow Teddy's mind, and I'd lay odds he'll crack under questioning."

Devon shook his head, then realized Connie couldn't see him. "He might clear you of Zane's murder, but it wouldn't change the fact that Eric killed the old man."

"It was a crime of passion," Connie argued. "Couldn't he plead self-defense? I mean, you got this kid shut in a dark closet listening to the old man brow-beating his daughter. Couldn't a lawyer argue that when Elise opened that door, Eric thought it was Truxal coming after him and fired in an instinctive act of self-defense? At most it'd be voluntary manslaughter, wouldn't it? And being underage, Eric'd get a short sentence, wouldn't he?"

"I doubt it," Devon said with regret. "Truxal fell in the hall, which means he wasn't the one to open the door. The jury would think Eric shouldn't have been in Elise's bedroom in the first place, that her father was right to punish his fifteen-year-old daughter for having sex, and Eric was wrong to kill him for any reason. If they feel inclined toward mercy, they might give him twenty years."

"Jesus Christ, Devon."

"That's the way I see it, Connie."

"If it comes to that, I'll confess to both murders and let Eric skate."

Devon felt redeemed in his faith in his brother. But he had to say, "With Eric out of the picture, your only motive's money. Add statutory rape to murder committed in the course of a theft, another murder to cover the first, and no jury's gonna deal you mercy."

"I'll do it just the same," he said.

"I doubt if Eric'll let you."

"Well, holy shit, Devon. What're you gonna do?"

"I don't know," he said.

"Can't you doctor your reports to say Kalinsky committed suicide and Truxal was killed by an unknown burglar? You sent Elvis packing. Did you get the receipt and Elise's coat out of my truck?"

"Yeah, I did."

"Burn 'em, Devon. Tell your boss you've hit a dead end and let the case get filed in one of those trash bins in the courthouse basement. Teddy Truxal won't be the first to get away with murder and it ain't likely he'll do it again. Can you see your way clear to doing that, man?"

"It won't only be Teddy who's getting away with murder."

"Eric's just a kid," Connie rasped.

Devon hated hearing the desperation in his brother's voice. Guardedly, he said, "Call me this same time tomorrow night."

"Same number?"

"Yeah."

"I'll do it, but I'm moving just so you won't have to lie if someone asks where we are."

"Appreciate it," Devon said.

Connie laughed bitterly. "This is a helluva fuck, ain't it?"

"Yeah," Devon said.

Connie hung up and Devon listened to the broken connection for a long time before he replaced the receiver. Then he switched off the stereo, which had fallen silent a long time before, turned off the light, and walked into the dark room where Samantha was waiting in bed.

"Think I'll go out for a drink," he said.

"Don't," she whispered.

"I'll have to face the lieutenant in the morning, Sam. I need to find some answers before then."

"Can't you find them here?"

He sat down on the edge of her bed and touched her cheek. "I wish I could."

"Maybe if we make love," she suggested softly, "you'll see everything more clearly afterwards."

He shook his head. "I don't want to use you like that."

"What else can I give you, Devon, other than accepting your pain when you need to get rid of it?"

"Is that what you think love is?"

"Partly," she said.

He shook his head. "That's what's wrong with the world: everybody's too quick to share their pain."

"Maybe it's all we've got," she said.

He laughed without joy. "When this is behind me, Sam," he said, standing up, "we'll find a way to share something worth having."

"Promise me one thing, Devon."

"What?"

"No mater what else happens, even if you lose your badge and are drummed out of the force in disgrace, don't put yourself in jail."

"Wouldn't you wait for me?"

"No," she said. "The man who came out wouldn't be the Devon Gray I love. He'd be more like his brother, and I know I couldn't handle his pain."

Devon thought of Laura alone in his father's house, probably drunk in front of the TV, listening to jokes she couldn't find funny. Knowing he didn't want to inflict that on Samantha, he said, "I promise."

Devon drove up the hill past the hospital and turned east to ascend the winding curves of Rim Road. To his left, the towering castles of El Paso's old-money sprawled in medieval splendor on their huge lots; to his right, the earth disappeared in an arroyo that deepened as he climbed until it became the edge of the mountain and the road lived up to its name, traversing the rim. He parked at the view point and sat idling his engine as he looked down at the lights of the city.

Half a million people need a lot of light. Every nimbus was either a streetlamp illuminating a residential block or thoroughfare, or it was a porch light left on for someone still prowling the streets. The clusters were constellations of convenience stores and gas stations still open, the dark ribbon intersecting the city was the river, and beyond it the blue lights of Juárez were dimmer and more scattered. Beyond Juárez, the desert stretched empty for three hundred miles to the City of Chihuahua. East of El Paso the plains stretched nearly empty the entire six hundred miles to San Antonio. The western vista was abruptly aborted by the rugged range of the Juárez Mountains and Cristo Rey, which had been called Muleskinners Mountain by the pioneers. The name was changed when a cross was erected on its peak in 1939. The sculpture was designed by Urbichi Soler, the same artist who designed the cross over Rio de Janeiro. Every Easter pilgrims climbed the long, winding road up Mount Cristo Rey to celebrate the Resurrection under the cross. Some of them climbed on their knees in penance or petition.

Devon knew El Paso well. Knew its history and its people. He had always considered himself a force for good, a husband of the city's safety, patrolling the barrier between the flock and the wolves when he'd been a cop on the beat. As a detective, his job had become the more difficult task of finding the wolves among the flock.

Connie, however, wasn't a killer. Maybe that was why Devon had chosen to work in homicide: it took him out of his brother's arena of petty thefts and shady deals. The disengagement, however, had only served to ricochet with greater force into the next generation. In an argument last summer, Eric had told Devon that in the same way doctors make their living off disease, cops make theirs off crime; and Devon had to concede that if you eliminated crime, he would lose his purpose in life. Now he suspected that by choosing to work in homicide, he had encouraged Eric's outlawry, increasing the ante in the game they were playing on the board set up by Eric's grandfather.

In the car next to Devon, a young couple was making out. He watched them idly a moment, realizing they were underage and therefore violating curfew. A couple like Eric and Elise must have been, seeking their illicit pleasures in public when their parents were home. Devon wondered what had happened to the old-fashioned protocols of courtship, at what point kids had decided life was too short to postpone any pleasure they could grab, in what decade the authority of their parents had become irrelevant. There were technological answers: automobiles and birth control, the thousand passionate kisses kids witnessed on TV and movie screens while growing up, those same screens teaching an apocryphal code of honor depicted by the glorification of men who broke the law. But the deeper answer lay in the fabric of the family.

The fathers had failed. Devon's father and Connie's. Elise's father and Teddy's. The mothers went along, colluding with their husband's violence by ceding power to an undeserving patriarch. No one could remember what a deserving patriarch was like. Connie's answer had been to become a pal to his son, a fellow comrade-in-arms against the system, but that hadn't worked either. As a father, he had been unable to teach Eric how to succeed in a game he'd lost.

It seemed men's most highly developed skill in the

modern world was how to run. As Connie had, catapulting himself into the criminality in an attempt to escape the moral consequences of burning his sister alive. As Teddy had, choosing murder over standing up to his father, then choosing it again when his plot implicated his sister. As Devon's father had, surrendering all sense of obligation to his self-righteous indulgence in anger. As Devon had, using a badge to shield himself from the responsibility of raising sons *and* daughters who had a father worthy of honor.

When a squad car pulled between Devon and the groping couple, he shifted into reverse and headed back down the mountain toward Smeltertown. In the dark cavern of the Rio Grande Valley, the white crosses over the graves of his parents leaned pathetically from their paltry foundations in the sandy ground. Devon stood above the grave of his father, wishing the old man were alive to hear what he had to say. But then his gaze fell on the small rectangle of his sister's stone between the long, narrow graves of his parents, and he guessed Rosemary had already spoken the words he had just now learned were needed: a plea for forgiveness, mercy from the lash of rage, and a prayer that, somehow, for the sake of the sisters, the brothers of the world could stand before the High Court of Justice and repent.

The Devon Gray whom Samantha loved walked into Rosa's Cantina at ten-thirty that Monday night and saw Teddy Truxal alone at the bar. Devon stopped at the jukebox, dropped a quarter in the slot, and punched the number for *El Paso*, then walked across the room with a smile for his prey.

Tulles laughed. "Why you always play that song, Devon?"

"I like it," he answered, sitting down next to Teddy and singing along with Marty Robbins: "Out in the West Texas town of El Paso, I fell in love with a girl named Elise."

Teddy jumped as if Devon had pricked him with a cattle prod.

"What're you drinking?" Devon asked, though Teddy's can of Coors was right in front of him.

"Nothing with you."

"Tecate," Devon told Tulles.

"I know," she said, the can already in her hand. She set a wedge of lime on top of the open beer and pushed it toward him. Her stretch pants tonight were orange, her blouse yellow, accenting the rot in her teeth when she grinned and asked, "Where's Connie hiding out? I haven't seen him all weekend."

"How the hell should I know?" Teddy muttered.

Both Tulles and Devon looked at him, then Tulles laughed. "I was asking Devon," she said. "Connie's his brother."

Teddy jerked around to stare hard.

Devon smiled. "An accident of birth."

Tulles laughed. "He's an accident, all right."

Devon sipped his beer, then asked her, "You got any Janis Joplin on that jukebox?"

"No, *hombre,*" she said sadly. "Mostly we have Mexican music. This is El Paso, you know, and it's mostly Mexican."

"*Cholos* in low riders," Devon agreed. "They're involved in most of my cases."

"Ah *sí?*" she smirked. "Gringos don't kill each other."

"Yeah, they do. But not for the same reasons."

"How is it different?" she asked.

"Mexicans kill for honor." Devon smiled. "Anglos mostly kill for money."

"There's a racist generalization," Teddy muttered.

"Take the case I'm working on now," Devon said, looking at Tulles but feeling Teddy perk up. "Two men were killed over a collection of coins."

"They must've been worth a lot," Tulles whispered.

"Not that much," Devon said. "Course the fence only paid half of what they were really worth."

"They always do that," Tulles said sagely.

"Yeah, but on top of that," Devon paused to sip his beer, "the go-between cut the take before handing it over, so the sucker committing the murders got ripped off all the way around."

Teddy smacked his empty can on the bar. "Give me another."

"You've had five already," Tulles frowned. "You gonna let me call a cab when you wanta go home?"

"What's it to you?" he snarled.

"I'm li'ble if I let a drunk walk out the door and I know he's gonna drive home. My friend here is a cop, *hombre,* so I gotta be careful."

"I know goddamned well what he is," Teddy said. "Give me another beer."

Devon nodded at Tulles, and her eyes flared as she caught on to what he was doing. *"Andale pues,"* she said, taking a Coors from the cooler and handing it over. "Is nothing to me."

Teddy popped the can and drank a long time.

Softly Devon said, "It must've hurt you to kill Zane, being as you liked the kid."

Teddy just stared at him.

"We found your prints on the gun," Devon said.

"You're lying," Teddy said.

Devon shrugged. "I just read it off the report, Teddy. If it isn't true, you'll have to take it up with the crime lab."

Teddy took another long swallow of beer. "You're fishing again."

"No, I'm off-duty now," Devon said. "Just shootin' the shit."

Teddy looked at him sideways. "Your brother's in as deep as I am."

"How do you figure?" Devon asked lightly.

"He sold the coins," Teddy said.

"That was inconclusive," Devon said. "We found the coins but we lost 'em again."

"What do you mean?"

"A patrolman found a fellow who admitted he'd bought the coins from a man with BORN TO LOSE tattooed on his arm. When we checked the tattoo parlors, we found out a dozen men got that same tattoo just last month. Given that the fellow could've gotten it anytime and not necessarily in El Paso, we didn't have much to go on. So the patrolman went back hoping to get a better description, but the man had split, taking the coins with him and not leaving a forwarding address." Devon smiled. "You know where that leaves us?"

"Where?" Teddy asked.

"With the family. Most murders, you know, are committed by someone close to the victim."

"So what's your theory?" Teddy asked with a smirk, though he was sweating now.

"Well, you know," Devon said in a conspiratorial whisper, "there was one detail I noticed when I first saw your father's body. Want to know what it was?"

Teddy nodded.

"His belt was unbuckled," Devon said, then shrugged. "At the time, I thought he was on his way to the can, but after I dug a little deeper, I decided he was taking his belt off to use it against your sister. Elise, I mean. I think *she* shot your father."

"You can't prove that," Teddy scoffed.

"You're right," Devon said.

Teddy relaxed a little. Devon sipped his beer. Tulles sang along with the jukebox under her breath.

Teddy stared at her, then looked at Devon and asked with disgust, "What're you doing here? Were you just driving by and saw my truck?"

"Something like that. I was driving around, trying to get a handle on how to close the case."

"I thought you're off-duty."

"A cop's never off-duty. It's a twenty-four-hour job." He smiled. "I'm getting tired and thinking of turning in my badge."

"You'd turn it in rather than arrest your brother, isn't that what you're saying?"

"Arrest him for what?"

"Have you even bothered investigating him?"

"For what?"

"Look in his truck."

"He's out of town," Devon said.

"Did he take his truck with him?"

"It's not at his house."

"It's in the parking lot," Teddy muttered, "at the foot of Santa Fe Street."

"No, it isn't," Devon said. "It was towed. I had to give the guy fifty dollars to hold it till Connie comes home."

"Didn't it occur to you he might not come home 'cause he's running from something?"

Devon shook his head.

Teddy glared at him.

The jukebox clicked into silence, and Devon asked, "You want to know what has crossed my mind?"

"I'm sure you're gonna tell me," Teddy said.

Devon nodded. "I've been thinking about a son whose father ruined his credit, stuck him with so many bills he was about to have his mortgage foreclosed. So this son, he figured it would solve all his problems if the father died. Not only would the old man not be running up debts in the son's name, but the son would get a share of the old man's insurance and whatever property he owned. So the son, he figured to hasten the inevitable, maybe thinking it would be best for the family all the way around, being as the old man had a habit of getting violent when he was drunk. And I heard from more than one source that he was rarely sober."

Teddy just stared at him, sweat beading on his upper lip.

"So the son," Devon said, leaning closer as if sharing a confidence, "left a shotgun primed in his sister's closet. He didn't intend for the sister to use it. He thought she was gonna be gone for the weekend. But you know what they say about the best laid plans . . ."

"What do they say?" Teddy whispered.

"Some tiny detail goes wrong," Devon said, "but that little detail snowballs until pretty soon innocent people get buried in the avalanche. I told you before that's what I thought happened with Zane."

"What do you think what wrong?" Teddy asked.

"The sister stayed home. When her father came in drunk and started abusing her again, she used the shotgun and killed him. That was the snowball. The avalanche was the brother's uncommon love for his sister. This family, you see, was so tight that nobody made a move without consulting the brother. Because the father was ineffective in any kind of masculine role, the brother had taken all that on. Even though he was still pretty young, in truth he was the patriarch of that family."

Teddy sat up a little straighter.

"So the brother," Devon said, "trying to protect his sister, returned the shotgun to the person he'd borrowed it from, that person being his sister's boyfriend, or who he thought was his sister's boyfriend. In the meantime, though, the sister had fallen in love with another man."

"Someone else's brother," Teddy said.

"What's pertinent," Devon said, "is that the sister's old boyfriend couldn't be relied on to protect a girl who'd cut him loose."

"That's right," Teddy said.

"So, telling himself he was motivated by love for his sister, the brother killed the boyfriend."

"Maybe he was," Teddy said. "Motivated by love for his sister."

"Maybe," Devon said. "But the night all this happened, the brother picked his sister up downtown. Once he had her in his car, he used some innocent-sounding ploy to get her to take her coat off, then he told her he intended to plant the coat in her new boyfriend's truck to frame him for murder. When the sister heard that, she took off running, hoping she could get to the old boyfriend in time to save his life. She didn't make it, but what she *did* do is give her new boyfriend an alibi for when her old boyfriend died. I don't think you want to hear how she did that."

"Statutory rape," Teddy hissed. "Connie's old enough to be her father."

Devon nodded. "Let's make a deal. You leave him out of it, and I'll leave her out of it."

Teddy stared at him.

"For killing just your father, Elise would've been put away

at least until she turns eighteen. But killing Zane upped the charge for both you and her to capital murder. We got your prints on the weapon, Teddy, which makes you the principal and Elise an accessory. If you're gonna fall once, since you did it for her, why not follow through and fall twice?"

"You could really keep her out of it?" Teddy whispered.

Devon nodded. "You can plea bargain for life. With good time, you might be out in twenty years, maybe less."

Teddy held his head in his hands and cried. Tulles watched from a distance. When he was quiet again, Devon asked, "You want to come downtown with me, Teddy?"

"Yeah," he said, wiping his nose with the back of his hand.

Devon winked at Tulles as he laid money on the bar to pay for the beer. She grinned and gave him a thumb's up, then he took hold of Teddy's elbow and escorted him out the door.

At three a.m., Lieutenant Dreyfus came into the detective's bullpen where Devon was finishing his report. Dreyfus was a bear of a man, rotund body topped with a thick neck and a florid face which at the moment was beaming with joy.

"You sneaky sonofabitch," Dreyfus yelled from the other end of the room. "If you weren't so goddamned good, I'd have your badge."

Devon gave him a smile, then looked down at his screen and typed an X into the closed box, filed his report and shut off his computer.

Dreyfus clapped a hand on his shoulder. "Let me buy you a drink, Devon."

"Bars are closed," he said, standing up and shrugging into his jacket.

"Hell's bells, we oughta do something to celebrate."

"I'm taking a vacation," Devon said.

"Where you going?"

"Acapulco."

"Alone?"

Devon shook his head.

"Takes a week to process a vacation request," Dreyfus grinned. "We'll have our drink tomorrow."

"I thought maybe you'd expedite the paperwork for me," Devon said.

Dreyfus threw an arm across Devon's shoulders as they walked out of the bullpen. "You know we gotta follow rules, Devon. That's why I love you so much. You're a supervisor's dream, always coming through with results without ever stepping across the line of the law. Makes me wonder how you do it."

"Think I'll call in sick tomorrow," Devon said.

Dreyfus laughed. "I'll buy you that drink 'fore you go on vacation. Don't think you're getting out of it."

"I wouldn't dare," Devon said.

Dreyfus laughed again. "I'm gonna call the mayor right now and tell him we got the press off our back. He'll prob'ly join us for a drink, maybe even front for champagne. Yeah, we'll have a party at the Camino Real. What d'ya think of that?"

Devon shrugged, waiting for the elevator to make his escape.

"Bring your lady friend," Dreyfus called over his shoulder as he hurried toward his office. "The one you're gonna take to Acapulco. We'll show her how proud of you we are!"

Devon watched Dreyfus disappear around a turn of the hall. Then the elevator opened and he stood face to face with Mrs. Truxal. Her face was pale without makeup, and her watery blue eyes were red from crying. She wore a baby blue sweatshirt and white polyester slacks over running shoes that looked brand new. Across the front of her sweatshirt, embroidered with gold thread among the lavender curlicue of morning glory were the words: WORLD'S BEST MOM.

He took a step back and she followed him. "I've just come from the jail," she said, her voice hoarse from crying.

Devon nodded then reached for her elbow to escort her toward the bench against the far wall, but she jerked away, obviously not wanting him to touch her. Gently, he said, "Let's sit down, Mrs. Truxal."

She looked at the bench, then took the few steps across the linoleum and sat down, leaning forward and hugging her voluminous black purse as she fought for control. He sat down beside her, careful to leave a distance between them.

"I saw Teddy," she finally said. "They let me see him, me and Wanda, for a few minutes before they took him away."

Devon nodded, though she wasn't looking at him.

"They told me you were here," she continued. "That if I wanted to speak to you, I had to come here."

He waited, then asked, "What was it you wanted to say to me, Mrs. Truxal?"

She looked at him then, her pale blue eyes beseeching for mercy as she stated, "I knew it all along."

"What did you know?" he coaxed.

"That Teddy had done it. I called him from the church just before we left for Cloudcroft. Elise said he'd asked me to call home, so I did. He told me that Ted had been going after Elise again, so Teddy shot him. Teddy said I should go on the retreat as if I didn't know, that he'd make it look like a burglar did it, and everything would be all right. I said I couldn't do that and he told me I had to, that if I didn't he'd go to jail. I couldn't let that happen. With Ted gone, I needed a man in my family."

She bowed her head and cried. Devon would have held her in an effort to ease her pain, but he knew she didn't want him to touch her. Finally she sat up and opened her purse, took a tissue out and wiped her eyes. "Wanda's outside in the car," she said, straightening the tissue as if she meant to use it again. "She told Teddy she wouldn't wait for him. Said she could've forgiven what he'd done to his father, but not what he'd done to Zane. Right to his face, she said, 'I'm not your wife anymore, Teddy.' Then she turned her back and walked out. She waited outside, and she drove me here, but she wouldn't come up with me. She said it was over for her, or will be as soon as she gets a divorce." She met Devon's eyes. "Can you believe that?"

He nodded, remembering Wanda's stance on tough love.

"What kind of wife would say that?" Mrs. Truxal pleaded. "I stood by my husband even when I knew he was wrong! That's what a wife does. For better or worse the marriage vows say. Now, when Teddy needs her, she turns her back."

Devon kept quiet.

Wadding the tissue into her fist, she snapped her purse closed. "I'll stand up for him" she said, sitting straight. "He's my son."

Knowing how badly she was hurting, Devon asked gently, "Have you ever stood up for your daughters?"

Slowly her head swiveled toward him until she was meeting his eyes. For a long moment, she stared at him in the shock of comprehension, then she sniffed and cleared her throat, but she didn't say anything.

Devon moved away to push the button for the elevator. "I think you should go home, Mrs. Truxal."

She watched as the elevator door opened. Then she gained her feet and walked inside. Her eyes bruised with confusion, she nodded just before the doors closed and left him alone.

Devon watched the elevator light indicate it had stopped in the lobby, then he pushed the button again. When the elevator opened, he got in by himself. The cables clanked, lowering him to the garage where the attendant tossed him a set of keys. "Got her all tanked up in bay seven, Detective Gray," he grinned. "Congratulations."

"Thanks," Devon said, catching the keys and walking away without a smile. The sedan in bay seven was just like all the others.

He drove to Samantha's apartment, let himself in with his key and walked through the dark to her bedroom, where he sat on the edge of her bed. When he turned on the lamp, she awoke and reached eagerly to hold him.

"It's over," he said into the comforting fragrance of her hair. "Truxal took the fall on both counts."

She met his eyes. "Eric?" she whispered.

"Got away with murder," Devon said.

They watched each other to catch the first nuances of what this new knowledge would weigh.

"Surely he'll see this as a chance to make good," she finally said.

"I hope so," Devon said.

"And Connie? Is he in the clear?"

"Till he fucks up again."

"Oh, Devon," she half-laughed. "Won't you ever quit being his keeper?"

"Not till one of us is dead," he answered.

She sighed, leaning against his chest.

"I've been thinking maybe I'll move out of the house," he said, feeling his way slowly. "Laura's looking for a job now, and that's gonna change things between her and Connie. Maybe if I'm not there, it'll give him a chance to come into his own."

Samantha leaned back with a smile. "Are you asking to move in with me, Devon?"

He nodded, "Figure we oughta give it a try before we take any vows."

Watching her laugh, he remembered Mr. and Mrs. Truxal and all the tragedies their union engendered. But he pushed their sorrow from his mind, reassuring himself that any children he had with Samantha would fare better because she wouldn't stand behind him when she thought he was wrong.

At nine-thirty the following night, Devon stood under the Marlboro sign and watched his brother and nephew cross the bridge from Juárez. Connie swaggered with exaggerated nonchalance while Eric strolled with a leonine shyness, flaunting to the world that they were riding the cusp of success. Moving eagerly to join them on the concrete decline, Devon wished with all his might they could stay in this moment together.